Longman Strategy Series for

GEPT

New Edition

朗文全民英檢

贏家策略 中級 Intermediate

聽力測驗

Listening Test

Jason Buddo & 謝璿蓁—著

LWAYS LEARNING

PEARSON

前言

聽力是許多台灣中學生的英文學習障礙,主要的原因多半是因為現階段基測與大學聯考出題方式是著重在讀和寫的部分,因此一般學校的課程設計就會比較忽略了聽力和口說的部分;再加上台灣尚未創造出優良的英文使用環境,學生的英語聽力就顯得比較弱。大部分的學生通常不是因為速度太快聽不清楚,就是聽不懂內容,如果你聽不懂內容便無法作答,也直接影響了口說的表達能力。

從累積多年教授全民英檢經驗中得知,幫助學生通過全民英檢聽力測驗的最佳捷徑就是「充分了解考試的題型與應答技巧」、「學習有效的準備策略」、「培養敏銳的聽力能力」以及「訓練作答的反應力」,才能在有限的時間內,快速地具備高分通過考試的能力。

很多學生在準備英語聽力考試的階段,只是買一些模擬試題反覆練習,直到聽得懂這些題目為止,這樣子是不對的。他們忽略了中級聽力測驗重點是在日常生活相關的內容,應該在平時就養成紮實的聽力基本功夫,例如熟練地掌握連音、消音與弱音現象,豐富生活中的基本詞彙、片語與慣用語和常用的句型。一旦奠定了良好的聽力基本功夫,考試時就可以快速地理解對話中上下文的關係、掌握住主旨與重要訊息,作答就變得輕而易舉。

這本書最大的特色在於,歸納出全民英檢聽力測驗的考題中最重要、必考的題型和解題訣竅,更提供了多樣主題的情境對話,運用適合全民英檢中級程度的字彙、片語與詳細的解析。目的是培養考生敏銳的聽力技巧與信心,希望你喜歡這本書;當然,最重要的是以優異的成績通過全民英檢中級考試。

Enjoy the journey!

Jason Buddo & 謝璿蓁

使用說明

一、本書的設計

1. 本書的主軸是根據全民英檢出題的趨勢、常見的考試題型與解題的關鍵訣竅而編寫的，內容包含了聽力考試三個部分，讀者能藉由本書培養聽力能力與作答的反應，使讀者不論遇到什麼樣的題型，都可以從容不迫地輕鬆作答、高分過關！

2. 本書依照課堂教學使用和自修學習者所需，分別提供兩種不同的學習計畫，不論是課堂教學使用或自修，都可以按照本書建議的進度和準備時間的長短，來調整適合的進度與份量。

3. 本書有 5 大特色：
   ① 13 類題型完整歸納
   ② 清晰易學解題策略
   ③ 解題的訣竅與技巧
   ④ 實用的字彙與片語
   ⑤ 最新全真模擬試題

二、本書的架構

本書的架構是根據全民英檢聽力測驗的三個部分設計的，每一個部分都為了培養學生具備高分通過考試的能力，提供了不同的學習技巧與訣竅。以下就這三部分簡單說明：

第一部分 看圖辨義

本書將看圖辨義中常考的題型歸納成人物、地方與物品三種類型，根據不同題型階段性地教授考生應該學會的聽力技巧，並且快速地找出正確的答案。在這個單元將會學到看圖辨義中的三種作答技巧，包含了預測題目、運用圖片聯想法與抓住關鍵字。如此一來考生就會分析圖片，找出和主題有關的單字和背景知識，並且會辨別相似音、同音異形字和多義字，與熟悉連音等等。

第二部分 問答

為了讓學生理解口語中不同情境常用的問句或直述句，進而快速選擇適當的回應，我們將最常出現的疑問詞、問題的句型和情境歸納成五個單元。每一個單元都依據不同的情境提供了常見的問句、句型範例與第二部分必學的聽力技巧，包含了辨認相似音字、同

音異形字、辨別正確的時態與單複數、正確的回應附加問句與附和句等等。

第三部分 簡短對話

為了讓考生聽得出對話的主旨、意圖、細節、推論與解決問題之道，本書將常考題型歸納成五個單元。透過每一個單元可以學習聽力的技巧，學到如何運用由上而下的思考方式、聽懂口語中的連音、省略音與弱化音、邊聽邊做筆記、做出推論等技巧，進而掌握對話整體的方向、細節及推斷言外之意。

三、課堂教學計畫

本書提供了兩種不同的課程計畫方便老師課堂上使用，您可以根據教學的時數或是學生的程度來調整課程進度。

Plan 1

課程週數：12 週完成
教學時數：每週上課總時數 4 小時（每週上課 2 次，每次 2 小時）
適合程度：適合大多數中等學生（教學速度適中）

週次	上課單元	
	第 1 堂課	第 2 堂課
Week 1	實力養成與應試要訣 Unit 1-1 辨別人物圖片	Unit 1-1 辨別人物圖片 題型實戰演練
Week 2	Unit 1-2 辨別地方圖片	Unit 1-2 辨別地方圖片 題型實戰演練
Week 3	Unit 1-3 辨別物件圖片	Unit 1-3 辨別物件圖片 題型實戰演練
Week 4	Unit 2-1 建議的回應	Unit 2-1 題型實戰演練 Unit 2-2 情境的回應
Week 5	Unit 2-2 情境的回應 題型實戰演練	Unit 2-3 地點的回應

週次	上課單元	
	第 1 堂課	第 2 堂課
Week 6	Unit 2-3 題型實戰演練 Unit 2-4 態度的回應	Unit 2-4 態度的回應 題型實戰演練
Week 7	Unit 2-5 意見的回應	Unit 2-5 題型實戰演練
Week 8	Unit 3-1 聽出主旨	Unit 3-1 聽出主旨 題型實戰演練
Week 9	Unit 3-2 聽出意圖	Unit 3-2 聽出意圖 題型實戰演練
Week 10	Unit 3-3 聽出細節	Unit 3-3 聽出細節 題型實戰演練
Week 11	Unit 3-4 聽出推論	Unit 3-4 聽出推論 題型實戰演練
Week 12	Unit 3-5 聽出問題與解決方式	Unit 3-5 題型實戰演練 Test 聽力測驗總複習

Plan 2

課程週數：8 週完成

教學時數：每週上課總時數 4 小時（每週上課 2 次，每次 2 小時）

適合程度：適合程度較好的學生（教學速度較快）

週次	上課單元	
	第 1 堂課	第 2 堂課
Week 1	實力養成與應試要訣 Unit 1-1 辨別人物圖片	Unit 1-1 辨別人物圖片 題型實戰演練

週次	上課單元	
	第 1 堂課	第 2 堂課
Week 2	Unit 1-2 辨別地方圖片 題型實戰演練	Unit 1-3 辨別物件圖片 題型實戰演練
Week 3	Unit 2-1 建議的回應 題型實戰演練	Unit 2-2 情境的回應 題型實戰演練
Week 4	Unit 2-3 地點的回應 題型實戰演練	Unit 2-4 態度的回應 題型實戰演練
Week 5	Unit 2-5 意見的回應	Unit 2-5 題型實戰演練
Week 6	Unit 3-1 聽出主旨 題型實戰演練	Unit 3-2 聽出意圖 題型實戰演練
Week 7	Unit 3-3 聽出細節 題型實戰演練	Unit 3-4 聽出推論 題型實戰演練
Week 8	Unit 3-5 聽出問題與解決方式	題型實戰演練 Test 聽力測驗總複習

四、自修計畫

本書提供了兩種不同的自修課程計畫供考生參考，您可以根據準備時間的長短、學習時數和不同的程度來調整自修學習的計畫。

Plan 1

課程週數：12 週完成

教學時數：每週自修總時數 4 小時

適合程度：適合大多數程度中等考生（學習速度適中）

週次	學習單元			
	第 1 小時	第 2 小時	第 3 小時	第 4 小時
Week 1	實力養成與應試要訣 Unit 1-1 辨別人物圖片	Unit 1-1 辨別人物圖片	Unit 1-1 辨別人物圖片	Unit 1-1 題型實戰演練
Week 2	Unit 1-2 辨別地方圖片	Unit 1-2 辨別地方圖片	Unit 1-2 辨別地方圖片	Unit 1-2 題型實戰演練
Week 3	Unit 1-3 辨別物件圖片	Unit 1-3 辨別物件圖片	Unit 1-3 辨別物件圖片	Unit 1-3 題型實戰演練
Week 4	Unit 2-1 建議的回應	Unit 2-1 建議的回應	Unit 2-1 題型實戰演練	Unit 2-2 情境的回應
Week 5	Unit 2-2 情境的回應	Unit 2-2 題型實戰演練	Unit 2-3 地點的回應	Unit 2-3 地點的回應
Week 6	Unit 2-3 題型實戰演練	Unit 2-4 態度的回應	Unit 2-4 態度的回應	Unit 2-4 題型實戰演練
Week 7	Unit 2-5 意見的回應	Unit 2-5 意見的回應	Unit 2-5 意見的回應	Unit 2-5 題型實戰演練
Week 8	Unit 3-1 聽出主旨	Unit 3-1 聽出主旨	Unit 3-1 聽出主旨	Unit 3-1 題型實戰演練
Week 9	Unit 3-2 聽出意圖	Unit 3-2 聽出意圖	Unit 3-2 聽出意圖	Unit 3-2 題型實戰演練
Week 10	Unit 3-3 聽出細節	Unit 3-3 聽出細節	Unit 3-3 聽出細節	Unit 3-3 題型實戰演練
Week 11	Unit 3-4 聽出推論	Unit 3-4 聽出推論	Unit 3-4 聽出推論	Unit 3-4 題型實戰演練

週次	學習單元			
	第 1 小時	第 2 小時	第 3 小時	第 4 小時
Week 12	Unit 3-5 聽出問題與解決方式	Unit 3-5 聽出問題與解決方式	Unit 3-5 題型實戰演練	Test 聽力測驗 總複習

Plan 2

課程週數：8 週完成

教學時數：每週自修總時數 4-6 小時

適合程度：適合程度稍好的考生（學習速度快）

週次	學習單元			
	第 1 小時	第 2 小時	第 3 小時	第 4 小時
Week 1	實力養成與應試要訣 Unit 1-1 辨別人物圖片	Unit 1-1 題型實戰演練	Unit 1-2 辨別地方圖片	Unit 1-2 題型實戰演練
Week 2	Unit 1-3 辨別物件圖片	Unit 1-3 題型實戰演練	Unit 2-1 建議的回應	Unit 2-1 題型實戰演練
Week 3	Unit 2-2 情境的回應	Unit 2-2 題型實戰演練	Unit 2-3 地點的回應	Unit 2-3 題型實戰演練
Week 4	Unit 2-4 態度的回應	Unit 2-4 題型實戰演練	Unit 2-5 意見的回應	Unit 2-5 題型實戰演練
Week 5	Unit 3-1 聽出主旨	Unit 3-1 聽出主旨	Unit 3-1 題型實戰演練	Unit 3-2 聽出意圖
Week 6	Unit 3-2 聽出意圖	Unit 3-2 題型實戰演練	Unit 3-3 聽出細節	Unit 3-3 聽出細節

週次	學習單元			
	第 1 小時	第 2 小時	第 3 小時	第 4 小時
Week 7	Unit 3-3 題型實戰演練	Unit 3-4 聽出推論	Unit 3-4 聽出推論	Unit 3-4 題型實戰演練
Week 8	Unit 3-5 聽出問題與解決 方式	Unit 3-5 聽出問題與解決 方式	Unit 3-5 題型實戰演練	Test 聽力測驗 總複習

五、學習小叮嚀

1. 要學好語言，一定要常常複習。語言不是看過學過就算了，一定要經常練習、反覆背誦，才會記得。

2. 每次學習完成之後，一定要額外再做兩次以上的練習，每次需維持 1-2 小時的複習與背誦。

3. 本書所提供的英語詞彙與語句，一定要有上下文情境的聯想，要能活用。

4. 複習時，請多利用 CD。一定要多聽多說。只有反覆地聽與說，才能夠真正熟練。

5. 學習與複習時，可以根據個人需求來安排與調整速度。

目錄

題型與策略

答案與解析

全民英檢中級測驗簡介

一、測驗能力說明

通過全民英語能力分級檢定測驗中級測驗者，英語能力相當於高中畢業的程度，具有使用簡單英語進行日常生活溝通的能力。需要具備這項語言能力者為一般行政、業務、技術、銷售人員、接待人員和旅遊從業人員等。

聽	在日常生活情境中，能聽懂一般的會話，能大致聽懂公共場所廣播、氣象報告及廣告等。在工作情境中，能聽懂簡易的產品介紹與操作說明，能大致聽懂外籍人士的談話及詢問。
讀	在日常生活情境中，能閱讀短文、故事、私人信件、廣告、傳單、簡介及使用說明等。在工作情境中，能閱讀工作須知、公告、操作手冊、例行的文件、傳真、電報等。
寫	能寫簡單的書信、故事及測驗心得等。對於熟悉且與個人經驗相關的主題，能以簡易的文字表達。
說	在日常生活情境中，能以簡易英語交談或描述一般事物，能介紹自己的生活作息、工作、家庭、經歷等，並可對一般話題陳述看法。在工作情境中，能進行簡單的問答，並與外籍人士交談溝通。

二、測驗項目說明

初 / 複試	各項測驗	通過標準	滿　分
初試	聽力測驗	兩項測驗成績總和達 160 分，且其中任一項成績不低於 72 分。	120
	閱讀能力測驗		120
複試	寫作能力測驗	80	100
	口說能力測驗	80	100

三、測驗時間說明

初 / 複試	分項能力	測驗題型	題數	總作答時間
初試	聽力	一、看圖辨義	15	約 30 分鐘
		二、問答	15	
		三、簡短對話	15	
	閱讀能力	一、詞彙和結構	15	45 分鐘
		二、段落填空	10	
		三、閱讀理解	15	
複試	寫作能力	一、中譯英	1 段	40 分鐘
		二、英文作文	1 篇	
	口說能力	一、朗讀短文	2~3 篇	約 15 分鐘
		二、回答問題	10	
		三、看圖敘述	1 篇	

實力養成與應試要訣

培養敏銳聽力的方法

如果你想要通過全民英檢聽力測驗並且擁有敏銳的聽力，首先要培養良好的學習習慣，在日常生活中訓練自己的聽力與專注力。學校和老師所教的課程非常有限，鼓勵你成為一位獨立的學習者，設立自己的學習目標，善用手邊容易取得的資源，讓自己的聽力更上一層樓。透過本書所教授的聽力技巧與應答訣竅，你可以學到如何培養出好耳力，再加上下列培養敏銳聽力的方法與五個應試要訣，你不但可以高分通過全民英檢聽力考試，也會在日常生活中感受到自己英文程度提升。

方法 ❶ 聽英語有聲書籍

購買有聲書籍，培養邊閱讀邊聽的習慣。然後進一步嘗試只聆聽有聲的部分，不依靠視覺上的閱讀理解來看看你聽懂了多少。藉由聽有聲出版品來增加英語的環境，可以熟悉英語的韻律、語調和正確的發音。找一本你喜歡的英文書，上網購買下載有聲的部分，為了節省一些錢，可以找幾個朋友一起分擔。另外也推薦你買市面上流行的小說讀本。這一類的書內容豐富有趣，又大量使用時下美國最流行的俚語與口語用法，可以提升我們閱讀的樂趣，又可以學到更多實用流通的詞彙。有些書本的兩側會提供關鍵字彙與慣用語的附註，因此學習起來十分輕鬆方便。

方法 ❷ 看電影學英文

看電影是一個練習聽力很棒的方法。租一部電影，選擇不看中文字幕，盡量練習看英文字幕。你還可以在網路上搜尋到數以萬計的電影劇本，你可能會發現在看電影之前，先閱讀電影腳本，會對你進一步聽懂電影很有幫助。透過看來自世界各地的影片，會幫助你熟悉不同國家的英文腔調。

方法 ❸ 看電視影集學英文

像看電影一樣，看電視影集對提高聽力的專注力與理解力也很有幫助。有一些節目，你可以在網路上找到電視劇本。因為電視影集的場景與內容都是取自於日常生活中，透過影集會讓我們熟悉各種對話的題材與回應，自然而然學習到正確的語調和連音，進一步強化考生的應答與理解言外之意的能力。電視影集我推薦《歡樂單身派對》(*Seinfeld*)、

《黑道家族》(*The Sopranos*) 和《六人行》(*Friends*)。對於卡通愛好者,《辛普森》(*The Simpsons*) 絕不會讓你失望。在你購買任何影集之前,可以先上 YouTube 網站查看每個影集的精彩花絮,來選擇你喜歡的。

方法 ❹ 聽網路廣播學英文

如果你想掌握最新時事新聞,可以收看英語新聞台,或是收聽英語廣播。你可以使用 iTunes 來訂閱下載網路廣播節目 (Podcasts) 和電台節目,如此一來不論你在什麼時間與地點,都可以隨時練習聽力。如果你覺得這些內容太困難了,可以試試專門為青少年或是兒童設計的網站,像是 Time for Kids 或是 National Geographic Kids 這一類的網站。

方法 ❺ 使用 Skype 上網聊天

透過 Skype 免費視訊通話,來結交外國網友。我建議你找一個想要學習中文的人當朋友,藉由互相學習對方的語言和認識文化來加深友誼,這樣你在語言的學習上就有個伴,更可以互相幫助。但是請記得:不要在網路上分享個人的私人資料,要保護自己的安全。

方法 ❻ 聽音樂學英文與善用英語學習網站

如果你只是想放鬆一下,聽聽音樂唱唱歌的話,可以在 YouTube 網站上搜索喜歡的音樂 MV。你還可以在任何搜尋引擎上,鍵入歌曲名稱和 lyrics(歌詞) 這個字,找出所喜歡歌曲的歌詞,你就可以一邊唱一邊學。

網路提供了相當豐富的學習資源,介紹一些你可能會喜歡的英語學習網站,來加強你的聽力能力。這些網站都是很棒的,不僅對你的聽力很有幫助,而且對閱讀、口語和寫作能力的提升,都相當有助益。

- www.esl-lab.com
- www.elllo.org
- www.manythings.org
- www.bbc.co.uk/worldservice/learningenglish
- www.eslfast.com
- www.voanews.com/learningenglish/home

方法 ❼ 評估自己的聽力能力

最重要的是你需要不定期的評估自己的聽力能力,想一想還有哪些弱點呢?應該如何改善呢?試著找出聽不懂的原因,然後做必要的調整。一般學生最常見的問題如下:

- 聽不懂關鍵字。

- 試著聽懂每個字,而錯過了語調和重音強調的位置。
- 因為不熟悉的單字而卡住,也許是不重要的字卻錯過了重要的內容。
- 聽不懂已經認識的單字。
- 不能理解不同的口音與英文腔調。

應試要訣

在準備考試期間也要注意以下的應試要訣,來提升自己的英語聽力能力,以高分通過全民英檢。

要訣 ❶ 豐富字彙量與慣用語

要聽懂對話中的內容,補充中級範圍相關的字彙與生活口語中的片語、俚語與慣用語是非常重要的一件事。鼓勵學生們要買一本中級英檢的單字書和片語書籍,還要藉由廣泛閱讀英語小說和英語學習雜誌來幫助自己累積字彙,並且多注意現代流行時事與熱門話題中的字彙和口語中慣用語的用法。

要訣 ❷ 辨別出易混淆的字

在聽力測驗中,易混淆字的辨別也是考題的重點,所以花時間學習辨別易混淆字是很重要的。因為一旦學會如何分辨相似音字、同形異音字、同音異形字等容易混淆的字,就不會聽錯語意或是誤解對話的內容。

要訣 ❸ 熟悉連音、弱音、消音與語調變化

在口語英文中,因為說話者的速度太快或是為了讓說話更加流暢,字的發音就會和字典中的 K.K. 音標不符合。最常見的變化有「連音」、「弱音」和「消音」的發音現象。在對話中有時候為了強調某些訊息,就會重讀 (stress) 某些字然後弱化功能字,而這一些被弱化的功能字中的某些子音就會被省略掉。所以常常聆聽英文歌曲、電影、電視影集與廣播就可以幫助自己提升英文聽力。

要訣 ❹ 融入文法觀念並聽出句型

有些人認為在聽力考試中文法是不重要的,這是錯誤的觀念。在聽力考試中,如果你聽不清楚時態或是單複數名詞時,你就無法選出正確的回應。如果你不知道附加問句和附和句的正確用法,那你就無法選擇正確的答案。對話中要聽出句型才可以了解正確的語意,更要聽得懂句子中的「轉折語」,如此才能幫助你推論出對話中的言外之意,所以熟悉常用句型對你的聽力測驗是很有助益的。

要訣 ❺ 了解語言情境、正式與非正式用語以及暗示語用法

在簡短對話中，如果我們聽得出對話的情境背景，就會幫助你了解對話者的身分與關係，更可以掌握住對話的主旨大意。因為對話者的身分關係不同，會有正式與非正式的不同用語。有時候對話者因為禮貌或是客氣的原因，也會用較迂迴或委婉的說法，如果你熟悉這些用法，可以幫助你更理解題目，進一步聽懂說話者的言外之意。

這本書所教授的技巧將幫助你克服所有聽力上的困難，希望你喜歡這本書，並且以優秀的考試成績過關！

題型與策略

看圖辨義

作答說明

以下是全民英檢中級聽力測驗第一部分的作答說明與題目範例。事先熟記作答說明與題型，考試時就可以略過作答說明，往下瀏覽題目，以提高得分。

第一部分：看圖辨義

共 15 題，試題冊上有數幅圖畫，每一圖畫有 1~3 個描述該圖的題目，每題請聽光碟放音機播出題目以及四個英文敘述之後，選出與所看到的圖畫最相符的答案，每題只播出一遍。

例 （看）

（聽）Look at the picture. What does the man want to do?

A. He is playing golf.

B. He wants to play golf.

C. He wants to cut the grass.

D. He wants to take a vacation.

正確答案為 B，請在答案紙上塗黑作答。

 1. 聽到 What does the man want to do? 可知本題是問「動作」。

2. 問句時態是用現在簡單式，選項 A 是表示現在正在打高爾夫球，所以與問句不合。

3. 關鍵字彙：play golf 是「打高爾夫球」，cut the grass 是「除草」，而 take a vacation 是「渡假」。

答案 B

應考策略

Step 1 快速瀏覽圖片（Scan the picture.）

一定要很快地找到圖片中的主題、辨別出圖片題型、掌握重點，然後預測題目。

Step 2 運用圖片聯想法（Apply the picture analysis skill.）

掌握和主題有關的單字和背景知識，就很容易聽出題目的主旨大意，也會很快理解題目內容。

Step 3 聽出關鍵字（Listen for key words.）

留意內容字，抓到主要名詞、動詞，就很容易把握內容大意。

Step 4 仔細聆聽選項（Listen carefully.）

仔細辨別相似音、同音異形字和多義字，熟悉連音與語調找出正確答案。

常考題型

一見到圖片時要能分辨出題型，根據不同題型找出圖片主旨，運用聽力技巧快速找出正確的答案。

本部分根據「看圖辨義」的常考題目，歸納成下列三種常考題型：

- 1-1　辨別人物圖片
- 1-2　辨別地方圖片
- 1-3　辨別物件圖片

1-1　辨別人物圖片

基本觀念

在「看圖辨義」中，最常考的題目就是有人物的圖片，我們將這類最常考的題型歸納為以下這五種：

1. **動作題**（Actions）
2. **細節題**（Details）
3. **推論題**（Inferences）
4. **比較題**（Comparisons）
5. **職業與工作題**（Occupations）

在遇到這種題型時，首先請仔細看圖片中出現的人數。題目通常會根據不同人數來出不同的題目。請注意以下可能的出題方式：

❶ 是**一個人**時，請注意他正在做的動作或是其穿著打扮，最常考的大多是**動作**、**細節**、**職業**或**身分地位**的相關問題。

❷ 是**兩個人**時，請留意這兩人的性別、圖上是否標示出姓名、兩人站立的**相對位置**等等，最常考的問題大多著重在他們**相同**或相異之處，或是他們之間的**身分關係**。

❸ 是**三個人**時，大部分都會標上他們的姓名，這一類題型多半是著重於**比較級**與**最高級**的問題，請留意**細節**方面的問題。

❹ 是**一群人**的話，請注意他們所在的場所、共同的動作與職業身分。如果其中**某人**和其他人有**明顯不同處**，則多為考題的焦點。

常見問題

1. What is the boy on the right doing?（在右邊的那個男孩正在做什麼？）
2. Which statement best describes Brenda?（哪一種敘述最適合描述布蘭達？）
3. What do these people have in common?（這些人有什麼相同點？）
4. What is the man's occupation?（這位男士的職業是什麼？）

作答技巧

▶ 預測題目（Prediction）

首先要學的技巧是看圖預測題目或是做合理的猜測，這樣做可以先判斷或預測接下來可能會聽到的內容。在聽題目之前，一定要很快地找到圖片中的主題、辨別出圖片題型、

掌握重點，然後預測題目。一旦你掌握和主題相關的背景資訊，當你在聽題目的時候，所需要聽到的新資訊就可以少一點，也會很快就辨識出正確答案。由於題目與下一題的時間空檔只有大約兩秒，所以速度一定要快。

題型介紹 ·······

題型 ❶ 動作題（Actions）

最常考的人物動作題型就是問圖片中發生什麼事情。例如：What is Jessie doing?（潔西正在做什麼？）這個問句的時態是用現在進行式，而這也是人物動作題中最常用的時態。然而，有時題目可能會用別的時態來問，所以一定要聽清楚每個問題所用的時態。一般而言，回答的時態會和問句的時態相同。

 範 例

Jessie

What does Jessie like to do when she gets home from work?

A. She is playing with her cats.

B. She likes to feed her cats.

C. She likes to play with her cats.

D. She was playing with her cats.

潔西下班回家後喜歡做什麼事情？

她正在和貓玩。

她喜歡餵貓。

她喜歡和貓玩。

她那時正和貓一起玩。

解析 1. 這個題目是用現在式，因此選項 A 和 D 不能選，因為選項 A 使用現在進行式，選項 D 是用過去進行式。

2. 看得出來，潔西並不是在餵貓，所以正確答案是 C。 答案 C

相關問句

1. What is the woman doing?（這位女士正在做什麼？）

2. Kyle is in a restaurant. What is the waiter doing?

（凱爾正在餐廳裡。服務生正在做什麼？）

3. Which sentence best describes what is happening in the picture?

（哪個敘述最適合描寫圖片中發生的事？）

題型 ❷ 細節題（Details）

考題常常會問到圖片裡面的細節問題，例如：地點、服裝、臉部表情、手勢和兩人之間的關係等等。所以聽到問題之前，一定要仔細觀察圖片。

範 例

Which of the following statements best describes this couple?

A. They like to walk in their neighborhood.

B. They love adventure.

C. It's a scenic place to hike.

D. They should watch their step.

下列哪項敘述最適合描寫這對情侶？

他們喜歡在家附近走路。

他們愛冒險。

那是一個適合健行的風景地。

他們應該要小心他們的腳步。

解析 1. 題目關鍵字為 best describes this couple，在仔細聆聽選項之後，要使用消去法，將不可能的選項消去，然後找出最好的答案。

2. 本題問有關爬山的字彙，neighborhood 是「附近」，adventure 是「冒險」，scenic place 是「風景優美的地方」，watch their step 是「當心步伐」，所以答案要選 B。 **答案** B

相關問句

1. Who isn't having a good time at the party?（在派對中，誰沒有玩得很愉快？）

2. Which sentence best describes the girl in the picture?

（哪一句最適合描述圖片中的女子？）

3. Nancy and Brad are spending the afternoon together. What is Nancy carrying?

（南西和布萊德一起度過一個下午。南西手上拿著什麼？）

題型 ③ 推論題（Inferences）

有些問題會要你根據圖片來推測原因、理由或接下來會發生的事情。這種問題要仔細看圖片，並且思考推論出最佳的答案。

  範 例

Why is this girl so excited?

A. She just found the exit.

B. She got an autograph.

C. She's going to sing with a rock star.

D. She can't stand rock stars.

為何女孩如此興奮？

她剛發現出口。

她拿到親筆簽名。

她要和一位搖滾明星一起唱歌。

她不能忍受搖滾明星。

解析 1. 問句疑問詞是 why，而關鍵字是 so excited，所以我們要推論她興奮的理由。

2. 關鍵字彙：exit 是「出口」、can't stand 是「受不了」。

3. 選項 A 是混淆題，所以最佳的答案是 B。 答案 B

相關問句

1. Why doesn't the boy want to go home?（為什麼男孩不想要回家？）

2. What do you think Eric is saying to the girl?（你想艾瑞克正對那位女孩說什麼？）

3. How do these moviegoers feel?（這些常看電影的人感覺如何？）

題型 ❹ 比較題（Comparisons）

有些題型是要你比較圖片中的人物，如果只有兩個人是考比較級，若有三個人以上則考最高級。請注意題目有可能要你比較圖片中人物的相似或相異點。

範 例

Who looks the most fashionable in this picture?

A. Tiffany does.

B. Vicky looks the most fashionable.

C. Tiffany is the least fashionable.

D. Rita enjoys fashion.

圖片中誰看起來最時髦？

蒂芬妮。

維奇看起來最時髦。

蒂芬妮是最不時髦的人。

瑞塔喜歡時尚。

解析 1. 問句的疑問詞是 who，關鍵字是 looks the most fashionable「看起來最時髦的」，所以是問圖片中的細節。

2. 三個人的題目一定要先留意圖中的名字，然後比較出三個人的相似處與差異點。

3. 選項 C 是混淆題，一定要分辨出 the most 和 the least 的差別。

4. 比較之後可知答案是 A。 **答案** A

相關問句

1. Who is the most outgoing person?（誰是最外向的人？）

2. What do these boys have in common?（這些男生的共同點是什麼？）

3. How might you describe these two children?（你會如何描述這兩位小孩？）

題型 ⑤ 工作職業題（Occupations）

關於工作職業方面的問題，也是常考的題型。所以有關工作職業的字彙都要很熟悉。

 範 例

What does this man do for a living?　　　**這名男子以什麼為生？**

A. He's a musician.　　　　　　　　　　他是個音樂家。

B. He likes playing the guitar.　　　　　　他喜歡彈吉他。

C. He's doing his homework.　　　　　　他正在做功課。

D. He makes a good living.　　　　　　　他生活過得很好。

解析　1. 要聽懂的關鍵字是 do for a living，所以我們知道本題是問「職業」。
　　　2. 選項 D 中，make a good living 是「過得很好」。　　　答案 A

相關問句

1. What is this man's occupation?（這位男士的職業是什麼？）

2. What is this man's job?（這位男士的工作是什麼？）

3. What might this man do at work?（這位男士可能是做什麼工作的？）

作答說明：每一圖畫有1到3個描述該圖的題目，每題請聽光碟放音機播出題目以及四個英語敘述之後，選出與所看到的圖畫最相符的答案。每題只播出一遍。

A Question 1

D Question 5

B Questions 2-3

E Questions 6-7

C Question 4

F Question 8

G Question 9

I Questions 12-13

H Questions 10-11

J Questions 14-15

1-2　辨別地方圖片

基本觀念

詢問有關地方圖片的問題，也是全民英檢的必考題型。本單元將這些常考類型的圖片歸納成以下四大種類：

1. **建築物題（Buildings）**
2. **交通題（Traffic）**
3. **事件題（Events）**
4. **景色題（Scenery）**

常見問題

1. Which statement best describes the picture?（下列哪一種說法最能描述此圖？）
2. Which description best matches the picture?（下列哪一個描述最符合這個圖片？）
3. Which statement does not match the picture?（下列哪一個說法不適合這個圖片？）
4. Which announcement would you most likely hear at this place?
   （你在這個地方最可能聽到哪一種廣播？）
5. Which statement is correct?（下列哪一種敘述是正確的？）
6. What is true about this picture?（關於這個圖片何者是對的？）
7. What does the picture tell you?（這個圖片告訴你什麼？）
8. What is happening in this picture?（在這張圖片中發生了什麼事？）

作答技巧

▶ 圖片聯想法

當你一看到圖片時，腦中要快速想出你所會的字彙，就像英文圖解字典一樣，在圖片中列出所有相關的英文單字。這項技巧可以幫助你聽懂題目所需要的詞彙，也會很快知道正確的答案。最重要的是如果圖片中出現你不會的單字，千萬不要浪費時間，只要想出你所知道的單字即可，記得不要先想中文，再翻譯成英文，請直接用英文思考。在接下來的題型當中，讀者可以學習用圖片來做聯想，熟悉這個作答技巧。

題型介紹

題型 ❶ 建築物題（Buildings）

當你看到一個圖片是大樓的平面圖、樓層圖或是房間內部的圖片時，心中要預備好可能
會考有關描述主題或者是在哪裡可以找到某個東西。這一類常考的主題有：房屋、百貨
公司、車站和商店。

範 例

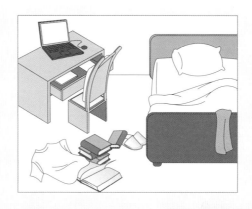

Which description best describes this bedroom?

A. It's clean and tidy.

B. It's messy.

C. It's a double bed.

D. There's a computer on the desk.

哪個敘述最能描述這個臥房？

乾淨又整潔。

髒亂。

雙人床。

書桌上有台電腦。

解析 1. 答案不可能是 A，因為臥室是髒亂的。

2. 如果你聽不懂選項 B 中 messy「髒亂的」這個字時，請繼續聽接下來的
兩個選項。圖中是一張單人床，所以選項 C 是不正確的。 圖中有一部電
腦，但是選項 D 並沒有形容這個房間，所以最好的答案是 B。　**答案** B

注意事項

要留意室內東西陳設的地方與相對位置，如牆上或門上所張貼的標語、招牌、文字或數
字都可能是命題的焦點。

相關問句

1. The woman is looking for her cat. Where is it?

（這名女子正在尋找她的貓。牠在哪裡？）

2. Where can I buy some boots?（我在哪裡可以買到靴子？）

3. Which description best describes this apartment?

（哪一個敘述最適合描寫這間公寓？）

▶ **圖片當中的重要詞彙**

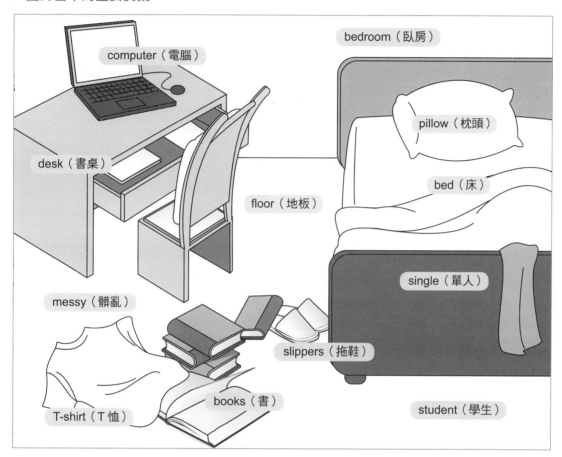

▶ **題型相關的單字與片語**

garage [gə`rɑʒ] (n.)	車庫	run-down [`rʌn͵daʊn] (adj.)	破爛的
driveway [`draɪv͵we] (n.)	車道	two-story house (n.)	兩層樓的房子
sidewalk [`saɪd͵wɔk] (n.)	人行道	floor [flor] (n.)	地板；樓層
yard [jɑrd] (n.)	院子	elevator [`ɛlə͵vetə] (n.)	電梯
fence [fɛns] (n.)	籬笆	escalator [`ɛskə͵letə] (n.)	手扶電梯
grand [grænd] (adj.)	豪華的	skyscraper [`skaɪ͵skrepə] (n.)	摩天大樓

題型 2 交通題 (Traffic)

我們的生活幾乎每天都和交通相關,所以這也是常考的主題。生活中常遇到的交通英文詞彙一定要會,例如:intersection (十字路口)、traffic (交通)、accident (事故)、cars being towed (汽車被拖走) 等等。

範 例

What is true about this picture?　　　　關於這張圖片的描述何者正確?

A. Traffic doesn't seem to be a problem.　　交通似乎不是個問題。

B. There's a traffic jam.　　　　　　　　現在塞車。

C. There was a traffic accident.　　　　　發生了交通事故。

D. The road is under construction.　　　　現在正在修路。

解析 1. 一聽到 What is true about this picture?,就知道要仔細聽每個選項,將不可能的答案先刪去。

　　　2. 關鍵字彙:traffic jam 是「塞車」、traffic accident 是「交通事故」、under construction 是「修路中」。

　　　3. 圖片是塞車的狀況,但我們不知原因,而選項 C 和 D 都有可能是造成塞車的原因,但是問題只是問此圖的狀況,所以最好的答案是 B。　　**答案** B

注意事項

請留意圖片中的交通狀況、交通號誌與車輛數目,還要注意圖片中是否有事故發生。

相關問句

1. How would you describe the traffic? (你如何描述交通狀況?)

2. How would you describe the road conditions? (你如何形容道路的狀況?)

3. Why is traffic congested on the freeway? (為什麼在高速公路上會塞車?)

▶ 圖片當中的重要詞彙

▶ 題型相關的單字與片語

traffic jam (n.)	塞車	road closed (phr.)	道路封閉
moving smoothly (phr.)	交通順暢	detour [`ditur] (n.)	繞道
construction [kən`strʌkʃən] (n.)	建設；建造	collision [kə`lɪʒən] (n.)	相撞
accident [`æksədənt] (n.)	事故	freeway [`frɪ͵we] (n.)	高速公路
congestion [kən`dʒɛstʃən] (n.)	擁擠	traffic light (n.)	交通號誌
transportation [͵trænspə`teʃən] (n.)	運輸工具	tow truck (n.)	拖吊車

題型 ❸ 事件題（Events）

常見的考題也包含了許多不同類型的室內和戶外活動，雖然大部分的圖片中都有人物出現，但是考題著重在事件發生的地點與細節上。

範 例

What is happening in the picture? 　　**圖片中正發生什麼事情？**

A. People are fishing in a river. 　　人們在河裡釣魚。

B. A boat race has begun. 　　划船比賽已經開始。

C. Ready, set, go! 　　預備、就位、開始！

D. The people look excited. 　　人們看起來很興奮。

解析 1. 聽到 What is happening...? 的關鍵問句時，就要分辨出這是事件題，是問事情的狀況。

2. 關鍵字彙：boat race 是「划船比賽」、Ready, set, go! 是「預備、就位、開始！」，所以選項 B 是最好的答案。　**答案** B

注意事項

要留意圖片中的事件發生原因與目的，也需要了解事件發生的人、事、時、地與物。

相關問句

1. Why would you go to this place?（你為什麼去這個地方？）

2. What do people do at a place like this?（人們都在類似這樣的地方做什麼事？）

3. What is about to happen in the picture?（圖片中即將發生什麼事？）

▶ 圖片當中的重要詞彙

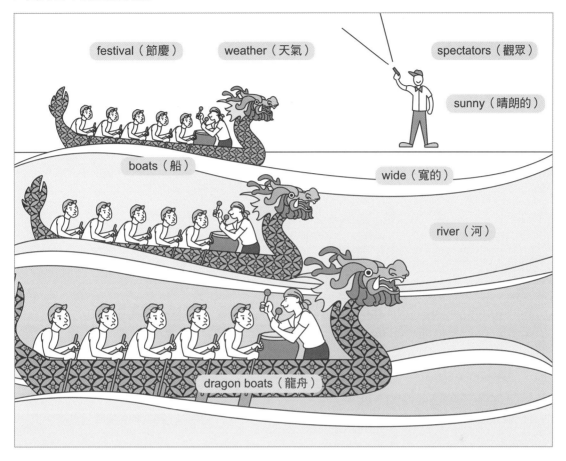

▶ 題型相關的單字與片語

stadium [ˋstedɪəm] (n.)	體育場	do a triathlon [traɪˋæθlɑn] (phr.)	三項運動
barbecue [ˋbɑrbɪkju] (n./v.)	烤肉	pond [pɑnd] (n.)	池塘
picnic [ˋpɪknɪk] (n.)	野餐	political rally (n.)	政治集會
concert [ˋkɑnsɚt] (n.)	演唱會	park [pɑrk] (n.)	公園
run a marathon (phr.)	跑馬拉松	bike race (n.)	自行車賽
wedding pictures (n.)	婚紗照	go hiking (phr.)	去登山健行

題型 ❹ 風景題（Scenery）

看到令人嘆為觀止的風景時，我們會想拍照留念，所以描述國家森林公園或是形容美麗風景的相關考題也是常考的問題。

 範　例

How would you describe this picture?　你會如何描述這張圖片？

A. People are fishing on the lake.　人們在湖上釣魚。

B. There's a lake with mountains in the background.　有一池湖水，背景有許多山。

C. People often vacation here.　人們常在這裡渡假。

D. A tribe used to live here by the lake.　有一個部落以前住在這裡的湖邊。

解析　1. 問句是考我們如何描述此圖，所以要用圖片聯想法來辨別圖中景物的名稱。

2. describe「描述」和 tribe「部落」是相似字，不要被混淆了。

3. 選項 C 和 D 都有可能出現於圖片中，但是依照圖片的情況，可知 B 是最佳的答案。

答案 B

注意事項

請留意圖片中的地點、人物，和人們來這裡的原因與從事什麼活動。

相關問句

1. What do most people like to do at a place like this?
（人們最喜歡來像這樣的地方做什麼？）

2. Why do people like to visit this kind of place?（為什麼人們喜歡來像這樣的地方？）

3. Would you recommend someone to visit here?（你會建議別人來這裡嗎？）

▶ 圖片當中的重要詞彙

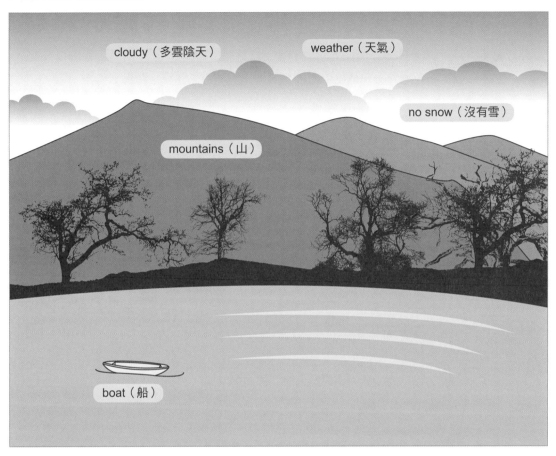

▶ 題型相關的單字與片語

lake [lek] (n.)	湖	countryside [`kʌntrɪˌsaɪd] (n.)	農村
mountain [`mauntṇ] (n.)	山	peaceful [`pisfəl] (adj.)	平靜的
valley [`vælɪ] (n.)	山谷	waterfall [`wɔtɚˌfɔl] (n.)	瀑布
beach [bitʃ] (n.)	海灘	river [`rɪvɚ] (n.)	河
ocean [`oʃən] (n.)	海洋	path [pæθ] (n.)	路徑
breathtaking [`brɛθˌtekɪŋ] (adj.)	令人屏息的	landscape [`lændˌskep] (n.)	景觀

題型實戰演練 ▶▶ 1-03

作答說明：每一圖畫有1到3個描述該圖的題目，每題請聽光碟放音機播出題目以及四
　　　　　個英語敘述之後，選出與所看到的圖畫最相符的答案。每題只播出一遍。

A Question 1

D Questions 4-5

B Question 2

E Question 6

C Question 3

F Questions 7-8

G Questions 9-10

I Questions 12-13

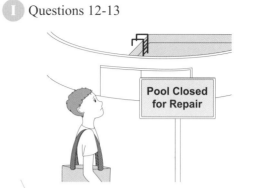

H Question 11

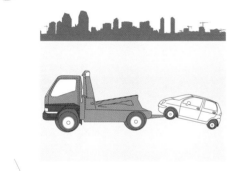

J Questions 14-15

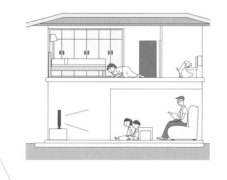

1-3 辨別物件圖片

基本觀念

物件圖片題型是大多數學生認為挑戰性較高的問題。也許是因為答案並不是非常明顯，題目也比較複雜一點，有時候要計算出價錢或是推算火車抵達的時間。加上答題的時間不變，所以難度會較高。物件圖片常見的主題包括：

1. **行程表與日曆**（Schedules and Calendars）
2. **地圖**（Maps）
3. **表格與圖表**（Charts and Graphs）
4. **購物項目**（Shopping Items）
5. **雜物項目**（Miscellaneous Items）
6. **天氣**（Weather）

常見問題

在看圖辨義中常考辨別物件的問句有以下這五種：

1. When can I make an appointment for this week?
   （這個星期我可以預約什麼時候？）
2. How much is the blouse?（這件女用上衣多少錢？）
3. Where is the clothing store located?（服裝店位於何處？）
4. Which train should Don take to get to Tainan before 2 p.m.?
   （唐要在下午 2 點前到台南，他應該搭哪一班火車？）
5. How's the weather today?（今天的天氣如何？）

學習過本單元的例子後，你將會用一個更寬廣的角度來看圖片中的物件，對題目的問句也會更了解，也會比較容易掌握關鍵字。

作答技巧

▶ 抓住關鍵字（Catching the Key Words）

當你快速瀏覽過圖片，找到主旨之後，就一定要仔細聆聽問題和答案選項，並且抓住關鍵字。每個選項中的關鍵字會幫助你刪去不相關的選項，找到正確的答案。即使你聽不懂問題，也可以藉由關鍵字找出和圖片相關聯的答案。

範　例

Which statement best describes the picture?　　**哪一項敘述最能描述該圖片？**

A.　A disastrous fire rages in a local zoo.　　恐怖的火災在當地的動物園肆虐。

B.　Someone started a fire.　　有人生火。

C.　Animals are running from a forest fire.　　動物從森林火災當中逃出。

D.　The animals are terrified of the fireworks.　　動物被煙火嚇到了。

解析　1.　不要因為聽到選項 A 中 disastrous「災難的」和 rages「肆虐」這兩個不熟悉的字就卡住而想要放棄，你一定聽得懂 zoo，所以可以判斷圖片中的背景並不是動物園，因此 A 不可選。

2.　你也許想大火的原因可能是有人施放煙火造成的，但圖片看不出有任何人，也無法辨別是否有人施放煙火，所以不可選 D。

3.　C 是正確答案，它很明顯地描述出圖片的狀況。　　 答案 C

題型介紹

題型 ❶ 行程表與日曆（Schedules and Calendars）

行程表和日曆當中包含了好多個訊息和時間、數字，要在很短的時間內讀懂並且回答問題不容易，但是只要看清楚圖片的類型、主要目的、標題或粗體字和時間數字，就不難回答，這類型的問題變化不多，大致上歸納為四種：

1.　**日曆（Calendars）**

2.　**每天的行事曆（Daily Planners）**

3.　**課表（Class Schedule）**

4.　**交通時刻表（Transportation Schedule）**

範 例

Bus Schedule Taichung to Taipei	Departs	Arrives
Bus 16	10:00	12:20
Bus 32	10:30	12:50
Bus 60	11:30	1:50
Bus 65	1:00	3:20

What bus should I take if I want to get to Taipei by 2 o'clock?

A. No bus arrives at 2 o'clock.

B. Bus #16 arrives in the early afternoon.

C. Bus #65 will get you there on time.

D. Bus #60 is your best choice.

如果我想要在兩點之前到達台北的話，應該要搭幾號公車？

沒有公車會在兩點抵達。

16 號公車在下午稍早時會抵達。

65 號公車會準時帶你到那裡。

60 號公車是你最佳的選擇。

解析 1. 問題是問「該搭哪部公車」，該抓住的關鍵字為 what bus 和 go to Taipei by 2 o'clock。

2. 請聽清楚 16 和 60，千萬不要搞混了。

3. 根據關鍵字找出在兩點之前到台北的火車，所以時間點最接近的答案是 D。

答案 D

相關問句

1. What are Jill's plans for tomorrow?（吉兒明天計畫做什麼？）

2. When can I make an appointment this week?（這週我可以預約什麼時候？）

3. On what date will Chris visit his family?（克里斯哪一天會去拜訪家人？）

關鍵字彙

plans [plænz] (n.)	計畫	on time (phr.)	準時
appointment [ə`pɔɪntmənt] (n.)	約定	around 2 o'clock (phr.)	兩點左右
schedule [`skɛdʒul] (n.)	時間表	be delayed (phr.)	被延遲
depart [dɪ`pɑrt] (v.)	離開	running late (phr.)	遲到
arrive [ə`raɪv] (v.)	抵達；到達	fit into my schedule (phr.)	符合我的時間表
available [ə`veləbḷ] (adj.)	有空的	date [det] (n.)	日期

題型 ❷ 地圖（Maps）

城市的街道圖是很常見的考題。一看到街道圖時，請做好準備可能會被問到某個特定地點的位置和其他地方的相對關係。如果是看到一張世界地圖或是某一個國家的地圖，就要留意和其他國家的相對位置或相異之處。

範 例

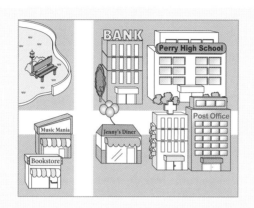

Where is the hospital?　　　　　　　　**醫院在哪裡？**

A. It's across from Music Mania.　　　　在音樂狂唱片行的對面。

B. It's between the post office and Jenny's　　在郵局和珍妮餐廳的中間。
Diner.

C. It's beside the park.　　　　　　　　在公園旁邊。

D. It's in front of the bank.　　　　　　在銀行前面。

解析 1. 問題是問醫院的「位置」，所以要注意和圖上其他建築物的相對位置。
2. 只要聽清楚方位用語，就可以找到答案是 B。　　　　**答案** B

相關問句

1. Where is the library?（圖書館在哪裡？）

2. Where is Hualien located?（花蓮的位置在哪裡？）

3. Can you give me directions to the bus station?（你可以指引我去公車站的方向嗎？）

4. Can you tell me how to get to the train station?（你可以告訴我該如何去火車站嗎？）

關鍵字彙

directions [dəˋrɛkʃənz] (n.)	方向	west [wɛst] (n.)	西方
is located (phr.)	位於	walk down the street (phr.)	順著街道走
get to (phr.)	到達	two blocks (n.)	兩個街口
north [nɔrθ] (n.)	北方	intersection [͵ɪntɚˋsɛkʃən] (n.)	十字路口

south [sauθ] (n.)	南方	take a right (phr.)	往右轉
east [ist] (n.)	東方	head north (phr.)	往北走

題型 ❸ 表格與圖表（Charts and Graphs）

最常考的圖表類型是家族樹，一定要弄清楚所有家庭成員的稱謂、名字與相互關係。圓餅圖和其他圖表也是常考題型，記得要留意英文數據的表達法，例如：比例和百分率的說法。

範 例

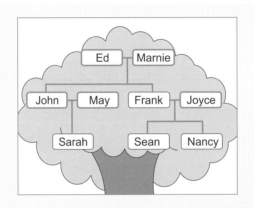

Which statement is true about this family tree? 關於這個家族樹的敘述何者正確？

A. Ed and Marnie have three grandchildren.　艾德和馬麗妮有三個孫子。

B. Sarah has two aunts.　莎拉有兩個姑姑。

C. Frank has one child.　法蘭克有一個小孩。

D. Frank's father-in-law is Ed.　法蘭克的岳父是艾德。

解析 由圖片得知此題目是問「家族樹」，要仔細聆聽選項並分辨家庭成員的關係。

答案 A

相關問句

1. What percentage of people drive a car?（有多少比例的人開車？）

2. Who is Janet's uncle?（珍妮特的叔叔是誰？）

3. What do people prefer doing the most on weekends?（週末時人們最喜歡做什麼事情？）

關鍵字彙

grandpa [`grændpɑ] (n.)	爺爺	grandchild [`grænd‚tʃaɪld] (n.)	孫子
grandma [`grændmɑ] (n.)	奶奶	grandson [`grænd‚sʌn] (n.)	男孫
son [sʌn] (n.)	兒子	granddaughter [`græn‚dɔtə] (n.)	孫女
daughter [`dɔtə] (n.)	女兒	cousin [`kʌzn̩] (n.)	堂或表兄弟姊妹

uncle [ˋʌŋkl] (n.)	叔叔	father-in-law (n.)	公公；岳父
aunt [ænt] (n.)	阿姨	mother-in-law (n.)	婆婆；岳母
quarter [ˋkwɔrtɚ] (n.)	四分之一	third [θɝd] (n.)	三分之一
half [hælf] (n.)	一半	percentage [pɚˋsɛntɪdʒ] (n.)	百分比

題型 ④ 購物項目（Shopping Items）

如果你看到購物商品項目時，心中一定要準備開始計算，因為一定會考和數字有關的問題。

請聽 CD，並分辨下列數字的讀音。 🎧 1-04

1.	thirteen [ˋθɝˋtin]	13	thirty [ˋθɝtɪ]	30
2.	fourteen [ˋforˋtin]	14	forty [ˋfɔrtɪ]	40
3.	fifteen [ˋfɪfˋtin]	15	fifty [ˋfɪftɪ]	50
4.	sixteen [ˋsɪksˋtin]	16	sixty [ˋsɪkstɪ]	60
5.	seventeen [ˏsɛvnˋtin]	17	seventy [ˋsɛvn̩tɪ]	70
6.	eighteen [ˋeˋtin]	18	eighty [ˋetɪ]	80
7.	nineteen [ˋnaɪnˋtin]	19	ninety [ˋnaɪntɪ]	90

請注意聽英文數字的結尾音如果是 ty 時，重音是放在第一音節。若是 teen 結尾的話，強調最後一個音節。

> ✎ 範 例

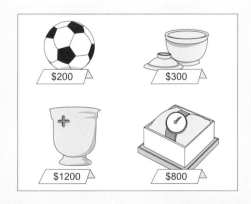

How much does the bowl cost?   **這個碗多少錢？**

A. It is cheaper than the ball.   它比球便宜。

B. It's only $200.   只要 200 元。

C. It costs $300.   300 元。

D. It's 50% off the regular price.   平時價錢的一半。

解析　1. 題目是問碗的「價錢」。
　　　2. 圖中得知碗是 300 元，答案要選 C。　　　　　答案 C

相關問句

1. Which item is the most expensive?（哪一個物品最昂貴？）

2. Which item is cheaper than the bowl?（哪一個物品比碗便宜？）

3. How much does the ball cost?（這顆球要多少錢？）

關鍵字彙

item [ˋaɪtəm] (n.)	項目	cheaper than (phr.)	比⋯便宜
cost [kɔst] (n.) (v.)	花費	cheapest (adj.)	最便宜的
can afford to buy (phr.)	買得起	most expensive (phr.)	最昂貴的
on sale (phr.)	特價	least expensive (phr.)	最不貴的
attractive [əˋtræktɪv] (adj.)	有吸引力的	more expensive than (phr.)	比⋯貴
It's a bargain! (phr.)	很划算！	not as expensive as (phr.)	不像⋯那麼貴

題型 ⑤ 雜物項目（Miscellaneous Items）

看到圖片中有很多雜物品項時，例如一張有擺設家具的房間，或是有很多遊樂器材的遊樂場。請先看過所有的物品與其他物品的相對位置，若是牆上有時鐘或是天空出現太陽或月亮，就可能會考時間問題，切記要熟悉時間的不同說法。

範　例

Which item is on the top left-hand corner of the desk?　　　**在書桌的左上角是什麼東西？**

　A. There are many items on the desk.　　　書桌上有許多東西。

　B. The watch is on the left side of the desk.　　　手錶在書桌的左邊。

C. The lamp. 　　　　　　　　　　　　燈。

D. Yes, the person is left-handed. 　　　對，那人是左撇子。

解析 1. 題目是問桌子「左上角的物品」。
2. 請留意 left-hand corner「左邊的角落」和 選項 D 中的 left-handed「左撇子」不一樣，所以答案是 C。　　　　　　　　　　答案 C

相關問句

1. Which item is on the bottom right-hand corner of the picture?
（圖片的右下角有什麼東西？）

2. What time is it?（現在是幾點？）

3. What's the midnight snack for tonight?（今晚的宵夜是什麼？）

關鍵字彙

a quarter after ten	十點十五分	ten to ten	九點五十分
a quarter to ten	九點四十五	ten after ten	十點十分
half past ten	十點半	ten o two	十點零二分

題型 ⑥ 天氣圖（Weather）

有關天氣和季節的題型也很常考，一定要知道如何描述不同的氣候條件和自然災害，也要會看天氣預測圖。

範 例

What's the weather like? 　　　　　天氣如何？

A. It's windy and rainy. 　　　　　　　多風有雨。

B. It's a balmy summer day. 　　　　　溫和的夏日。

49

C. It's foggy.   多霧的。

D. It's going to clear up soon.   不久就要放晴了。

 1. 題目是問「天氣」。

2. 要聽懂的關鍵字為 balmy「溫和的」、foggy「多霧的」、clear up「轉晴」。

3. 從圖片可知是下雨的天氣，所以答案選 A。   答案 A

【相關問句】

1. What is the best day for a bike ride?（哪一天是騎自行車的好日子？）

2. What might someone say about this kind of weather?
    （這樣的天氣人們可能會說什麼？）

3. Which season is this?（這是什麼季節？）

【關鍵字彙】

rainy [ˋrenɪ] (adj.)	下雨的	typhoon [taɪˋfun] (n.)	颱風
sunny [ˋsʌnɪ] (adj.)	晴朗的	smog [smɑg] (n.)	煙霧
foggy [ˋfɑgɪ] (adj.)	多霧的	pollution [pəˋluʃən] (n.)	污染
windy [ˋwɪndɪ] (adj.)	有風的	climate change (n.)	氣候變化
flood [flʌd] (n.)	水災	It's pouring.	下大雨。
earthquake [ˋɝθˏkwek] (n.)	地震	It's raining cats and dogs.	下傾盆大雨。
balmy [ˋbɑmɪ] (adj.)	溫和的	It's sprinkling.	下毛毛雨。

作答說明：每一圖畫有1到3個描述該圖的題目，每題請聽光碟放音機播出題目以及四個英語敘述之後，選出與所看到的圖畫最相符的答案。每題只播出一遍。

A Question 1

D Question 5

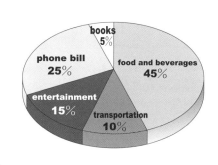

B Questions 2-3

Dentist Schedule						
	May 3 Mon.	May 4 Tue.	May 5 Wed.	May 6 Thur.	May 7 Fri.	May 8 Sat.
1:00-2:00	Mr. Hill	Mr. Fong		Surgery		Surgery
2:00-3:00	Kim	Mr. Song	Andrew	Surgery	Winnie	Surgery
3:00-4:00	Kevin	Sam	Mrs. Li	Tiffany	Mrs. Hu	Surgery
6:00-7:00	Mrs. Lin	Surgery	OFF	Rita		OFF
7:00-8:00	Mr. Chen	Surgery	OFF	Mr. Wu	William	OFF

E Question 6

C Question 4

Weather Forecast		
Mon.	Rainy	
Tue.	Rainy	
Wed.	Sunny	
Thur.	Sunny	
Fri.	Cloudy / light showers	

F Questions 7-8

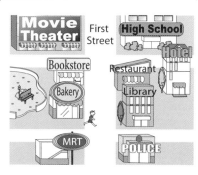

G Question 9

H Questions 10-11

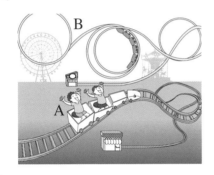

I Question 12

J Question 13

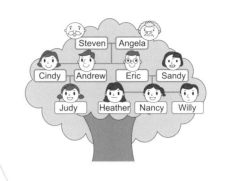

K Question 14

L Question 15

第一部分聽力答題技巧複習

學習完第一部分，你是否已經學會了在「看圖辨義」這個部分的所有答題技巧呢？請在你已經學會的方格中打勾。

看圖辨義的答題技巧	✔
1. 聆聽題目之前，我會先辨別圖片的題型，並且預測題目。	
2. 聆聽題目之前，我會分析圖片，找出相關聯的字彙與片語，同時留意圖片中的人名、標誌、招牌或是數字。	
3. 聆聽題目之前，我會確認題目題數與圖片的配對。	
4. 聆聽題目時，我會聽清楚題目的指示和問句的疑問詞。	
5. 聆聽題目時，我會快速地掌握主旨、抓到關鍵字、刪去不相關的選項，並且找到答案。	
6. 聆聽題目時，我會仔細辨別相似音、同音異形字和多義字。	
7. 聆聽題目時，我可以聽懂連音，與句子中的重音。	
8. 聆聽完題目之後，我會快速地找到答案，當機立斷，不耽誤下一題的時間。	

問答

作答說明

以下是全民英檢中級聽力測驗第二部分的作答說明與題目範例。事先熟記作答說明與題型，考試時就可以略過作答說明，往下瀏覽題目，以提高得分。

第二部分：問答

共 15 題。每題請聽光碟放音機播出的英語問句或直述句之後，從試題冊上 A、B、C、D 四個回答或回應中，選出一個最適合者作答。每題只播出一遍。

例 （聽）I like your haircut.　　　　　（看）A. Usually once a month.

　　　　　　　　　　　　　　　　　　　　B. I cut it.

　　　　　　　　　　　　　　　　　　　　C. Thanks.

　　　　　　　　　　　　　　　　　　　　D. My hairdresser is cute.

正確答案應為 C，請在答案紙上塗黑作答。

解析 本題是讚美別人的直述句，回應別人的最佳方式是感謝。　　　**答案** C

應考策略

Step 1 快速瀏覽選項（Scan the choices.）

很快地看過四個選項，並從中找出共同點，以便預測題目的主題。請留意選項中的時態，如果出現兩種以上的時態，那麼時態就可能是考題的關鍵。

Step 2 聆聽題目並且辨別題型（Identify the type of question.）

仔細聽清楚題目，分辨出題目是疑問句或是直述句，辨別出題目的意圖，如此一來就可以輕鬆掌握答題的方向。

Step 3 掌握關鍵字（Listen for key words.）

聽清楚關鍵字，特別注意「主詞」、「動詞」和「受詞」，並且確認句子的時態與名詞的單複數。

Step 4 善用刪去法（Rule out answers you know are not correct.）

將與題目主題無關的選項、相似音字的陷阱、同音異義字和不可能的選項先刪除，以增加答對的機率。

Step 5 選出正確的答案（Choose the correct answer.）

找出最符合題目的回應，在答案卡上正確的答案劃記。

常考題型

此部分的題目型態有兩大類：疑問句與直述句。疑問句的部分包括了 Yes/No 問句、Wh-問句（Who, What, When, Where, Why）和 How 問句。而直述句的部分主要是考題目的「主旨」、「目的」與「意圖」。

本部分根據常考題型的回應方向，歸納成下列五種：

- ■ 2-1 建議的回應
- ■ 2-2 情境的回應
- ■ 2-3 地點的回應
- ■ 2-4 態度的回應
- ■ 2-5 意見的回應

2-1 建議的回應

基本觀念

提出建議是常考的題型之一，因為在我們的日常生活中，常常會提供自己的意見給別人。例如出去遊玩時，我們需要聽別人的建議。當朋友或家人有困難或要做重要的決定時，都會想要聽聽我們的意見。在這個單元當中，我們將要學習一些常見的提出建議方式和對方可能的回應方式。以下要介紹兩種提出建議的主要方式，第一種是以問句來表示，第二種是直述句。請參考下面的範例：

範例 1

Why don't we get something to eat?   **我們何不吃點東西？**

A. Sure, turn up the heat.   好啊，把溫度提高一點。

B. Where do you want to go?   你想要去哪裡呀？

C. I ate beef and noodles for lunch.   我午餐吃牛肉麵。

D. We really don't need to buy a heater.   我們真的不需要買暖氣。

解析 1. 關鍵字是 get something to eat「吃點東西」，也就是對接下來要做的事情提出建議。

2. 運用刪去法可得知選項 C 不是答案。

3. 選項 A 和 D 中 heat「高溫」、heater「暖氣」是相近音，是測試你是否專心聽，也非正確答案。由這句的語意得知選項 B 是正確答案。 **答案** B

範例 2

Let's go to the travel agency to book our flight.   **讓我們去旅行社預訂機票。**

A. I can buy a book for the flight.   我可以買一本書在飛機上看。

B. I'm afraid of flying.   我害怕坐飛機。

C. That sounds like a good idea.   這聽起來像一個好主意。

D. It's next to the post office.   它是在郵局的旁邊。

解析 1. 這題考是否聽懂了關鍵動詞 book「訂票」的意思。

2. 選項 A 中的 book 是名詞，所以不選。

3. 選項 B 和 D 和題目的意思不符合。選項 C 才是最恰當的。 **答案** C

▶ 提出建議的句型與回應

在英語中，提出建議的句型有很多種，有可能用直述句，也有可能用問句來表達，以下介紹一些常考的建議句型，和可能的應答方式。每一個句型提供了正面的（+）與負面的（-）回應方式，如此可以培養學生迅速理解句子的語意功能，與快速地選出答案的作答能力。

1 直述句（Statements）

1. **Let's** go see a movie.	（**讓我們**去看場電影。）	
+	Great idea!	（好主意！）
	What movie do you want to see?	（你想看什麼電影？）
	That sounds good.	（聽起來不錯喔。）
-	I don't think I can go.	（我想我不能去。）
	I'll take a rain check.	（改天，下一次吧。）
	I'm broke.	（我破產了。）

2. **You'd better** not work so hard.	（你**最好**不要工作得那麼辛苦。）	
+	You're right.	（你說得對。）
	I should take a break.	（我應該休息一下。）
	I appreciate your concern.	（我很感謝你的關心。）
-	I have to finish this project.	（我必須要完成這計畫案。）
	I have no choice.	（我別無選擇。）
	If I don't, I won't finish on time.	（如果我不這樣做，就無法按時完成。）

3. You **ought to** visit your grandmother more often.	（你**應該**更常去看你的外婆。）	
+	I know I should.	（我知道我應該這樣。）
	Yes, I should go see her soon.	（是的，我應該很快就會去看看她。）
	How about we visit her next week?	（我們下個星期去看她怎麼樣？）
-	I'm too busy right now.	（我現在太忙了。）
	I can't find the time.	（我沒有時間去。）
	Maybe next week.	（也許下個星期吧。）

4. You **ought not to** disturb him when he's sleeping.	（當他正在睡覺時，你**不應該**去打擾他。）	
+	Whatever you say.	（你說什麼都好。）
	I agree.	（我同意。）
	I wouldn't think of it.	（我才不會這樣想。）

-	It's okay.	（沒關係。）
	I disagree.	（我不同意。）
	Don't worry about it.	（不要擔心。）

5.	**If I were you, I would** find a new job before I quit.	（**如果我是你，我會**在離職前先找到新工作。）
+	That's a good idea.	（這是一個好主意。）
	I think you're right.	（我覺得你說的對。）
	Yeah, that's the smart thing to do.	（是啊，那是聰明的做法。）
-	But I can't stand this job.	（但是，我不能忍受這個工作。）
	No, I'm going to quit today.	（不，我今天就要辭職。）
	Mind your own business.	（別管閒事。）

6.	**I suggest** you listen to your teachers.	（我**建議**你聽老師們的話。）
+	I know.	（我知道。）
	I like your suggestion.	（我喜歡你的建議。）
	They do know what's best for me.	（他們確實知道什麼對我最好。）
-	Not this time.	（這次不行。）
	I have to make my own decisions.	（我得自己做決定。）
	You must be joking!	（你在開玩笑吧！）

7.	You **could** date my sister.	（你**可以**和我姐姐約會。）
+	That would be awesome.	（那將會很棒。）
	Are you pulling my leg?	（你在開玩笑嗎？）
	Are you serious?	（你是說真的嗎？）
-	I don't think that's a good idea.	（我想這不是個好主意。）
	Not in a million years.	（門都沒有！）
	Dream on!	（你作夢！）

8.	We **should** visit the museum before we leave.	（離開前，我們**應該**要參觀博物館。）
+	Yes, we should.	（對，我們應該要。）
	Why didn't I think of that?	（為什麼我沒有想到這一點？）
	Now you're talking!	（這才像話！）
-	I don't think we have time.	（我覺得我們沒有時間。）
	Maybe some other time.	（也許改天吧。）
	Museums are so boring.	（博物館那麼無聊。）

59

9. We **shouldn't** eat so much junk food.　　（我們**不應該**吃這麼多垃圾食物。）

+ I know.　　（我知道。）

　You're right.　　（你說得對。）

　I am getting chubby.　　（我越來越胖了。）

- It's so delicious.　　（真好吃。）

　I can do whatever I want.　　（我可以做任何我想做的事。）

　Speak for yourself.　　（那只不過是你自己一廂情願的想法。）

❷ 問句（Questions）

1. **Why don't** we take a taxi?　　（我們**何不**搭計程車？）

+ Good idea!　　（好主意。）

　Yeah, it's too far to walk.　　（是啊，走路去太遠了。）

　Why not?　　（為什麼不呢？）

- No, let's take a bus.　　（不，讓我們坐公車吧。）

　It's too expensive.　　（太貴了。）

　Bad idea.　　（爛點子。）

2. **What about** going to Orchid Island for vacation?　　（我們去蘭嶼渡假**好不好**？）

+ Great suggestion!　　（很棒的建議！）

　That's a fine suggestion.　　（這是一個很好的建議。）

　That's one idea.　　（這是一個好想法。）

- I'll have to think about it.　　（我要想一想。）

　I don't think so.　　（我可不這麼認為。）

　I'd rather go abroad this summer.　　（我寧願今年夏天出國去玩。）

3. **How about** we meet at 8 o'clock?　　（我們八點見面**怎麼樣**？）

+ I'll see you then.　　（到時候見。）

　That's fine by me.　　（這個時間我可以。）

　No problem. See you then.　　（沒問題。到時候見。）

- How about 7:30?　　（七點半，怎麼樣？）

　Sorry, I can't make it that early.　　（對不起，我沒辦法那麼早。）

　I'm busy then.　　（那個時間我正在忙。）

作答技巧

技巧 ❶ 辨別相似音（Pronunciation Pairs）

英文中有一些字拼法相近，就連發音也聽起來很像，如果聽錯了就會造成誤解，請參考下面這個有趣的例子。

A: Is your locker huge like mine?	A：你的置物櫃和我的一樣大嗎？
B: No! She's not huge!	B：不！她不是很大！
A: What?	A：什麼？
B: My girlfriend is slim!	B：我的女朋友很纖細！
A: I said *locker*.	A：我是說置物櫃。
B: Oh, I thought you said *lover*.	B：哦，我以為你是說情人。

在全民英檢中級聽力測驗中，相似音的考題是很常見的題目。這些相似音的字組聽起來很像，一不小心就會弄錯，造成選錯答案的情況，因此一定要學會辨別相似音。除此之外，也要將整個句子的文法架構列入考量，如此就會更清楚知道這個字是否為片語，或者該字的詞性為何，減少因為聽錯字而誤解的機率。

▶ 常見的相似音字組 🎧 **1-06**

1.	assistant [əˋsɪstənt] (n.) 助理	assistance [əˋsɪstəns] (n.) 協助
2.	back [bæk] (n.) 背部	bike [baɪk] (n.) 腳踏車
3.	ball [bɔl] (n.) 球	bowl [bol] (n.) 碗
4.	bud [bʌd] (n.) 花苞	bird [bɝd] (n.) 鳥
5.	cars [kɑrz] (n.) 車子	cards [kɑrdz] (n.) 牌；卡片
6.	cheap [tʃip] (adj.) 便宜的	jeep [dʒip] (n.) 吉普車
7.	cooler [ˋkulɚ] (n.) 冰桶	color [ˋkʌlɚ] (n.) 顏色
8.	cup [kʌp] (n.) 杯子	cop [kɑp] (n.) 警察
9.	door [dor] (n.) 門	more [mor] (adj.) 更多的
10.	eight [et] (n.) 八	late [let] (adj.) 遲的
11.	facts [fækts] (n.) 真相	fax [fæks] (n.) 傳真
12.	fair [fɛr] (adj.) 公平的	far [fɑr] (adj.) 遠的
13.	free [fri] (adj.) 免費的	three [θri] (n.) 三
14.	glass [glæs] (n.) 玻璃杯	class [klæs] (n.) 班級
15.	gull [gʌl] (n.) 海鷗	girl [gɝl] (n.) 女孩

16.	hard [hɑrd] (adj.) 硬的	heart [hɑrt] (n.) 心
17.	hat [hæt] (n.) 帽子	hot [hɑt] (adj.) 熱的
18.	hear [hɪr] (v.) 聽到	hire [haɪr] (v.) 雇用
19.	hurt [hɜt] (adj.) 受傷的	heart [hɑrt] (n.) 心
20.	hut [hʌt] (n.) 小草屋	hurt [hɜt] (v.) 受傷
21.	key [ki] (n.) 鑰匙	keep [kip] (v) 保持
22.	move [muv] (v.) 移動	movies [muvɪz] (n.) 電影
23.	pen [pɛn] (n.) 筆	pan [pæn] (n.) 煎鍋
24.	planes [plenz] (n.) 飛機	plans [plænz] (n.) 計畫
25.	please [pliz] (adv.) 請	police [pəˋlis] (n.) 警察
26.	price [praɪs] (n.) 價錢	prize [praɪz] (n.) 獎品
27.	saw [sɔ] (v.) 看見的過去式	sew [so] (v.) 縫合
28.	sea [si] (n.) 海	she [ʃi] (n.) 她
29.	sell [sɛl] (v.) 賣	shell [ʃɛl] (n.) 貝殼
30.	send [sɛnd] (v.) 寄	sign [saɪn] (v.) 簽名；(n.) 標誌
31.	sick [sɪk] (adj.) 生病的	thick [θɪk] (adj.) 厚的
32.	skirt [skɜt] (n.) 裙子	shirt [ʃɜt] (n.) 襯衫
33.	suck [sʌk] (v.) 吮吸	sock [sɑk] (n.) 襪子
34.	taxes [ˋtæksɪz] (n.) 稅	taxi [ˋtæksɪ] (n.) 計程車
35.	trunk [trʌŋk] (n.) 後車箱	truck [trʌk] (n.) 卡車
36	two nights [tu naɪts] (n.) 兩晚	tonight [təˋnaɪt] (n.) 今晚
37.	vote [vot] (v.) 投票	boat [bot] (n.) 船
38.	walk [wɔk] (v.) 走路	work [wɜk] (n.) 工作
39.	way [we] (n.) 方式	away [əˋwe] (adv.) 離開
40.	won't tell [wont tɛl] 不會說	hotel [hoˋtɛl] (n.) 飯店

當你學習本書時，請練習在對話內容中標示重點，提醒自己該注意的地方，例如單字的詞性或是片語用法。請參考以下例子：

1. Why not vote for Mr. Wang this year?（為什麼今年不選王先生呢？）

   解析 boat 不能當作動詞，所以這個字應該是 vote「投票；選舉」。

2. Should we make another bowl of fruit salad?（我們應該要再做一碗水果沙拉嗎？）

   解析 不可能是一「球（ball）」沙拉，所以一定是一「碗（bowl）」沙拉。

3. Let's see if we can sell these at the beach. （看看我們是否可以在沙灘上賣這些東西。）

解析 情態動詞 can 之後只能接現在簡單式動詞，不能接名詞，所以我們知道這個字是 sell「賣」而不是 shell「貝殼」。

4. How about buying him that nice shirt?（買那件不錯的襯衫給他怎麼樣？）

解析 我想你不會買給男生 skirt「裙子」吧，所以一定是 shirt「襯衫」。

技巧 ❷ 辨別容易混淆的同形異音字（Homographs）

在聽力測驗中，同形異音字也常造成學生們的困擾。同形異音字就像是中文的破音字，也就是拼法一樣，但是唸法不一樣，意思也完全不同。請在聽 CD 之前，先試著自己唸出下面的句子與單字。

請聽 CD，並辨別下列的單字發音。 🎧 **1-07**

I know this might sound like a **minute** problem, and you may be **content** to just overlook it, but if you want to **perfect** your reading, I must **object**.

▶ 常見的同形異音字組 🎧 **1-08**

	單字	詞性	音標	意思		單字	詞性	音標	意思
1.	bow	(v.)	[baʊ]	鞠躬	8.	excuse	(v.)	[ɪkˋskjuz]	允許離開
		(n.)	[bo]	弓			(n.)	[ɪkˋskjus]	藉口
2.	close	(v.)	[kloz]	關上	9.	lead	(v.)	[lid]	領導
		(adj.)	[klos]	接近的			(n.)	[lɛd]	鉛
3.	conflict	(v.)	[kənˋflɪkt]	衝突	10.	minute	(n.)	[ˋmɪnɪt]	分鐘
		(n.)	[ˋkɑnflɪkt]	爭執			(adj.)	[maɪˋnjut]	微小的
4.	content	(n.)	[ˋkɑntɛnt]	內容	11.	moderate	(adj.)	[ˋmɑdərɪt]	適度的
		(adj.)	[kənˋtɛnt]	滿意的			(v.)	[ˋmɑdə͵ret]	減輕
5.	desert	(v.)	[dɪˋzɝt]	遺棄	12.	object	(v.)	[əbˋdʒɛkt]	反對
		(n.)	[ˋdɛzɚt]	沙漠			(n.)	[ˋɑbdʒɪkt]	事物
6.	dove	(n.)	[dʌv]	鴿子	13.	perfect	(adj.)	[ˋpɝfɪkt]	完美的
		(v.)	[dov]	跳水（過去式）			(v.)	[pɚˋfɛkt]	使完美
7.	drawer	(n.)	[drɔr]	抽屜	14.	produce	(n.)	[ˋprodjus]	農產品
		(n.)	[ˋdrɔɚ]	畫者			(v.)	[prəˋdjus]	生產

單 字	詞性	音標	意思	單 字	詞性	音標	意思
15. read	(v.)	[rid]	閱讀	18. tear	(v.)	[tɛr]	撕破
	(v.)	[rɛd]	閱讀 (過去式)		(n.)	[tɪr]	眼淚
16. record	(n.)	[ˋrɛkəd]	唱片	19. wind	(v.)	[waɪnd]	纏繞
	(v.)	[rɪˋkɔrd]	記錄		(n.)	[wɪnd]	風
17. resume	(v.)	[rɪˋzjum]	恢復	20. wound	(n.)	[wund]	傷口
	(n.)	[͵rɛzjuˋme]	簡歷		(v.)	[waʊnd]	纏繞 (過去式)

 範例 1

What would you like on your dessert?	**你的甜點上面想要放什麼？**
A. I like many things that live in the desert.	我喜歡很多生長在沙漠中的東西。
B. I recommend the Sahara desert.	我推薦撒哈拉大沙漠。
C. How about some chocolate sauce?	來一些巧克力醬好嗎？
D. I had the carrot cake.	我吃了胡蘿蔔蛋糕。

 1. 這題考的是單字，測試是否聽懂問句的關鍵字 dessert「甜點」，千萬不要以為是 desert「沙漠」。

2. 選項 A 和 B 都是在說沙漠的事所以不可選。此題答案要選 C。 **答案** C

 範例 2

She left the party for no apparent reason.	**她沒有明顯的理由就離開了派對。**
A. My parents weren't there, either.	我的父母也不在那裡。
B. She should have turned right.	她剛剛應該要右轉的。
C. Maybe she was tired.	也許她累了。
D. It'll end around midnight.	大約到午夜的時候就會結束了。

 1. 要聽懂的字是 apparent「明顯的」，它和選項 A 的 parents 聽起來相似，但是意思差很遠。

2. 題目中的 left 是動詞「離開」的意思，而不是「左邊」，所以選項 B 不考慮。

3. 選項 D 和題目不相關，也不對。選項 C 表達出對題目的回應最合理，所以答案選 C。 **答案** C

作答說明：每題請聽光碟放音機播出一英語問句或直述句之後，從試題冊上A、B、
C、D四個回答或回應中，選出一個最適合者作答。每題只播出一遍。

1
A. Where is it?
B. Which girl are you talking about?
C. I don't have any paper.
D. I'm too shy.

2
A. Is she okay?
B. I know. I should go.
C. I heard he loves it there.
D. He works 40 hours a week.

3
A. Oh, I like this skirt.
B. I'm not in the mood.
C. Sure, I'll read it.
D. I prefer the black one.

4
A. That's a great idea!
B. Yes, I went there last summer.
C. My parents have been there.
D. I can take a vacation in July.

5
A. I don't have much extra money.
B. I want to learn how to speak French.
C. Yes, I should swim more.
D. The XL size T-shirts are too big.

6
A. We had dumplings last night.
B. I'll set the table.
C. I'm glad you could make it for dinner.
D. Yes, her room is a dump.

7
A. Okay, I'll start work on Monday.
B. Yes, you're a lot like me.
C. I agree. I can find a better job.
D. Sure, I'll take it home.

8
A. You're right. It'll be safe there.
B. I don't think it's better.
C. We should be safe inside.
D. But I don't love her.

9
A. Yeah, I went yesterday.
B. I hate having nightmares.
C. We can eat some stinky tofu!
D. I often go to the night market.

10
A. Are you crazy?
B. It's difficult to say good-bye.
C. I've never been there.
D. No, her neck feels fine.

2-2 情境的回應

基本觀念

在考試當中，有關情境的題型有很多種，大部分都是發生在日常生活中的情境，例如：去銀行辦事，或是打電話給朋友等等。在日常生活中，要試著練習將每天所聽到的事情翻譯成英文，只要養成這個習慣，便可以快速學會很多實用的英文片語和句型，不論是在準備考試，或是用英文溝通，都會有很大的幫助。

範例 1

Why are you late this morning?	**你今天早上為什麼遲到了？**
A. I ate a sandwich for breakfast.	我早餐吃了一個三明治。
B. Sorry, I'm late.	對不起，我遲到了。
C. Don't tell the boss.	不要告訴老闆。
D. I was caught in traffic.	我遇上塞車了。

解析 1. 本題的疑問詞是 why，所以答題關鍵在於找出最合理的理由。
2. 選項 D 的答案最佳，因為有提供遲到的原因，選項 A 中的 ate「吃」和 late「遲到」是混淆字。　　　　**答案** D

範例 2

I ran into my ex-girlfriend in the lobby.	**我在大廳遇到我的前女友。**
A. Did you say sorry?	你有說對不起嗎？
B. I'm sure she was surprised to see you.	我肯定她看到你一定很驚訝。
C. She's in college now.	她現在在唸大學。
D. They have very cozy couches.	他們有非常舒適的沙發。

解析 1. 本題的關鍵字是 ran into「巧遇」和 ex-girlfriend「前女友」。
2. 巧遇到前女友的心情應該是驚訝與尷尬，所以合乎邏輯的正確回應是 B。其他選項都不合理。　　　　**答案** B

作答技巧

技巧 ❶ 時間和時態的表達（Time Expressions and Tenses）

英文的「時態」是和中文語法最不一樣的地方，所以英文動詞會因為事件發生的時間而變化，也就是說，我們只要聽清楚時態，就會明白事件發生的時間，也會更了解說話者的意思。在聽力考試當中，最常考的題型就是「時態和時間的表達」。一旦你熟悉了所有的時態與時間用語，你就會發現選出正確的答案很容易。讓我們來看看下面的例子。

▶ 現在簡單式的表達法

現在簡單式大部分是用在 ❶ 陳述現在的事實、習慣、態度、想法、觀念和感受等等。
❷ 大自然的變化與不變的真理。
❸ 也可以表示未來的計畫或安排。

相關例句

1. I work **every** morning until 11 a.m.（我每天早上工作到上午 11 點。）
2. **Do** they **have** your consent?（他們是否得到你的允許？）
3. **Don't** you think her excuse is ridiculous?（你不覺得她的藉口很荒謬嗎？）
4. Allan **doesn't** smoke anymore.（艾倫不再抽煙了。）

範 例

It's not appropriate for Nancy to call so late.	**南西這麼晚打電話來是不恰當的。**
A. I'll let her know tomorrow.	我明天會讓她知道。
B. I didn't call Nancy.	我沒有打電話給南西。
C. She already knows it's appropriate.	她已經知道這是恰當的。
D. You're right. She should try to call later.	你是對的。她應該試著晚一點再打電話。

解析 1. 這個敘述是用現在式的時態，表明南西這麼晚打電話的習慣或事情是不恰當的。

2. 選項 B 不正確，因為是南西打電話來的。選項 C 如果是用 inappropriate「不恰當」的話，就是正確的答案。

3. 選項 D 要她更晚打電話，只會將問題更加惡化，所以不正確。正確的回應是 A。

答案 A

▶ 進行式的表達法

現在進行式是用來表示 **❶** 現在正在進行的動作或是即將要發生的事情。

❷ 表示已經排定的未來計畫。

【相關例句】

1. You're not supposed to be writing your essay **now**.（你不應該現在寫你的論文。）

2. Henry is studying finance **right now**.（亨利現在正在研讀金融。）

3. She's assisting customers **at the moment**.（她此刻正在協助客戶。）

4. I don't enjoy hanging around with them because they are **always** complaining.
（我不喜歡和他們在一起，因為他們總是在抱怨。）

【範　例】

They're announcing the winners now.	他們現在正在宣布優勝者。
A. They should tell them to stop whining.	他們應該告訴他們要停止抱怨了。
B. I was surprised that Jeremy won.	我感到驚訝的是傑若米贏了。
C. I hope we win!	希望我們會贏！
D. Okay, I'll make the announcement.	好的，我會宣布。

【解析】 1. 由現在進行式的時態我們可以得知，目前正在宣布，而名單尚未揭曉，所以選項 A 和 B 都不對。

2. 要聽清楚 winners「優勝者」和 whining「抱怨」是兩個不同的字。

3. 選項 D 中出現了和題目相近的字 announcement「宣布」，千萬不要上當，正確答案是 C。 【答案】 C

▶ 過去簡單式的表達法

過去簡單式大部分是用在 **❶** 描述過去時間所發生的事情或變化。

❷ 表達過去的習慣。

【相關例句】

1. She got engaged **last** month.（她上個月訂婚了。）

2. These immigrants arrived **yesterday**.（這些移民的人昨天剛到。）

3. I visited my homeland about five years **ago**.（我大約 5 年前回到祖國參觀。）

4. Stanley didn't like mushrooms **before**.（史坦利以前不喜歡蘑菇。）

範　例

We couldn't access the computer files last night.	**昨晚我們無法打開電腦檔案。**
A. You should have called me.	你應該打電話給我的。
B. Did you save the files?	你存檔了嗎？
C. My computer got hit by a harmful virus.	我的電腦中了具有傷害性的病毒。
D. Stop accessing those computer files.	停止使用那些電腦檔案。

解析 1. 從題目中的 couldn't「不能」和 last night「昨晚」可得知是過去發生的事，所以接話者最好提出建議或是詢問更詳細的細節。

2. 選項 B、C、D 都不合理，選項 A 是提出問題解決的方法，所以是正確的答案。

答案 A

▶ 過去進行式的表達法

過去進行式是用在 ❶ 過去的某一段時間內，正在進行的動作。

❷ 過去習慣性的動作或狀況。

相關例句

1. **While** I was running errands around town, I bumped into my old professor.
   （當我在城裡辦事時，巧遇了我以前的教授。）

2. What **were** you doing **when** the typhoon hit?
   （當颱風來的時候，你正在做什麼？）

3. I **wasn't** listening while my spouse **was** talking to me.
   （我的配偶和我說話時，我正好沒在聽。）

4. We **were** studying at the library **when** the earthquake struck.
   （地震發生的時候，我們正在圖書館唸書。）

範　例

While Sam was sleeping in class, someone stole his iPod.	**山姆在課堂上睡覺時，有人偷了他的 iPod。**
A. Have they found them?	他們有找到他們嗎？
B. You should wake him up now.	你應該現在就叫醒他。
C. Maybe someone just borrowed it.	也許只是有人借去玩一下。
D. I have the same iPod.	我有相同的 iPod。

1. 要聽懂的關鍵字是 was sleeping「睡覺」和 stole「偷」，由這兩個關鍵字我們知道事情是當山姆在睡覺時發生的。

2. 題目中 his iPod 是單數名詞，所以選項 A 中的 them 是錯誤的。選項 B 和 D 都不合理，正確的答案是 C。

3. 關鍵字彙：wake up 是「叫醒」、effective 是「有效率的」。 C

▶ 未來簡單式的表達法

未來簡單式是用在 ❶ 表示未來會發生的動作。

❷ 未來習慣性的動作或狀態。

❸ 表示承諾、決心或預言會發生的事。

相關例句

1. I'll be here **tomorrow** morning.（明天早上我將會在這裡。）

2. I **hope** the **next** translator is better.（我希望下一位翻譯的人更好。）

3. Your website **will** be finished **in three days**.（你的網站將在三天內完成。）

4. We're **going to** see a movie **later**.（我們等一下就要去看一場電影。）

範 例

I'll consult with Craig and call you later tonight.	**我諮詢過葛瑞格之後，今晚稍晚打電話給你。**
A. I waited for your call.	我那時正等待著你的來電。
B. I'll be expecting your call.	我將會等你的電話。
C. Thanks, I'll be waiting for Craig's call.	謝謝，我將會等葛瑞格的電話。
D. I wouldn't insult Craig if I were you.	如果我是你的話，我才不會侮辱葛瑞格。

解析 1. 要聽懂的關鍵字是 consult with「和…諮詢」和 later tonight「今晚稍晚」。

2. 由文法句型來看，我們得知說話者的時間安排次序，所以選項 A 指的是過去的時間，因此不合理。

3. 選項 C 不合理，選項 D 中的 insult「侮辱」是 consult「諮詢」的相似音，所以不可選，因此答案要選 B。 答案 B

▶ 現在完成式的表達法

現在完成式是用在 **❶** 表示以前就開始且一直持續到現在的動作。

　　　　　　　　　❷ 描述發生在過去不確定的動作或狀態。

相關例句

1. **Has** there **ever been** a tug-of-war contest at school?
（學校以前曾經辦過拔河比賽嗎？）

2. The government **has become** more interested in designing satellites.
（政府對衛星設計更有興趣了。）

3. We **haven't finished** the composition **yet**.（我們還沒有寫完作文。）

4. I've **had** three tests **so far this week**.（這個星期到目前為止我已經考了三次試了。）

範　例

Jasmine has talked to several psychologists about her problem, but no one seems to know how to help her.	潔思美已經和好幾個心理醫生談論她的問題，但是似乎沒有人知道如何幫助她。
A. That's good news.	這真是個好消息。
B. Psychologists can teach her how to handle her anxiety.	心理學家可以教她如何處理她的焦慮。
C. She should call and make a reservation.	她應該打電話預約。
D. I can recommend a great psychologist.	我可以推薦一個很棒的心理醫生。

解析 1. 要聽懂的關鍵字是 psychologist「心理醫生」。當我們聽到別人的困境或是難題，我們直接的反應大多是表示同情或是提供解決之道。

2. 選項 A 不合理，選項 B 對她一點幫助也沒有，選項 C 中的 call and just 和 psychologist「心理醫生」聽起來很像，但是答案不合理。正確答案是 D。

3. 關鍵字彙：anxiety 是「焦慮」、recommend 是「推薦」。　　**答案** D

▶ 現在完成進行式的表達法

現在完成進行式是用於 **❶** 表示動作在過去開始，現在仍持續進行中，未曾間斷。

　　　　　　　　　　❷ 正在進行但是尚未完成的動作。

相關例句

1. We've **been going** to that spa **for five years**.（我們去那家水療會館已經 5 年了。）

2. What **have** they **been doing for the last hour**?（他們前一個小時在做什麼？）

3. James **has been playing** basketball **since he was** 12 years old.
   （詹姆斯從他十二歲起就開始打籃球了。）

4. She**'s been chatting** online too much **lately**.（她最近太常上網聊天了。）

範 例

I've been waiting for two hours, and Mr. Wilson still hasn't arrived.	我已經等了兩個小時，但是威爾遜先生還沒有來。
A. There's likely a long line in customs.	在海關那裡可能排了很長的隊伍。
B. I'm sorry you had to wait so long.	很抱歉讓你等這麼久。
C. He's a light traveler.	他是一個行李簡便的旅客。
D. The High Speed Rail doesn't run very late.	高鐵不會行駛到很晚。

解析 1. 選項 C 描述了威爾遜先生的旅行方式，而選項 D 提供了細節，但是兩者都和題目無關。

2. 選項 B 使用了過去式動詞 had，表示等待時間已經結束了，題目是用現在完成式，所以我們可以得知還在等威爾遜先生，所以不可選 B。

3. 選項 A 是猜測威爾遜先生還沒來的原因，為合理的答案。

4. 關鍵字彙：customs 是「海關」的意思。　　　　　　　**答案** A

技巧 ❷ 同音異形字（Heterographs / Homophones）

除了前面單元中的相似音字和同形異音字，我們還需要知道一些常見的同音異形字。這些字雖然讀音相同，但是拼法不同，所以意思也不同。下面是考試中可能會出現的同音異形字。

▶ 常見的同音異形字組

1.	[et]	eight (n.) 八	ate (v.) 吃的過去式
2.	[ˋbɛrɪ]	berry (n.) 野莓	bury (v.) 埋葬
3.	[bord]	board (v.) 登機	bored (adj.) 無趣的
4.	[baɪ]	buy (v.) 買	by (adv.) 經過
5.	[faɪnd]	find (v.) 找到	fined (adj.) 被罰錢的
6.	[flaʊr]	flour (n.) 麵粉	flower (n.) 花
7.	[gɛst]	guest (n.) 客人	guessed (v.) 猜的過去式
8.	[hɪr]	hear (v.) 聽到	here (adv.) 這裡
9.	[haɪr]	hire (v.) 雇用	higher (adj.) 更高的

10.	[ɪts]	its (pron.) 它的	it's 它是
11.	[nju]	new (adj.) 新的	knew (v.) 知道的過去式
12.	[no]	know (v.) 知道	no (adv.) 不
13.	[noz]	knows (v.) 知道	nose (n.) 鼻子
14.	[lɛd]	lead (n.) 鉛	led (v.) 領導的過去式
15.	[pis]	peace (n.) 和平	piece (n.) 片
16.	[sin]	scene (n.) 場景	seen (v.) 看的過去分詞
17.	[saɪd]	side (n.) 旁邊	sighed (v.) 嘆氣的過去式
18.	[stil]	steal (v.) 偷竊	steel (n.) 鋼鐵
19.	[tel]	tail (n.) 尾巴	tale (n.) 傳說
20.	[θru]	through (prep.) 穿越	threw (v.) 丟棄的過去式
21.	[wet]	wait (v.) 等待	weight (v.) 稱重量
22.	[ˋwɛðɚ]	weather (n.) 天氣	whether (conj.) 是否
23.	[wɪtʃ]	witch (n.) 巫婆	which (pron.) 哪一個
24.	[huz]	whose (pron.) 誰的	who's 誰是

 ● 在例 (6) 和 (9) 當中，某些字典可能會將字尾 r 和 er 的發音分別標示為 [r] 與 [ɚ]，但是其實在口語中，r 和 er 可說是發一樣的音。

● 在例 (22) 和 (23) 當中，某些字典會把字首 wh- 的發音標成 [hw]，但其實在口語中，[h] 的音幾乎不會發出來。

 範例 1

We should board the plane.	**我們應該要開始登機了。**
A. I'm starting to get bored, too.	我也開始感到厭倦了。
B. Did they call our seat numbers?	他們已經叫我們的座位號碼了嗎？
C. It didn't take long.	它沒有花很長的時間。
D. Put your seatbelt on, please.	請繫上安全帶。

 1. 選項 A 中的 bored「感到厭倦」和 board「登機」是同音異形字，意思不對，所以不選。

2. 選項 C 和 D 都和搭飛機有關，但不是最佳的回應。

3. 本題要聽出來的關鍵字是 board「登機」，我們從此句得知接下來該做的事就是去登機，所以選項 B 的答案最合理。

答案 B

範例 2

Have you seen my camera?

A. Can you take our picture, please?

B. Yes, it's so cute.

C. No, maybe you left it at the restaurant.

D. Yeah, that was a great scene.

你有沒有看到我的相機?

可以請你幫我們拍照嗎?

是,它是如此可愛。

沒有,也許你將它遺留在餐廳了。

對,那真是很棒的一幕。

解析 1. 選項 A、B、D 都和拍照有關,但不是最佳的回答。

2. 本題是用現在完成式的時態,詢問對方是否看見相機在哪裡,選項 C 提供
了相機下落的可能線索,所以是正確的答案。 **答案** C

作答說明：每題請聽光碟放音機播出一英語問句或直述句之後，從試題冊上A、B、
C、D 四個回答或回應中，選出一個最適合者作答。每題只播出一遍。

1
A. I might join one near my house.
B. Yes, I love the aerobics classes they offer.
C. It's open only on the weekends.
D. No, I often get caught in traffic.

2
A. Was it the 10th of July?
B. You can still change the date.
C. Maybe she felt the same way.
D. Dates are quite nutritious.

3
A. Yes, a pirate hit him in the nose.
B. Yes, but he can't afford new ones.
C. No, he never saw a pirate.
D. The quality is often very poor.

4
A. No way!
B. He should try working in finance.
C. That's a cool name.
D. You should try a different shampoo.

5
A. I think I qualify for some of them.
B. How much are they?
C. Yes, but I'm not interested in designing ships.
D. I prefer living in an apartment.

6
A. It's good for your skin.
B. Because I'm a rebel.
C. I don't want the boss to hear me.
D. My doctor says it's good for me.

7
A. I think they wanted a different present.
B. Yes, I hope he'll like it.
C. It's about how to increase consumer spending.
D. I couldn't tell.

8
A. Yeah, I need to take a leak.
B. I do.
C. My employer is giving me a lot of pressure.
D. Yes, it's been an easy week.

9
A. How did you know it was Fay?
B. I fainted, too.
C. I can't remember where we met.
D. I had the same feeling.

10
A. No, it's all nonsense to me.
B. Yes, I have some.
C. I think it's a great idea.
D. Sorry, I didn't.

2-3 地點的回應

基本觀念

在問有關地方或是方向與位置的問題時，疑問詞不一定是用 where。除了常見的 where 問句，還有用 what 和 how 開頭的問句，甚至連 Yes/No 問句也是很常見的問題型態。

範例 1

Where is my bank book?

A. I think I saw it on the kitchen counter.

B. It's on Arthur Street.

C. Try the new bookstore.

D. They're on your desk.

我的銀行存摺在哪裡？

我想我在廚房的櫃檯上看過。

它在亞瑟街上。

試試新的書店。

它們在你的桌上。

解析 1. 題目中是用單數 is，而選項 D 中的主詞用複數 they're，所以不正確。選項 B、C 的回應都不合理。

2. 題目是問銀行存摺在哪裡，而四個選項中都含有地點，但只有選項 A 是正確的。 **答案** A

範例 2

Is the baseball field far from here?

A. Yes, they have four baseball fields.

B. It's just up ahead.

C. No, we don't have one here.

D. Sorry, I don't play very well.

棒球場離這裡遠嗎？

是的，他們有 4 個棒球場。

它就在前方。

不，我們這裡一個也沒有。

對不起，我打得不好。

解析 題目是問距離，所以要做出最適當的回答，只有選項 B 表示出方位，其他的選項都不合理。 **答案** B

▶ 常見表示地點和方位的字彙與介系詞

where [hwɛr] (adv.)	在哪裡	in [ɪn] (prep.)	在裡面
what [hwɑt] (adv.)	什麼	at [æt] (prep.)	在 (表示小的地方)
near [nɪr] (adj.)	附近	by [baɪ] (prep.)	在旁邊
closc to (prcp.)	在附近	behind [bɪˋhaɪnd] (prep.)	在後面

far [fɑr] (adj.)	遠的	in front of (prep.)	在前面
between [bɪ`twin] (prep.)	在兩者之間	across from (prep.)	穿過；對面
beside [bɪ`saɪd] (prep.)	在…旁邊	right [raɪt] (adj.)	右邊的
next to (prep.)	在旁邊	left [lɛft] (adj.)	左邊的
under [`ʌndə] (prep.)	在下面	adjacent [ə`dʒesənt] (adj.)	緊鄰著
over [`ovə] (prep.)	越過	catty corner [`kætɪ `kɔrnə]	斜對面的

相關例句

1. **Where can I find the nearest** bank?（我在哪裡可以找到最近的銀行？）
2. **Where** are my keys?（我的鑰匙在哪裡？）
3. **Where's the** peanut butter?（花生醬在哪裡？）
4. **What's on** the table?（桌上擺了什麼東西？）
5. **How far** is it to the library?（到圖書館有多遠？）
6. Taiwan is **located** east of the Taiwan Strait.（台灣是位於台灣海峽的東邊。）
7. They plan to **situate** a new bus stop near my house.
   （他們計畫在我家附近蓋一個新的公車站。）
8. Is the restaurant **close to** here?（餐廳距離這裡近嗎？）

作答技巧

技巧 ❶ 附加問句（Tag Questions）

附加問句是一個敘述句，再加上一個肯定或是否定的短問句。當我們不確定某件事，想反問對方，或是想得到對方的認同時，通常就會使用附加問句。它們看起來可能很簡單，但是其實回答起來有點複雜。

▶ 附加問句的句型結構
一般而言，在肯定的敘述句之後加上否定的問句。反之在否定敘述句要加上肯定的問句。

肯定敘述句 +	否定問句 -	否定敘述句 -	肯定問句 +
I passed the test, （我通過了考試	**didn't** I? 不是嗎？）	**I won't pass** the test, （我將不會通過考試	**will** I? 我會嗎？）

▶ 附加問句的用法
❶ 在敘述句中使用的動詞是 be 動詞，後面短問句也要用相同的 be 動詞。
❷ 在敘述句中使用的是情態助動詞，後面短問句也要用相同的情態助動詞 (can, could, should, would, might 等等)。

❸ 在敘述句中使用的是一般動詞或者 do / does / did 的話，後面短問句就用 do / does / did。

❹ 在敘述句中使用的是完成式時態（有 have / has / had + p.p.）的話，後面短問句就用 have / has / had。

肯定敘述句＋否定問句	否定敘述句＋肯定問句
be 動詞	
You're coming, **aren't** you? （你要來了，不是嗎？）	You **aren't** coming, **are** you? （你不要來了，是嗎？）
He's happy at university, **isn't** he? （他在大學很快樂，不是嗎？）	He **isn't** happy at university, **is** he? （他在大學不快樂，是嗎？）
They're into jazz, **aren't** they? （他們欣賞爵士樂，不是嗎？）	They **aren't** into jazz, **are** they? （他們不欣賞爵士樂，是嗎？）
情態助動詞	
I **can** come, **can't** I? （我可以來，不是嗎？）	I **can't** come, **can** I? （我不可以來，是嗎？）
We **should** bring dessert, **shouldn't** we? （我們應該帶甜點，不是嗎？）	We **shouldn't** bring dessert, **should** we? （我們不應該帶甜點，是嗎？）
She'd tell the truth, **wouldn't** she? （她應該要說實話的，不是嗎？）	She **wouldn't** tell the truth, **would** she? （她不應該說實話的，是嗎？）
一般動詞或 do / does / did	
I forgot, **didn't** I?（我忘記了，不是嗎？）	I **didn't** forget, **did** I?（我沒有忘記，是嗎？）
You eat meat, **don't** you? （你吃肉，不是嗎？）	You **don't** eat meat, **do** you? （你不吃肉，是嗎？）
They smoke, **don't** they? （他們抽煙，不是嗎？）	They **don't** smoke, **do** they? （他們不抽煙，是嗎？）
完成式時態	
Mandy's **finished** her homework, **hasn't** she?（蔓蒂已經寫完功課了，不是嗎？）	Mandy **hasn't finished** her homework, **has** she?（蔓蒂還沒有寫完功課，是嗎？）
You've **cleaned** the bathroom, **haven't** you?（你已經打掃浴室了，不是嗎？）	You **haven't cleaned** the bathroom, **have** you?（你還沒有打掃浴室，是嗎？）
They've already **left**, **haven't** they? （他們已經離開了，不是嗎？）	They **haven't left** yet, **have** they? （他們還沒有離開，是嗎？）

▶ 附加問句的回答

附加問句的回答方式是要根據事情的真相來回答，而不是問句的肯定或否定的方式。也就是說，你的回答會反應出實際的現況，所以不管短問句是出現 did you 或是 didn't you，都不會影響回答的答案。

附加問句	實際情況	回答
Jason isn't late again, is he? （傑森沒有再遲到了，是嗎？）	他沒有遲到	No, he isn't. （對，他沒有。）
	他遲到了	Yeah, he's late. （是的，他遲到了。）
	他遲到了	I'm afraid he is. （恐怕是的。）
Ken forgot about the meeting, didn't he? （肯忘記要開會，不是嗎？）	他沒有忘記	No, he didn't. （不，他沒有忘記。）
	他忘記了	Yes, he forgot again. （是的，他又忘記了。）
	你不知道	How would I know? （我怎麼會知道？）
Sara solved the riddle, didn't she? （莎拉解開謎語了，不是嗎？）	她沒有解開	No, she didn't. （不，她並沒有。）
	她解開了	She sure did. （她當然解開了。）
	她解開了	You bet she did. （她肯定解開了。）

在聽力考試中，你可能不知道該句中的敘述是否為真，所以只要試圖找出不矛盾的答案即可。請記住，在否定的回答中，都是用像 isn't、weren't、didn't 的字眼。而肯定的答案中，出現的字眼大多是像 is、were 或是 did 這樣的字眼。然而，這並非總是如此，也會有例外的情況發生。

範例 1

Karen isn't from Taipei, is she?	**卡倫不是從台北來的，是嗎？**
A. Yes, she took care of many victims.	是的，她照顧了很多受難者。
B. No, he's from Tainan.	不，他從台南來。
C. No, Karen's from Taipei.	不，卡倫是來自於台北。
D. No, she's from Taichung.	不，她是從台中來。

1. 選項 A 的意思和題目不相關，選項 B 的主詞是 he，所以錯誤。

2. 選項 C 也不對，No 的後面要接 she isn't from Taipei 意思才通順。

3. 只有 D 補充說明了細節，是正確的答案。 **答案** D

範例 2

Your stepfather's a diplomat, isn't he?	你的繼父是一個外交官，不是嗎？
A. Yes, he cleaned the mat.	是的，他清理過地墊了。
B. No, he's a Taiwanese diplomat.	不是，他是一個台灣的外交官。
C. Yes, he works for the Taiwanese government.	是的，他為台灣的政府工作。
D. Yes, he fell down the steps.	是的，他從樓梯上摔下。

 1. 本題考的是單字 diplomat「外交官」，如果前面這個敘述句是正確的，選項 B 就不應該用 No 來回答，因為 No 的後面應該接否定的 isn't。

2. 選項 A 和 D 的時態和語意都不對。 **答案** C

範例 3

It isn't that risky, is it?	這並不是很危險，是嗎？
A. No, it's very risky.	不，這是非常危險的。
B. Yes, it's terribly risky.	是，它非常危險的。
C. Yes, it's not risky.	是，這不冒險。
D. I'm not buying that compact disc.	我不買那 CD 光碟。

解析 1. No 的後面要接 isn't 才對，Yes 的後面要接肯定的，所以選項 A 和 C 是錯誤的。

2. 選項 D 的 compact disc「CD 光碟」和 risky「危險的」聽起來相似，但意思差很遠，千萬不要弄錯。 **答案** B

技巧 ❷ 辨別單數和複數名詞（Singular & Plural Nouns）

另一種測試聽力能力的方法，就是看是否有仔細聽清楚名詞的單數或複數，聽錯的話，意思就會相差很遠。

範例 1

Should we be concerned that a criminal escaped?

A. I've seen better days.

B. Yes, we need to find them right away.

C. We can always find another one.

D. Yes, we should. Let's call the police for assistance.

我們應該在意一位罪犯逃脫嗎？

我也曾風光過。

是的，我們必須要馬上找到他們。

我們永遠可以再找另一個。

是的，應該。讓我們打電話報警求助。

解析 1. 題目清楚地表明是一位罪犯，選項 B 是用 them 所以不對。

2. 選項 A 和 C 的語意不對，合理的答案是 D 。 **答案** D

範例 2

I don't think these applicants are suitable for the job.

A. I think she'll do a wonderful job.

B. We can always try other suits.

C. Then what kind of fruit should we use?

D. Then we should keep looking.

我認為這些應徵者都不適合這份工作。

我認為她會表現得很出色。

我們總是可以試試其他西裝。

那麼我們應該要用哪一種水果呢？

那麼我們應該繼續尋找。

解析 1. 題目的關鍵字是複數 these ，選項 A 中用 she'll 所以不對。

2. 選項 B 意思不對，suits「西裝」和 suitable「適合」是發音相近的字，不可選。

3. 選項 C 語意不符。

4. 選項 D 提出了合理的解決之道，所以為正確答案。

5. 關鍵字彙：applicants 是「應徵者」、suitable 是「合適的」。 **答案** D

題型實戰演練

作答說明：每題請聽光碟放音機播出一英語問句或直述句之後，從試題冊上A、B、
C、D四個回答或回應中，選出一個最適合者作答。每題只播出一遍。

1. A. Yes, there's one close to our house.
   B. No, there aren't many places to rest in town.
   C. We should take a taxi downtown.
   D. Perhaps we should make a reservation.

2. A. No, she's from Taichung.
   B. Yes, she works there.
   C. Yeah, she was born and raised there.
   D. She enjoys living there a lot.

3. A. She's meeting new students at the airport.
   B. She'll be back late tonight.
   C. She drove her own car.
   D. I'll see her tomorrow at the game.

4. A. The scenery there is magnificent.
   B. We usually vacation in July.
   C. We went to Green Island.
   D. We enjoy spending time in Kenting.

5. A. No, this is a safe town.
   B. Yes, he's the sexy man sitting over there.
   C. It's due to arrive next week.
   D. Yes, I enjoy my life very much.

6. A. The offer will not last long.
   B. It's about another kilometer.
   C. Only three more kilograms.
   D. We can stay there until dark.

7. A. Check the boxes.
   B. I'm glad you found it.
   C. Try calling her mother.
   D. She lost her love handles.

8. A. It beats me what the caller said.
   B. I don't foresee any problems.
   C. I'm not sure what's on his mind.
   D. It's lipstick.

9. A. They're living in Italy now.
   B. Aisle 12.
   C. They're driving me nuts.
   D. They're hiding in the bushes.

10. A. You have many fond memories of that place.
    B. Where are you going to put it?
    C. That's a splendid idea.
    D. I don't think Jake wants one.

2-4　態度的回應

基本觀念

在日常生活中，我們常常會表達自己的態度和意見，不管這些態度是正面或是負面的，都是用來表達個人的情緒或對事情的看法。在本單元中，你不僅會學到不同態度的表達方式，還會學到如何快速地刪去錯誤不合理的選項，找出正確的答案。

範例 1

I have a feeling I'm going to ace this test.　　**我有一個感覺，我將會高分通過這個考試。**

A.　Are you sure you have an ace?　　你確定你有一張王牌？

B.　You sound pretty confident.　　聽起來你非常有自信。

C.　I'm sorry to hear that.　　很抱歉聽到這件事。

D.　You should have studied harder.　　你應該更努力用功。

解析 關鍵字是 ace「表現突出」，說話者很明顯地表示出充分的信心，所以最好的答案是 B。　　**答案 B**

範例 2

I'm not sure we can beat this team.　　**我不確定我們可以打敗這一隊。**

A.　That's not a nice thing to do.　　做這件事情不好。

B.　I'm sure they won't.　　我相信他們不會。

C.　I know we can beat them.　　我知道我們可以打敗他們。

D.　I hold them in high esteem.　　我非常尊敬他們。

解析 1. 關鍵字是動詞 beat「打敗；擊敗」。this team「這一隊」和 esteem「尊重」發音相近，不要聽錯了。

2. 說話者表示出不確定的態度，所以最佳的回應是 C。　　**答案 C**

▶ 態度

以下是表達積極和消極態度的例句。學會之後，就可以很快地分析出選項是持正面或是負面的態度，快速找出正確答案。

正面的態度（Positive Attitudes）	負面的態度（Negative Attitudes）
She has a positive attitude. （她有積極的態度。）	She has a negative attitude. （她有消極負面的態度。）
Kenny's in a good mood. （肯尼的心情很好。）	Kenny's in a bad mood. （肯尼心情不好。）
He's a real upbeat person. （他是一個真正樂觀的人。）	He's so down all the time. （他一直都很消沉。）
I'm so thankful. （我很感激。）	I deserve more than that. （我值得更好的。）
I'm so blessed. （我備受祝福。）	I must be cursed. （我肯定被詛咒了。）
I need to forgive her. （我需要原諒她。）	I wish she would get out of my life. （我希望她可以走出我的生命。）
I'm going to encourage him. （我要鼓勵他。）	Leave me alone. （我要獨處。）
What a gorgeous view. （如此華麗的景色。）	This place is a dump. （這個地方是個垃圾堆。）
She's very easygoing. （她非常隨和。）	She has a bad temper. （她的脾氣不好。）
My friends are very reliable. （我的朋友們都非常可靠。）	I can't rely on my friends. （我不能依靠我的朋友們。）
Henry is very generous. （亨利非常慷慨。）	Henry is terribly stingy. （亨利非常吝嗇。）
My sister is brave. （我的姐姐很勇敢。）	My sister is chicken. （我的姐姐是膽小鬼。）
If at first you don't succeed, try, try again. （如果一開始沒成功，你要一試再試。）	I quit. （我放棄了。）

作答技巧

技巧 ❶ 提出補充說明或解決之道（Additional Information）

請記住，在這個部分的考試，是要求你對於所聽到的問句或者直述句，選出一個最好的回答或者回應。有時候答案可能會是一個補充說明或解決的方式與建議。

範例 1

I've had enough of my neighbors.

A. I can hear their TV all night.

B. You should find some time to talk with them.

C. You shouldn't eat so much when you visit them.

D. They sound very hospitable.

我已經受夠了我的鄰居們。

我一整晚都可以聽到他們的電視聲。

你應該找一些時間與他們談談。

當你去拜訪他們的時候，不應該吃這麼多。

他們聽起來非常好客。

解析 關鍵字是 had enough of「受夠了某人」，說話者表達出受不了的感覺，選項 A 應該是說話者接下來會說的事，回應的方式可以是表示同情或提出解決之道，所以選項 B 是最佳答案。 **答案** B

範例 2

You ran that red light, ma'am.

A. I run every day.

B. Sure, I might buy that red one.

C. I need to see your driver's license.

D. I'm so sorry. I didn't even see it.

這位女士，妳闖紅燈了。

我每天都跑步。

當然，我可能會買紅色的那一個。

我需要看看你的駕駛執照。

我非常抱歉，我沒有看到它。

解析 關鍵字是 ran that red light「闖紅燈了」，說話者的語氣聽起來像是正要開紅單的警察，選項 C 應該是警察會說的話，面對這個情況你最好表達出悔意，所以選項 D 是正確的。 **答案** D

題型實戰演練 ▶▶ 1-12

作答說明：每題請聽光碟放音機播出一英語問句或直述句之後，從試題冊上A、B、
C、D 四個回答或回應中，選出一個最適合者作答。每題只播出一遍。

1 A. You ought to visit them this weekend.
B. So do I.
C. Don't eat too many.
D. Let's challenge them to a game of beach volleyball.

2 A. It should be a piece of cake.
B. Sam should be okay by himself.
C. Yes, I prepared a lot for it.
D. I'm taking the exam next week.

3 A. No, my train comes today.
B. Maybe you should cancel the barbecue.
C. I don't think it did.
D. You enjoy dancing in the rain, don't you?

4 A. Yes, cycling can make a difference.
B. They're easy to make.
C. I don't think we should call now.
D. I believe you're right.

5 A. You're right. I shouldn't be.
B. You're right.
C. We're totally different.
D. Think more positively.

6 A. I'm so proud of her.
B. I told you she was a good cook.
C. When will she write it?
D. She always wanted to move there.

7 A. I already sent the fax.
B. I know. I need a vacation.
C. I might vacation there this summer.
D. You're right. I should relax.

8 A. The weather should clear up.
B. That's great news.
C. What are we going to do?
D. You're right. I'm sitting too much.

9 A. I wish we could have stayed another week.
B. They were too sweet.
C. Don't call me Honey!
D. We'll be going to Japan for a week.

10 A. I do, too.
B. There's a significant difference in quality.
C. I am, too.
D. I'm glad we resolved the differences.

2-5　意見的回應

基本觀念

還有一種常見的題型是要你提出看法或意見來回應問題，或是別人提出他們的看法，要你以贊成或反對的方式來回應。在這個單元，我們將會介紹各種不同的意見表達方式和常見的回答方式。

範例 1

Do you think they'll lay off any more staff?	**你認為他們會解雇更多的員工嗎？**
A. I think our staff works well together.	我想我們的員工一起工作得很好。
B. Yes, I think we can lay them here.	是的，我認為我們可以把他們放在這裡。
C. I hope not.	希望不會。
D. We shouldn't count our chickens before they hatch.	不要高興得太早。

解析 1. 題目是問對裁員的看法，因為是壞消息，所以選項 C 的答案最好。

2. 關鍵字彙：lay 是「放置」、lay off 是「裁員」、staff 是「員工」。

3. Don't count your chickens before they hatch. 是諺語，意思是「不要過早指望」，選項 D 就是引用此諺語的說法。　**答案** C

範例 2

What's your thought on the existence of aliens?	**你對外星人的存在有什麼看法？**
A. I think they should exit this place immediately.	我覺得他們應該立即離開這個地方。
B. I should talk to my priest.	我應該要和我的牧師談談。
C. They run a lot of good businesses in town.	他們在鎮上經營了許多不錯的生意。
D. I don't think there is any proof that they exist.	我不認為有他們存在的任何證據。

解析 1. 選項 A 的 exit「離開」和 existence「存在」是混淆字，千萬不要上當。

2. 題目是問對於外星人存在的意見，表示同意或不同意都可以，所以正確答案為 D。

3. 關鍵字彙：existence 是 (n.)「存在」、proof 是「證據」、exist 是 (v.)「存在」。　**答案** D

▶ 意見的表達方式

有很多不同的方式來表達意見，不管是表達個人的意見或是回應他人的意見時，最佳的回應方式就是表明贊同或是反對。

相關例句

1. **In my opinion**, her complaints aren't ridiculous.（在我看來，她的抱怨一點都不離譜。）

2. **It's my feeling (that)** we should open our own studio.
   （我的感覺是，我們應該開我們自己的工作室。）

3. **I feel (that)** he sometimes gets too emotional.（我覺得他有時太過情緒化了。）

4. **I believe** he's a very immoral man.（我相信他是一個非常沒有道德的人。）

5. **I loved** her voice.（我喜歡她的聲音。）

6. **I liked** it a lot.（我非常喜歡它。）

7. **I enjoyed** the exhibition.（我很欣賞這個展覽。）

8. **I think** your ideas are wonderful.（我覺得你的想法棒透了。）

9. **I thought** the play was boring.（我以為這齣戲很無聊。）

10. **I don't think** the mountain is too steep.（我不覺得這座山太陡了。）

11. **I say** it's a great idea.（我說這是一個好主意。）

12. **I didn't mind** taking the bus.（我不介意坐公車。）

作答技巧

技巧 ❶ 表達贊成與反對的附和句

表示同意和不同意的意見是考試中常看到的題型，也是我們每天幾乎都會說的話。當你在表達贊成或反對朋友、家人的意見時，請練習用英語思考，一旦你越來越熟悉這類表達方式，此類問題對你而言將會易如反掌。

▶ 附和他人的意見

當我們要附和或贊成前面所說過的話時，就會運用附和句。

附和句：❶ 可分為「肯定附和句」和「否定附和句」。

　　　　❷ 表達方式有兩種：

　　　　　　A. 平裝句 (肯定用 too；否定用 either)

　　　　　　B. 倒裝句 (肯定用 so；否定用 neither/nor)

肯定句	肯定附和句	肯定附和句（倒裝句）
主詞＋ be 動詞 / 一般動詞 ...	主詞＋ be 動詞 / 助動詞＋ too.	So ＋ be 動詞 / 助動詞＋主詞 .
否定句	**否定附和句**	**否定附和句（倒裝句）**
主詞＋ be 動詞 / 一般動詞＋ not ＋ ...	主詞＋ be 動詞 / 助動詞＋ not, either	Neither ＋ be 動詞 / 助動詞＋主詞 .

例 I went to Thailand this summer. He went to Thailand, too.（平裝句）

I went to Thailand this summer. So did he.（倒裝句）

（今年夏天我去了泰國。他也去了泰國。）

例 Mandy doesn't play online games. I don't, either.（平裝句）

Mandy doesn't play online games. Neither do I.（倒裝句）

（蔓蒂不玩線上遊戲，我也不玩。）

說明 否定倒裝附和句中，因為 neither 已經有否定的意思，所以不用再加 not。

▶ 以下介紹肯定和否定的附和句：

敘述句	附和句
be 動詞	
I'm totally frustrated right now.（我現在完全受挫。）	So is she.（她也是。）
Judy is eager to go to America this summer.（茱蒂渴望今年夏天去美國。）	So is Tiffany.（蒂芬妮也是。）
He's not an only child.（他不是獨生子。）	Neither am I.（我也不是。）
情態助動詞	
Joyce can play the piano.（喬依思會彈鋼琴。）	So can Mandy.（曼蒂也會。）
He should exercise more.（他應該多運動。）	So should I.（我也應該。）
He shouldn't eat too much junk food.（他不應該吃太多垃圾食物。）	Neither should I.（我也不應該。）
一般動詞或 do / does / did	
I ordered steak.（我點了牛排。）	So did Barbie.（芭比也是。）
He does yoga almost every week.（他幾乎每個星期做瑜珈。）	So do I.（我也是。）
He doesn't enjoy dancing.（他不喜愛跳舞。）	I don't, either.（我也不喜愛。）

完成式時態

Oscar has done his homework. （奧斯卡已經寫完功課了。）	So have I. （我也是。）
I've run a marathon. （我已經跑過馬拉松了。）	So has my brother. （我弟弟也是。）
He hasn't finished his report. （他尚未完成他的報告。）	Neither have I. （我也還沒。）

（學習小筆記）

「have + p.p.」表示完成式，附和句要用 So have I. 而不是 So do I。

（○）He's finished his laundry. **So have I.**

（×）He's finished his laundry. **So do I.**

（他已經洗好他的衣服了。我也是。）

（○）She's been busy all afternoon. **So have I.**

（×）She's been busy all afternoon. **So do I.**

（她已經忙了一整個下午了。我也是。）

▶ 其他表示贊成的說法

以下是其他常見的表達方式，用來表示贊成或是同意別人的意見與看法。有時候語氣還會加上一點熱情或是活力來回應別人。

敘述句	表示贊成的附和句
We need more determined people. （我們需要更有決心的人。）	Exactly! （沒錯！）
We should make extra copies. （我們應該多複印幾份。）	Yes, of course. （是的，當然。）
The concert was very entertaining. （這個演唱會真是非常具有娛樂性。）	Yes, it was splendid. （是的，很精彩。）
Jonathon got fired. （喬納森被開除了。）	Yes, I know. （是的，我知道。）
It's time for a coffee break. （喝咖啡的休息時間到了。）	I agree. （我同意。）
Let's go out for dinner. （我們出去吃晚飯吧。）	Sounds good. （聽起來不錯。）

(續下表)

Fear slowly suffocates a person.
（恐懼會慢慢讓人窒息。）

That's a good point.
（這是一個很好的論點。）

Teachers should be paid more.
（教師應該獲得更多的薪水。）

Yes, I couldn't agree more.
（是的，我非常同意。）

Steinbeck was one of the best American writers.
（史坦貝克是美國最好的作家之一。）

You're absolutely right.
（你是絕對正確的。）

I need a vacation.
（我需要渡假。）

That's just what I was thinking.
（這正是我所想的。）

What we need is a hero.
（我們需要的是一個英雄。）

You hit the nail on the head!
（你說得非常中肯！）

This place is awesome!
（這個地方真棒！）

You can say that again!
（我同意你的說法！）

敘述句	表示勉強贊成的附和句
This work is boring. （這項工作真是無聊。）	Yes, I'm afraid so. （是的，恐怕是這樣。）
He said we need to work overtime. （他說我們需要加班。）	I must say he's right. （我必須說他是對的。）
Heather told me I should get plastic surgery. （海瑟告訴我，我應該要去做整形手術。）	I have to agree. （我不得不同意。）

▶ 表示不贊同的意見

當你不同意別人的意見或說法時，可以使用下面的句子來禮貌性地表達自己的意見，使用這些禮貌性的用語是很重要的。

敘述句	表示不贊成的禮貌附和句
I don't smoke. （我不抽煙。）	I do. （我抽呀。）
Kelly has a crush on you. （凱莉迷戀你。）	I don't think so. （我不認為如此。）
He doesn't show much sportsmanship. （他並沒有表現出運動家的精神。）	I disagree with you. （我不同意你的看法。）
Collin is a lazy employee. （柯林是一個懶惰的職員。）	I have to disagree. （我不同意。）
Global warming isn't a serious problem. （全球暖化問題並不嚴重。）	I'm afraid I disagree with you. （我恐怕不同意你的看法。）

(續下表)

I think Iain Banks wrote that novel.
（我想是伊恩・班克斯寫那本小說的。）

Perhaps, but I don't think so.
（也許吧，但我不這樣認為。）

Does he like me?
（他喜歡我嗎？）

I'm not too sure.
（我不太清楚。）

The acting in this movie was terrible.
（這部電影的戲演得很糟糕。）

Do you think so?
（你是這樣認為的嗎？）

I think we're going to lose the election.
（我想這次選舉我們會輸。）

I'm afraid you are mistaken.
（恐怕你錯了。）

They're going to offer new employees five-year contracts.
（他們將提供為期五年的合約給新員工。）

I can't go along with that.
（我不贊同這個做法。）

當你不同意別人的意見或說法時，若對方是和自己很熟的朋友，就可以使用比較直接的話來表達自己的意見。

敘述句	表示不贊成的直接附和句
They're sold out. （他們賣光了。）	You can't be serious? （你不是認真的吧？）
I think your girlfriend is a transsexual. （我覺得你的女朋友是變性人。）	You've got to be kidding me. （你是在開我玩笑吧。）
They're only interested in making a quick buck. （他們只對快快撈一筆有興趣。）	I totally disagree. （我完全不同意。）
The Chicago Cubs will win this year. （今年芝加哥小熊隊將會贏。）	Don't be ridiculous. （別說笑了。）
This shirt is so rad. （這件襯衫是這麼酷。）	You're nuts! （你瘋了！）
Professional athletes should get paid more money. （職業運動員應該得到更多的報酬。）	Rubbish! （胡說八道！）

作答說明：每題請聽光碟放音機播出一英語問句或直述句之後，從試題冊上A、B、
C、D 四個回答或回應中，選出一個最適合者作答。每題只播出一遍。

1
A. Yes, she loves that band.
B. Are you sure?
C. It costs NT$1,200 a bottle.
D. It was a nice birthday gift.

2
A. So do I.
B. Don't kick it too hard.
C. I'm sorry I don't know how to play.
D. How are your classes?

3
A. It didn't take too long to move everything.
B. I think we'll see it soon.
C. It's one of the best I've seen in a while.
D. Let's go to the seven o'clock show.

4
A. I'm not sure why it strays from home.
B. That's a great idea.
C. We can't afford another child.
D. Maybe someone at the animal shelter can pick it up.

5
A. No, she didn't lose it.
B. I haven't met her.
C. There's a good chance she will.
D. Yes, I don't think she'll win.

6
A. I love horror movies.
B. It was out of this world.
C. I prefer to watch movies at home.
D. Her movie theater used to be a pub.

7
A. No, I don't think Gary will tell us.
B. I'm sure he'll be jealous.
C. No, he always gets jealous.
D. Yes, I think he should remain in jail.

8
A. I won't spend much money.
B. Probably for about five days.
C. We went to Holland.
D. Let's try a week in Kenting.

9
A. That's not my responsibility.
B. It was delicious.
C. It's a beautiful place to visit.
D. I thought it helped us collect the data we needed.

10
A. I can't, either.
B. So do I.
C. He should have ducked sooner.
D. He's on a diet now.

第二部分聽力答題技巧複習

學習完第二部分，你是否已經學會了在「問答」這個部分的所有答題技巧呢？請在你已經學會的方格中打勾

問答的答題技巧	✔
1. 在參加聽力測驗之前，我已經熟悉各種問題的題型及可能的回應方式。	
2. 聆聽題目之前，我會快速瀏覽四個選項，找出共同點或是不同之處，並且預測題目的主題和問句的方向。	
3. 聆聽題目時，我可以清楚地分辨題目是問句或是直述句，並且聽清楚問句的疑問詞。	
4. 聆聽題目時，我已經學會分辨相似音字組、同音異形字和同形異音字。	
5. 聆聽題目時，我會留意句子中所使用的時態與名詞中單複數的用法。	
6. 聆聽題目時，我知道附加問句和附和句的表達法，與適當的回應方式。	
7. 聆聽題目時，我聽得出說話者的意圖和態度，並且知道如何掌握語調與語意關係，也知道如何回應。	
8. 聆聽完題目之後，我知道如何刪去答非所問、錯誤時態、發音混淆與人稱不正確的選項，正確地找出答案。	

簡短對話

作答說明

以下是全民英檢中級聽力測驗第三部分的作答說明與題目範例。事先熟記作答說明與題型，考試時就可以略過作答說明，往下瀏覽題目，以提高得分。

第三部分：簡短對話

共 15 題。每題請聽光碟放音機播出一段對話及一個相關的問題後，從試題冊上 A、B、C、D 四個選項中選出一個最適合者作答。每段對話及問題只播出一遍。

例 （聽） W: What is your problem?

M: Excuse me?

W: I checked out your Facebook page.

M: So?

W: So I mean nothing to you?

M: What are you talking about? I didn't write anything like that.

W: I know, but you haven't indicated that we're in a relationship.

M: Give me a break!

Question: How does the man feel?

（看） A. He's tired and needs a break.

B. He felt fine.

C. A little annoyed.

D. He doesn't write much on Facebook.

解析 1. 本題情境是一對情侶的對話，內容是女方在抱怨她不滿意她男朋友的事情，題目是問男方的感覺。

2. 答題線索是在於最後一句：Give me a break!，這句話透露出男方覺得這是小事，感到不耐煩，所以正確答案是 C。

3. 關鍵字彙與慣用語：indicate「註明；說出」、in a relationship「有對象；正在交往中」。

答案 C

應考策略 ⋯⋯

Step 1 快速瀏覽選項（Scan the choices and make predictions.）

一定要很快地看過四個答案選項，找出相同點，利用選項中的訊息來預測題目主題與對話內容。

Step 2 仔細聆聽對話並掌握主旨（Listen carefully for the gist.）

利用「由上而下」的思考模式，掌握對話的主題、目的與主旨大意。經由對話者的身分關係來推測出對話的情境。

Step 3 運用邊聽邊做筆記技巧來聽出細節（Take notes to remember details.）

根據對話內容快速地寫下文字、符號、日期或數字，以便幫助自己找出正確的答案。

Step 4 推論出不熟悉的字或內容（Infer the meaning of difficult words.）

運用上下文的大意、舉例、對比字或同義字來推測出不熟悉的字或內容，並且仔細辨別說話者的目的，推論出暗喻之意。

Step 5 完整地聽完對話（Keep listening.）

遇到聽不懂的字或細節，請不要放棄，繼續聽完對話，並找出正確答案。有時候你聽不懂的部分，並不影響你作答。

常考題型 ⋯⋯

一聽到對話要能分辨出情境，了解對話者的關係，判斷對話的目的與推論結論。我們將常考的題型，歸納成五大類，依照各種題型傳授不同的聽力技巧來幫助考生，培養得高分的耳力。

本部分根據「簡短對話」的常考題目，歸納成下列五種常考題型：

- 3-1 聽出主旨
- 3-2 聽出意圖
- 3-3 聽出細節
- 3-4 聽出推論
- 3-5 聽出問題與解決方式

3-1　聽出主旨

基本觀念

第三部分最基本也是最重要的題型之一，就是問有關對話中的主旨大意。主旨大意是指對話中的重點或主題。這一類型的問題應該很容易回答，因為並不需要聽懂對話中每一個字或是細節，就可以作答。換句話說，只要聽懂了一個或兩個關鍵字，就可以幫助你推斷出對話的主旨大意。

範例

M: I think this apartment is suitable for us.	我認為這個公寓很適合我們。
W: I'm not so sure.	我不太確定。
M: The location is close to our work, and it's certainly big enough.	這個地點離我們工作的地方很近，而且它一定夠大。
W: You're right, but I'm afraid it's too close to that temple.	你說得對，但是我怕它離那家廟太近。
M: It shouldn't be too much of a problem.	那應該不是太大的問題吧。
W: Have you ever lived close to a temple before?	你住過寺廟的附近嗎？
M: No, but you're probably right. We should keep looking.	沒有，但也許妳是對的。我們應該要繼續找。
Q: How do the man and the woman feel about the apartment?	這位男士和女士覺得這個公寓怎麼樣？

A. They both feel it's a decent choice.	他們都覺得這是一個不錯的選擇。
B. They agree not to rent it.	他們同意不租它。
C. The man disagrees with the woman.	這位男士不同意這位女士的看法。
D. They both prefer living close to a temple.	他們都偏愛居住得離寺廟近一點。

解析 1. 本題情境為兩人在討論是否要租下這個公寓，題目是問他們的看法。答案的線索是在於男方的最後一句話：We should keep looking. 得知他們不會租這個公寓，答案要選 B。

2. 關鍵字彙：suitable for someone 是「適合某人」、temple「寺廟」、decent「還不錯的」。

答案 B

相關問句

1. What are the speakers talking about?
   （說話者正在談論什麼？）

2. Where are the speakers now?
   （說話者現在在哪裡？）

3. What is the woman's job?
   （這位女士的工作是什麼？）

4. Which occasion is this?
   （這是哪一種場合？）

5. Why is the man so upset?
   （為什麼這位男士這麼難過？）

6. Is the woman expressing a positive or negative opinion?
   （這位女士是否表達出肯定或是否定的意見？）

7. What is the relationship between the two speakers?
   （這兩位說話者是什麼關係？）

8. How do the man and woman feel about the apartment?
   （這位男士和女士覺得這個公寓怎麼樣？）

作答技巧

▶ 由上而下的思考方式（Top-down Processing）

當我們聽到一件事情時，腦中會有兩種訊息思考的模式，一種是由上而下（top-down processing）的思考方式，另一種是由下而上（bottom-up processing）的思考方式。前者彷彿是從空中往下鳥瞰全圖，後者則像蓋房子一樣由地基向上。換句話說，如果我們要運用有關身分、關係情境與背景方面的訊息，來理解這件事情的涵義時，由上而下的思考模式就很重要。例如當你的朋友要告訴你有關她和她男友的事情時，你會因為他們之間的關係，而在腦中形成某些預期的主題或是以前所發生的事件，之後你可能會預期她又要抱怨了，此時你是從這個觀點來聆聽這段對話。換句話說，你是從上往下去思考這段談話，了解大意。

由下而上的聽力處理模式是專注聽出細節中關鍵的字和片語，然後將所聽到的細節元素串連起來，以便了解整個內容。例如當你的朋友正在告訴你要如何到他台南的公寓時，你需要專注於細節的部分，像是街道的名稱、左轉或右轉，或是他公寓的門牌號碼。

想要有很敏銳的聽力，需要靠這兩個聽力處理模式的相互合作。有時候考生必須要先聽懂足夠的細節來判斷對話的主旨或主題；有時聽懂了主旨，處理細節的部分就會輕而易舉。

如果你覺得要聽懂對話中的每個字才可以作答的話，那麼你可能會因為聽不懂某些字或因為細節太多而感到沮喪，之後就放棄了。千萬不要掉入這個困境中，請一定要繼續聽下去。在某些情況下，細節並不重要。有時候你不需要內容的細節就可以抓到大概的主題或是主旨。若是有些部分聽不懂，請繼續聆聽，並試著去預測或是猜測整個對話的大意，或是用上下文的意思來推論。除此之外，對話中所強調的字眼或是重音的位置，往往透露出重要的訊息，以此就可以判斷出答案。

聽對話之前，心中要預備回答下列幾個問題：

1. **Who is speaking?**
   （誰在說話？）
2. **Where are they?**
   （他們在哪裡？）
3. **Why are they having the conversation?**
   （為什麼他們會進行這段對話？）

1. Who is speaking? （誰在說話？）	
相關問句	**可能的答案**
Who are the speakers in the conversation? （在這段對話中的說話者是誰？）	• They are teacher and student. （他們是老師和學生。） • Boss and clerk. （老闆和職員。）
Which statement is true about the speakers? （有關說話者的敘述那一項是正確的呢？）	• They are friends. （他們是朋友。） • This is the first time they've met. （這是他們第一次見面。）
What is the relationship between the speakers? （說話者之間是什麼關係？）	• They are father and daughter. （他們是父親和女兒。） • Boyfriend and girlfriend. （男女朋友。）

2. Where are they?
（他們在哪裡？）

相關問句	可能的答案
Where are the speakers? （說話者在哪裡？）	• They're at an airport. （他們在機場。） • At a movie theater. （在電影院。）
Where might David probably be at this moment? （這一刻大衛可能在哪裡？）	• He might be at a bank. （他可能在銀行。） • At an embassy. （在大使館。）
Where is the man most likely to be? （這位男士最有可能在哪裡？）	• He's likely at a museum. （他可能是在博物館。） • He's probably hiking in the mountains. （他可能正在山裡健行。）

3. Why are they having the conversation?
（為什麼他們會進行這段對話？）

相關問句	可能的答案
What is the main topic of the conversation? （對話的主題是什麼？）	• They're talking about their vacation. （他們正在談論他們的假期。） • Buying vitamins. （購買維他命。）
Why are the speakers having this conversation? （說話者為什麼會進行這段對話？）	• They're deciding where to eat dinner. （他們正在決定要去哪裡吃晚飯。） • The woman lost the keys to her apartment. （這名女士弄丟了她公寓的鑰匙。）
What is the purpose of this conversation? （這段對話的目的是什麼？）	• The man is asking for directions. （這名男子正在問路。） • The woman is ordering a book online. （這位女士正在網路上訂購一本書。）

作答說明：每題請聽光碟放音機播出一段對話及一個相關的問題後，從試題冊上A、B、
　　　　　C、D四個選項中選出一個最適合者作答。每段對話及問題只播出一遍。

1
A. They're in a coffee shop.
B. They're at a grocery store.
C. They're in an embassy.
D. They're in a license bureau.

2
A. She's trying to find a new love.
B. She wants the man to get some dessert.
C. She's trying to order some apple pie without ice cream.
D. She's trying not to gain any more weight.

3
A. It's the boy's birthday party.
B. It's a barbecue.
C. It's Chinese New Year.
D. It's the boy's graduation ceremony.

4
A. She got her electricity and water bills reduced.
B. People helped restore things back to normal after an earthquake.
C. She received useful training.
D. Now she can watch her favorite TV show.

5
A. He's a dentist.
B. He's a nurse.
C. He's a cosmetic surgeon.
D. He's a salesman.

6
A. They're old friends.
B. They're neighbors.
C. They're doctor and patient.
D. They're dog trainers.

7
A. The ball she bought broke.
B. The man said she can't return the merchandise.
C. The clerk won't buy the lady a new bowl.
D. She wants to speak to the manager.

8
A. They're discussing the woman's promotion.
B. They're talking about their weekend plans.
C. They want to improve their work conditions.
D. They're talking about their responsibilities at work.

9
A. They're in Tokyo.
B. They're in the shade, probably under a tree.
C. They're at an amusement park.
D. They're at a shopping mall.

10
A. They're talking about an impressive tornado that hit town.
B. They're talking about their newest album.
C. They're deciding where to get a drink.
D. They're talking about the concert they just attended.

3-2 聽出意圖

基本觀念

推測意圖題在考試中很常見，這個題型主要是考辨別說話者的目的、意圖或是接下來會做的事。

範 例

M: That scared the living daylights out of me.	那真是把我嚇得魂飛魄散。
W: Do you need any help?	你需要幫助嗎？
M: No, it's okay. I've had flat tires before.	不，沒關係。我以前有過爆胎的情況。
W: Be careful.	小心一點。

Q: What is the man likely to do next?	**這位男士接下來可能會做什麼？**
A: Adjust his retirement fund.	調整他的退休基金。
B: Change a tire.	換輪胎。
C: Wait for the woman to finish.	等待這位女士來完成。
D: Turn the lights back on.	重新再開燈。

解析
1. 本題是在談論剛剛出的狀況，題目是問這位男士會怎麼處理。
2. 選項 A 中的 retire「退休」和 tire「輪胎」是相似音，非正確答案。
3. 答題線索是 No, it's okay. I've had flat tires before. 這句話透露出他不需要幫忙，因為根據以前的經驗，他知道應該如何處理，所以答案是 B。
4. 關鍵字彙與慣用語：That scared the living daylights out of me.「那真是把我嚇得魂飛魄散。」、flat tires「爆胎」。

答案 B

相關問句

1. What does the woman **plan** to do?（這位女士打算做什麼？）
2. What **will** the couple **likely** do next?（這對夫妻接下來可能會做什麼？）
3. What **will** the man **probably** do?（這位男士可能會做什麼？）
4. How **will** the speakers get to the mall?（說話者要怎麼到購物商場？）
5. What is the man **going to** do?（這位男士將會做什麼？）

作答技巧

▶ 弱音、連音、消音與變音（Connected Speech）

很多人會抱怨簡短對話的速度太快，來不及聽清楚。然而，一旦看到印出來的對話內容，才發現原來自己都能理解。這是因為講話是一連串的聲音，沒有明確的句子和句子之間的停頓，再加上某些字連在一起時就有弱音、連音、消音和變音的現象，所以有時聽不懂字義。

當學生聽不太懂對話的主旨大意時，就無法推論說話者的意圖，也因為如此，在辨別弱音、連音、消音和變音時就會有困難。請看以下這些相似的發音詞組：

- is really / Israeli
- for a coffee / photocopy
- in her office / inner office

其實考試時或者外國人所說的英語都是連在一起發音的，而不是逐字逐句地說英文。此外，英語句子中的某些單字會以較高的音調、較長的時間與較大的音量說出，相反的有些單字的發音就必須輕、短、快，這兩種重讀和弱讀的單字就形成了句子的節奏。

英語是一個非常注重韻律和節奏的語言，需要重讀的重音位置往往就是說話者要強調的關鍵字。在說話句子裡有內容字（content words）和功能字（function words）兩種，所謂的內容字也就是關鍵字，用來表達語意的字詞，因此說話時會加上重音。功能字通常在句子中扮演的角色比較沒那麼重要，因此輕輕帶過即可。請考生掌握以下兩個原則：

❶ 重音加在主要的內容字（content words）上，包括動詞、名詞、形容詞、副詞、指示代名詞和所有格代名詞。

❷ 功能字（function words）不加重音，包括人稱代名詞、介系詞、定冠詞、連接詞、助動詞和 be 動詞。

❶ 弱音

有些弱讀的字並不是只有輕唸而已，你還必須熟悉其弱讀的發音。以下的功能字在句子中大都是以弱讀的形式唸出，要聽懂道地的英語發音，就要熟悉這些句子中的弱讀發音！

單字	重讀發音	弱讀發音	單字	重讀發音	弱讀發音
a	[æ]	[ə]	have	[hæv]	[həv] [əv]
am	[æm]	[əm] [m]	her	[hɜ]	[ə] [hə]
an	[æn]	[ən] [n̩] [n]	him	[hɪm]	[ɪm]
and	[ænd]	[ɛnd] [ənd] [ən] [n̩d]	of	[ɑv]	[əv] [ə]
			or	[ɔr]	[ər]
at	[æt]	[ət] [ɪt]	that	[ðæt]	[ðət]
are	[ɑr]	[ər] [ə]	than	[ðæn]	[ðən]
as	[æz]	[əz]	them	[ðɛm]	[ðəm]
because	[bɪˋkɔz]	[ˋbɪkəz]	to	[tu]	[tə]
can	[kæn]	[kən]	was	[wɑz]	[wəz]
for	[fɔr]	[fə] [fər]	were	[wɜ]	[wə]
from	[frɑm]	[frəm]	you	[ju]	[ju] [jə]
had	[hæd]	[həd]	your	[jur]	[jə]
has	[hæz]	[həz] [əz]			

❷ 連音

連音在口語中是很普遍的現象，也往往是某些考生的障礙。下面介紹兩種連音的方式。

❶ 一個句子中，當前面字的子音遇到下一個字的母音時，發音自然會連起來，例如：kind of, cup of tea, work out, not at all 等等。

❷ 在一個句子中，以字母 h 或 th 為首的代名詞及助動詞，位於句中非重音節的位置時，h 和 th 常不發音（被弱化發音了）。例如：call her, told them, give him 等等。因此造成第一個單字的最後子音會跟第二個單字的開頭母音連結在一起發音。

請聽 CD ，注意下列粗體字的發音，並注意其弱音與連音的現象。 🎧 2-02

1. I'm kind **of** [ə] tired.

2. We need **to** [tə] find **a** [ə] bathroom.

3. Have **you** [jə] finished?

4. I'll try the fish **and** [n] chips, please.

5. She **can** [kən] speak English better than I can.

6. Which **have** [əv] you seen?

7. I'm looking **for** [fər] my keys.

8. I thought she said **that** [ðət] it was okay.

9. I'll buy **some** [səm] at the store on my way home.

10. How **do** [də] you do?（第二個 do 是重音）

11. He'll call **her** [ɚ] tomorrow night.

12. I told **them** [ðəm] not to call after 10 o'clock.

❸ 消音

在英語口語中，常常會因為句子的輕重音，或是要強調某些關鍵字的關係而弱化了部分的音，有時甚至因為說話速度太快，部分子音或母音的發音會省略不發。聽得懂消音字會幫助你更了解對話的內容。學會了這個技巧，不僅對你的聽力有助益，而且還會幫助你說話更自然流利。

▶ **常見例子**

序號	單字	有 schwa 的音	省略的 schwa 音
1.	chocolate	[ˋtʃakəlɪt]	[ˋtʃak(ə)lɪt]
2.	interesting	[ˋɪntərɪstɪŋ]	[ˋɪnt(ə)rɪstɪŋ]
3.	camera	[ˋkæmərə]	[ˋkæm(ə)rə]
4.	vegetable	[ˋvɛdʒətəbl̩]	[ˋvɛdʒ(ə)təbl̩]
5.	memory	[ˋmɛmərɪ]	[ˋmɛm(ə)rɪ]
6.	family	[ˋfæməlɪ]	[ˋfæm(ə)lɪ]
7.	preference	[ˋprɛfərəns]	[ˋprɛf(ə)rəns]
8.	favorite	[ˋfevərɪt]	[ˋfev(ə)rɪt]

編註 schwa 就是「非中央元音」，也就是不在重音節的母音。

如果單字結尾的音是 [t] 或 [d] 時，緊接在後的單字如果是子音開頭的字時，在說話很快的情況之下，[t] 和 [d] 的聲音往往會被省略。

請聽 CD 並且留意這些爆裂音如何被省略。 **2-03**

1.	This is the la<u>st s</u>ong.	[læst sɔŋ]	→ [læs sɔŋ]
2.	That's a fa<u>st c</u>ar.	[fæst kɑr]	→ [fæs kɑr]
3.	<u>Se</u>n<u>d M</u>ike an invitation.	[sɛnd maɪk]	→ [sɛn maɪk]
4.	He showed a lot of ki<u>nd</u>ness.	[ˋkaɪndnɪs]	→ [kaɪnɪs]

Exercise 1 **2-04**

請練習唸出下面的句子，並在被省略 [t] 或 [d] 的發音字母下面畫線。然後再聽 CD，比較你的和外國老師的發音。

1. The children seemed a little restless.
2. When does the next movie start?
3. I told them to stand the chairs against the wall.
4. I need to wind down after a long day.
5. We should do our best to assist the police.
6. The tourist stayed with us for two days.
7. We'll have the party in the vacant lot beside the school.
8. She spoke to us about her blindness.
9. Lend Danny your car tonight.
10. Didn't Frank tell you?

當 [t] 的聲音是出現在縮寫型式的 can't 時，後面如果也是緊接著子音的話，也會出現消音的現象。由於對話中常有這個情形，所以增加了考試的難度。

Exercise 2 **2-05**

請聽下面句子，並且圈出正確答案，然後對照後面的答案。

1. I (can / can't) prove who stole the parcel.
2. Why (can / can't) they go?
3. You (can / can't) call me anytime you want.
4. We (can / can't) wait outside.
5. (Can / Can't) they hear us from the back?
6. I (can / can't) help you this afternoon.
7. She (can / can't) finish before she goes home.
8. Hank (can / can't) compete in the race.
9. We (can / can't) perform without them.
10. (Can / Can't) they ask for a temporary extension?

④ 變音

當你在看電影或是聽英文歌時，你會發現為了配合句子的語調、速度或流暢而產生變音的現象。以下介紹一些常見的例子：

請聽 CD ，並且留意這些字的發音。 🎧 **2-06**

序號	標準英文 (Standard English)	縮減形式 (Reduced Form)	例句 (Example)
1.	because	cuz	I'm in trouble **cuz** of you.
2.	bet you	betcha	I **betcha** this movie sucks.
3.	could have + 子音	kuda	She **kuda** told me how she felt.
4.	could have + 母音	kudav	We **kudav** ordered out.
5.	did you	didja/didya	**Didya** call her last night?
6.	don't you	doncha	Why **doncha** eat meat?
7.	get you	getcha	I'll **getcha** a drink.
8.	give me	gimme	**Gimme** a thousand bucks.
9.	going to	gonna	We're **gonna** pass this test.
10.	got you	gotcha	I **gotcha** a little present.
11.	has to	hasta	He **hasta** stay home and study.
12.	have to	hafta	They **hafta** finish the report today.
13.	how are you + 動名詞	howarya	**Howarya** doin'?
14.	I don't know	I dunno	**I dunno** what she meant.
15.	kind of + 子音	kinda	It's the **kinda** novel you'd like.
16.	kind of + 母音	kindav	I like that **kindav** entertainment.
17.	let me	lemme	**Lemme** see.
18.	lot of + 子音	lotta	I have a **lotta** time on my hands.
19.	lot of + 母音	lottav	We have a **lottav** ice cream.
20.	ought to	oughta	You **oughta** visit your mom.
21.	should have + 子音	shoulda	You **shoulda** called her.
22.	should have + 母音	shouldav	We **shouldav** opened a pub.
23.	want to	wanna	I **wanna** go scuba diving.
24.	what are you + 動名詞	whatcha	**Whatcha** doin' tonight?
25.	what do you + 動詞	whaddaya	**Whaddaya** wanna watch on TV?

題型實戰演練　▶▶ 2-07

作答說明：每題請聽光碟放音機播出一段對話及一個相關的問題後，從試題冊上A、B、
　　　　　C、D 四個選項中選出一個最適合者作答。每段對話及問題只播出一遍。

1　A. Plan a wedding.
　　B. Call a wedding planner.
　　C. Call and change the appointment.
　　D. She likes to plan weddings.

2　A. They'll go buy some ice cream.
　　B. They'll fix what's broken.
　　C. They'll finish watching the movie.
　　D. They'll go swimming.

3　A. A five-star hotel.
　　B. A hotel by the beach
　　B. A beach hut.
　　D. A villa just like last year.

4　A. Stop the dog's bleeding.
　　B. Go somewhere else to hike.
　　C. Take the dog to a veterinarian.
　　D. Look for the dog's owner.

5　A. She'll pay with her credit card.
　　B. She'll leave without the purchase.
　　C. She'll borrow some cash.
　　D. She'll write a check for the perfume.

6　A. Beef and noodles and some chicken butts.
　　B. Fried chicken and some stir-fried vegetables.
　　C. Some noodles and stir-fried vegetables.
　　D. Two bowls of today's special.

7　A. A skirt.
　　B. A sandwich wrap.
　　C. A shirt with a scary design.
　　D. A bracelet.

8　A. They'll study for an exam.
　　B. They'll redecorate a kitchen.
　　C. They'll visit the man's parents.
　　D. They'll likely help the man's parents next Saturday.

9　A. Find a job.
　　B. Ask his girlfriend to marry him.
　　C. Tell his girlfriend to wait a little longer.
　　D. Call his parents and tell them that they're right.

10　A. They'll take a taxi.
　　B. They'll take a bus.
　　C. The woman will ride her scooter.
　　D. It'll probably take them twenty minutes to get there.

3-3 聽出細節

基本觀念

有關細節的問題是最常見的題型，因為我們的日常生活中充滿了各式各樣的小細節，像是幾點離開家、吃什麼、口袋裡有多少錢等等。我們不可能為了考試而準備生活中每一個小細節。不過本單元將要教導一些技巧，幫助考生處理細節方面的題型。

範例

M: What kind of workout are we going to do today, Miss Chen?	陳小姐，我們今天要做的是什麼樣的健身？
W: Well, I'd like to get rid of these flabby arms.	嗯，我想要擺脫這些軟趴趴的蝴蝶袖。
M: Sounds like a good plan.	聽起來像是一個好計畫。
W: My arms look horrible.	我的手臂慘不忍睹。
M: I think they look okay.	我認為看起來還好。
W: Oh, they jiggle like jello.	哦，他們像果凍一樣搖來晃去。
Q: Where is this conversation likely taking place?	這個對話可能在哪裡發生？
A: In a grocery store.	在一家雜貨店。
B: In a health club.	在一個健身俱樂部。
C: At an office.	在一個辦公室。
D: At a doctor's office.	在醫生的辦公室。

解析 1. 本題的內容是在談論今天要做的運動和原因，題目是問對話發生的地點。

2. 答題的線索在 workout 和 get rid of these flabby arms，所以我們知道最有可能的地方就是在健身房，答案選 B。

3. 關鍵字彙：workout「運動；健身」、get rid of「擺脫；消除」、flabby arms「蝴蝶袖；手臂上的贅肉」、jiggle「抖動」、jello「果凍」。 答案 B

作答技巧

▶ 做筆記（Note Taking）

❶ 邊聽邊做筆記

考試時總是有一些問題讓人感到困惑，因為有些對話提到很多細節，這些細節可能是重要的，也有可能是不重要的，要看是否和問題有關。當某項細節是回答問題的關鍵點，而你又沒有聽清楚時，你就會希望有機會再聽一次對話。為了避免這種情況發生，你必須要學會一邊聽對話，一邊做筆記的技巧。建議你現在就開始練習，這個技巧不但會幫助你記錄關鍵的細節，找到正確的答案，還會提高你聆聽對話時的專心度。無疑地，這個習慣會提升你腦中「由下而上」的聽力技巧。

當你做筆記時，最重要的是要聽清楚完整的句意。如果你只專注在所有過多的小細節上，可能會沒有留意到某些特殊的字眼，例如轉折語或是重要的句型，那麼就會聽錯意思。正如我們前面提到的，最好是靈活地運用「由上而下」和「由下而上」這兩個技巧。

考試時，一定要在聆聽對話之前先瀏覽答案選項。如果答案選項提到某些細節，如時間、日期和數量時，切記聆聽時一定要寫下來，並專注於細節的部分。另一方面，如果答案選項大多出現主旨大意的話，請務必專注於整體的對話意義與情境，來幫助自己通盤了解。以下為兩個專注在不同地方的例子。

▶ **專注細節的選項**

A. In two weeks.（在兩個星期後。）

B. In two months.（在兩個月後。）

C. He's leaving early to find an apartment.（他提早離開去找公寓。）

D. In the middle of February.（在 2 月中旬。）

▶ **專注主旨大意的選項**

A. They're talking about where to vacation.（他們正在談論要到哪裡渡假。）

B. They're talking in a restaurant.（他們正在一家餐廳聊天。）

C. They're talking about hotels.（他們正在談論飯店的事情。）

D. The woman prefers five-star hotels.（這位女士偏愛五星級飯店。）

參加正式考試時，可以做筆記寫下重點或關鍵字，從現在開始學會利用做筆記來訓練更好的耳力。

❷ 做筆記的訣竅

以下介紹一種實用的做筆記方法。首先，快速瀏覽答案選項，然後預測可能會考的題目。

範例 1 ✏️

A. Eight thirty.	*(What time?)*
B. He's been swimming all morning.	*(What has he been doing?)*
C. About twelve thirty.	*(What time?)*
D. It's time for lunch.	*(What is it time for?)*

基本上，由上述這個範例得知選項 A 和 C 是相似的，都是問時間。當選項中有兩個或三個答案相似時，你就要大膽地假設，題目是考有關時間方面的問題。

當然在考試的時候，我們沒有時間寫下完整的題目與對話內容，所以只要寫下關鍵字即可。若有些字你不會寫或者是拼不完整，你還可以運用一些簡易的符號或是圖來表示，只要自己看得懂即可。

請參考下面的範例來練習做筆記，並且看看你是否可以根據筆記快速地找到答案。

M: It's time for lunch. You boys have been swimming since half past eight.	午餐時間到了。你們這些孩子從八點半就游泳到現在。
W: Wow! We've been swimming for four hours?	哇！我們已經游了 4 個小時了？
M: You're like fish.	你們和魚一樣。
W: We're hungry fish!	我們是飢餓的魚！
Q: What time is it now?	現在幾點了？

Note Taking

WHEN   8:30, swimming 4 hours
WHAT   swimming, fish
TIME FOR lunch

從筆記中我們很快就知道答案是 C。

範例 2

A. It's a farewell party.　　　　　　　(What kind of party is it?)
B. She's tall with long hair.　　　　　(What does the woman look like?)
C. She's got a sweet smile.　　　　　(What does the woman look like?)
D. She's looking for a boyfriend.　　 (What is she looking for?)

同樣的，要先瀏覽選項找出共同點，選項 B 和 C 相似，由此可預測題目可能會考有關這個女孩長相方面的細節。

M: This is great music.　　　　　　　音樂真棒呀。
W: I'm so glad I came to Lisa's farewell party.　我很高興來參加麗莎的歡送會。
M: Hey, who's the cute girl over there?　嘿，那邊那位可愛的女孩是誰？
W: You mean the tall one with long hair?　你是說那個長髮的高個兒女孩嗎？
M: Well, she's nice too, but I was referring to the one beside her.　嗯，她也不錯，但是我是指在她旁邊的那個。
W: That's my sister!　　　　　　　　那是我妹妹耶！
M: She's got a sweet smile.　　　　她的笑容很甜美。
W: And a boyfriend, too.　　　　　而且她也有男朋友。

Q: Which statement best describes the woman who the man is checking out?　下列那一項敘述最符合這位男士正在看的女孩？

Note Taking

WHAT KIND　farewell party
LOOKS LIKE　tall long hair / sweet smile, sister
LOOKING FOR　X

從筆記中我們得知他們說到兩位女孩，但是從 *I was referring to the one* 這句話告訴我們，他是在說另一個，所以答案是 C。一旦你養成邊聽邊做筆記的習慣後，你會發現你的聽力變敏銳了，選出正確的答案也輕而易舉。

相關問句

細節的題型可以包括各式各樣不同的主題，以下是一些常見的主題和問題：

主題	常見問題
時間	1. What time is it now? （現在幾點？） 2. How soon will Kevin arrive? （凱文多快會到？） 3. What time does the next train leave? （下一班火車幾點離開？） 4. When will the party begin? （派對何時開始？） 5. How often does the man like to go jogging? （這位男士喜歡多久去慢跑一次？）
日期	1. When was the man born? （這位男士什麼時候出生？） 2. When will the woman arrive in Kaohsiung? （這位女士何時會到高雄？） 3. When does the man plan to be gone? （這位男士計畫何時離開？） 4. When does school start? （學校什麼時候開學？） 5. What are the dates for the music festival? （音樂嘉年華是什麼時候？）
數量	1. How much will the man pay? （這位男士將會付多少錢？） 2. How much will the woman save? （這位女士將會存多少錢？） 3. What size screen will they buy? （他們將要買多大尺寸的螢幕？） 4. How many students were sick? （有多少個學生生病了？） 5. How big is the department store? （這個百貨公司有多大？）

主題	常見問題
地點	1. Where will the couple meet? （這對夫婦會在哪裡見面？） 2. Where does the conversation take place? （這段對話是在哪裡發生的？） 3. Where are the speakers? （說話者在哪裡？） 4. Where is the man going this evening? （這位男士今晚要去哪裡？） 5. Where is Jacob from? （雅各是從哪裡來的？）
原因	1. Why is Elaine late? （為什麼依蓮遲到了？） 2. Why will the man call his mother? （這位男士為什麼會打電話給他的母親？） 3. Why are the speakers in a hurry? （為什麼說話者這麼匆忙？） 4. Why does this man want to change jobs? （為什麼這位男士想換工作？） 5. What's the reason for the delay? （是什麼原因延誤了？）
人物	1. Whose classroom is at the end of the hall? （誰的教室在走廊盡頭？） 2. What is the man's occupation? （這位男士的職業是什麼？） 3. Whose bag was left at the theater? （誰的包包留在戲院？） 4. Who is talking to the media? （誰正在對媒體說話？） 5. Who is the man talking to? （這位男士正在對誰說話？）

作答說明：每題請聽光碟放音機播出一段對話及一個相關的問題後，從試題冊上A、B、
　　　　C、D四個選項中選出一個最適合者作答。每段對話及問題只播出一遍。

1
A. Go see Gary.
B. Study at the library.
C. Take a biology test.
D. Have dinner with a friend.

2
A. It will rain tomorrow.
B. It's sunny.
C. It's raining.
D. They prefer sunny days.

3
A. She'll go with Mike.
B. Mike will drive.
C. She'll take a bus with Mike.
D. She'll take a taxi with Mike.

4
A. She heard them walking down the stairs.
B. She hurt her ankle.
C. She probably won't play tomorrow.
D. She hurt herself walking down the stairs.

5
A. She'll pay for three shirts.
B. She'll pay only NT$715.
C. She'll pay NT$290 each.
D. She'll pay NT$750.

6
A. His salary isn't very good.
B. He doesn't like his boss.
C. Because he wants more benefits.
D. His colleagues are awful.

7
A. The woman wanted to find an MRT station.
B. The woman wants to see Taipei 101.
C. The woman will take the MRT.
D. The woman is very close to Taipei 101.

8
A. She's from America.
B. She's from Canada.
C. She's vacationing in Taiwan.
D. She's living in Ireland.

9
A. At ten after one.
B. It's 1 o'clock.
C. At ten to ten.
D. At 2 p.m.

10
A. She likes fruit tea.
B. She'll buy a passion fruit tea.
C. She usually buys pearl green tea.
D. She won't buy any tea.

3-4 聽出推論

基本觀念

闡釋與推論題型主要是在問說話者的觀點、態度及言外之意等等。考生必須根據對話中所得到的資訊進行推論或下結論；換句話說，在對話中並沒有明確地說明原因或是結果，你必須要自己判斷結果或是聽出弦外之音。假設你看到你的鄰居太太手上拿著高爾夫球桿在她先生的車子後面追著跑，你可以推論出，這位妻子可能很生氣；但也可能是因為這位先生要去打球，但是忘了帶他的球桿；或者是有人偷了她丈夫的車子等等。像這一類的題型，我們必須要仔細聆聽對話的上下文意思，並且在四個選項答案中，選出最符合對話細節內容的推論。

範 例

M: Hey, where are you going?	嘿，妳要去哪裡？
W: Oh, I need to go photocopy this.	哦，我需要去影印這個。
M: While you're there, can you buy some A4 paper for me?	妳到那裡時，可以幫我買一些 A4 的紙嗎？
W: Sure.	當然可以。

Q: Where will the woman most likely go?	這位女士最有可能去哪裡？

A. She's going to a coffee shop to read the paper.	她將要去一家咖啡廳看報紙。
B. Somewhere to take pictures.	去某個地方拍照。
C. She's likely a photographer.	她可能是位攝影師。
D. To a photocopy store.	去影印店。

 1. 本題情境是男方想要知道女方要去何處，對話內容為男方請求女方幫忙買 A4 尺寸的紙。

2. 答題線索為 I need to go photocopy this. 和 can you buy some A4 paper for me 這兩句話，我們可以推論出，這位小姐是要去影印店，答案選 D。

3. 注意 photocopy「影印」和 for a coffee「為了一杯咖啡」聽起來相近，不要搞錯。請不要只聽細節的字彙，別忘了還要試著去了解這些細節透露出什麼訊息。

4. 關鍵字彙：photocopy「影印」、photographer「攝影師」。 D

作答技巧

▶ 做出推論

通常要求你做出推論的考題不是問你其中特定某個字的意思，就是要你推論出整個對話的重點。這裡要教你如何做出兩種推論：（A）推論出某些特定字或不熟悉的字的正確意思；（B）推論出對話的結果與結論。

A 特定字或不熟悉的字

❶ 從上下文的大意

遇到聽不懂的字，可以由對話中的上下文大意來推論出這個字的意思。

範 例

W: I have no idea what to buy for my mother.	我不知道該買什麼東西給我媽媽。
M: How about some *cosmetics*?	買化妝品怎麼樣？
W: That's a great idea. She enjoys looking her best, and she needs more help hiding her wrinkles.	這真是一個好主意。她喜愛呈現出最好的一面，而且她需要更多的東西幫忙蓋住她的皺紋。
M: Do you know what brand she likes?	妳知道她喜歡什麼品牌嗎？
W: No. I'll have to stop by her place to see what she has.	不知道，我必須要順道經過她家，去看看她有什麼。
M: By the way, I like the lipstick you're wearing.	對了，我喜歡妳擦的口紅。
W: Are you flirting with me?	你在勾引我嗎？
M: Uh...	嗯 ...

推論

由下面兩點可推論出 cosmetics 的字義：

＊ enjoys looking her best

＊ she needs more help hiding her wrinkles

想想女人通常會怎麼做來打扮自己，隱藏自己的皺紋呢？由此可推論出是化妝品。

Q: What is the woman going to buy for her mother?	這位女士將會為她的母親買什麼東西？

A. Some clothes.	一些衣服。
B. She'll go to her mother's place first.	她會先去她母親的家。
C. Some make-up.	一些化妝品。
D. A popular brand of lipstick.	一個受歡迎牌子的口紅。

 1. 本題情境是女方想要買禮物送給媽媽，而男方是幫她服務的店員。

2. 即使你不知道 cosmetics 這個字，你也可以由對話上下文推論出女人通常用什麼東西來幫助自己變好看，答題關鍵在 She enjoys looking her best, and she needs more help hiding her wrinkles.

3. 關鍵字彙：cosmetics「化妝品」、wrinkle「皺紋」、brand「品牌」、lipstick「口紅」、flirt with someone「和某人調情；勾引某人」。 答案 C

❷ 從對話中的例子猜測

遇到聽不懂的字，有時候對話中所舉的例子會暗示這個字的意思。

 範　例

M: So tell me about your new boyfriend.	那和我談談妳的新男友吧。
W: He loves going to parties and inviting friends over to his place.	他喜歡參加派對，和邀請朋友去他家。
M: He sounds quite *gregarious*.	他聽起來非常熱衷社交。
W: He is. I think he's in about three clubs at school.	他是，我想他在學校大概參加了 3 個社團。

推論

由下面兩點可推論出 gregarious 的字義：

* loves going to parties

* inviting friends over to his place

* in about 3 clubs

想想喜歡參加派對、邀請朋友到家中和參加三個社團的人，應該是熱愛社交的人，所以可推論出 gregarious 是「熱愛社交的」。

Q: What does the man think of the woman's boyfriend?	這位男士認為這位女士的男朋友如何？

A. He thinks her boyfriend is generous.　　他認為她男朋友很大方。

B. He thinks she's in love.　　他認為她正在戀愛。

C. He thinks they met at a school club.　　他認為他們是在學校社團認識的。

D. He thinks the man is very sociable.　　他覺得這名男子很善於交際。

 1. 本題情境是兩人在談論女方的新男朋友，題目是問男方覺得這位女士的新男朋友如何。

2. 答題關鍵是 He loves going to parties and inviting friends over to his place. 和 He sounds quite gregarious. 你可以藉由喜愛參加派對、邀請朋友來家裡和參加社團等例子，來猜想 gregarious 是什麼意思。如果你認為大概是接近 sociable「愛社交的」或是 outgoing「隨和的」這些字眼的話，你的推論就是正確的。

3. 關鍵字彙：invite someone over「邀請某人來」、gregarious「熱愛社交的」、sociable「擅長交際的」。　　答案 D

❸ 對比

此外，對話中常會出現一些對比的字眼，藉由對比的方式會幫助你猜出某些單字的意思。

 範 例

W: How do you like your new apartment?　　你喜歡你的新公寓嗎？

M: The location is nice, but my room is ***stuffy***.　　地點是不錯，但我的房間通風不好。

W: Really?　　真的嗎？

M: Yeah, maybe it's because I can't open my windows. Your room is more airy and better ventilated.　　是啊，也許是因為我無法打開窗戶。妳的房間比較有風，也較通風。

W: Ask your landlord if you can change apartments.　　問你的房東看看是否可以換別的公寓。

M: It's worth a try.　　值得一試。

推論

男生說這位女生的房間比較有風又通風，可見男生的房間和女生的房間相反，也就是說沒有風，由此可知 stuffy 是「通風不好」的意思。

Q: What can you infer about the man's apartment?	你可以推測出這名男子的公寓是怎麼樣的情況呢？
A. It has a lot of stuff in it.	裡面有很多東西。
B. It's too small.	它太小了。
C. The windows provide enough ventilation.	他的窗戶幫助通風。
D. His room is not very breezy.	他的房間不太有風。

解析
1. 本題情境是兩位熟識的人在談論男子的公寓，題目是要推論出該名男子的公寓如何。

2. 答題關鍵是：my room is stuffy 和 Your room is more airy and better ventilated.，如果你不知道 stuffy 是什麼意思的話，可以和這名女子房間對比，猜測出大概是沒有風或是不通風的意思。

3. 關鍵字彙：stuffy「空氣不流通的」、airy「有風的」、ventilated「通風的」、breezy「有微風的」。

答案 D

❹ 反義字

有時候我們可以藉由反義字猜測出某些單字的意思。

 範 例

M: How did you hear about this restaurant?	妳是怎麼知道這家餐廳的？
W: My professor recommended it.	我的教授推薦的。
M: The food here is **nasty**.	這裡的食物很難吃。
W: Really? I think it's quite tasty.	真的嗎？我覺得相當好吃。
M: Would you like my portion?	妳要吃我的份嗎？

推論

如果這名女子認為是美味的食物，而這名男子卻持不同看法時，那麼你就可以推斷出 nasty 是美味的反義字。

Q: How does the man feel about the food?	這位男士覺得食物如何？
A. He doesn't like it.	他不喜歡它。
B. The professor recommended the restaurant.	是教授推薦的餐廳。
C. He would like another portion.	他想要另外一份。
D. He feels the same way as the woman does.	他和這位女士感覺一樣。

1. 本題情境是兩位朋友在一家餐廳用餐，對話內容是談論對於這家餐廳食物的看法。

2. 答題關鍵是在 It's nasty.（男子的想法）和 Really? I think it's quite tasty.（女子的想法），由此我們可以推論出他們兩個人對食物的感覺不同，該名男子覺得食物不美味。

3. 關鍵字彙：nasty「難吃的」、portion「一份；一客」。

 A

B 對話的結果與結論

除了要學會推論出不懂的單字意思之外，還要知道如何推論出對話的結果或是結論。如果你能迅速辨別對話中說話者的身分、關係與談話觀點，並且掌握住對話中的主旨大意與上下文關係，就很容易判斷出結論。

範 例

W: What seems to be the problem?	看起來是什麼問題？
M: I'm not sure. He just seems so weak. The poor guy can barely walk.	我不知道。牠好像非常虛弱，可憐的傢伙幾乎無法走路。
W: He looks pretty friendly.	牠看起來相當友善。
M: He won't bite you.	牠不會咬妳。
W: Did he eat any food that he shouldn't have?	牠有沒有吃任何不應該吃的食物呢？
M: He probably got into the neighbor's trash. He ran away this morning for about an hour.	牠可能去鄰居的垃圾裡找食物。今天早上牠跑出去一個多小時。

推論

當你聽到這些片語和短語：can barely walk、won't bite you、got into the neighbor's trash、ran away this morning，你想到了什麼呢？應該是小狗之類的寵物吧。

Q: What is the woman's occupation?	這位女士的職業是什麼？
A. She's a doctor.	她是一位醫生。
B. She's examining the man's son.	她正在替這位男士的兒子做檢查。
C. She's a veterinarian.	她是位獸醫。
D. She's the man's neighbor.	她是這位男士的鄰居。

解析 1. 本題情境是兩人在談論寵物受傷的問題，對話內容是這名男子在敘述他的寵物的狀況給女方聽，題目是問女方的職業。

2. 答題關鍵是在女方說話的觀點與態度，由 What seems to be the problem? 和 Did he eat any food that he shouldn't have? 可以推測她應該是獸醫。

3. 關鍵字彙：barely「幾乎不能」、get into the trash「在垃圾堆中翻找食物」、run away「離家」。

答案 C

相關問句

主題	常見問題
職業	1. What is the man's occupation? （這位男士的職業是什麼？） 2. What does the man do for a living? （這位男士靠什麼維生？） 3. What's the man's job? （這位男士的工作是什麼？）
感覺與態度	1. How do you think the woman feels? （你認為這位女士的感覺是什麼？） 2. Which word best describes how the woman feels? （哪一個字最能形容這位女士的感覺？） 3. Why is the woman so nervous? （為什麼這位女士這麼緊張？）
地點	1. Where is this conversation likely taking place? （這段對話最有可能在哪裡發生？） 2. Where are the speakers probably talking? （說話者可能在哪裡交談？） 3. Where will the speakers meet later? （說話者等一會兒在哪裡見面？）
關係	1. What is the relationship between these two speakers? （這兩個說話者是什麼關係？） 2. Is this couple dating right now? （這一對正在交往中嗎？） 3. Who are the speakers? （說話者是誰？）

主題	常見問題
意見	1. Which statement best describes the man's opinion? （哪一項敘述最能說明這個人的意見？） 2. What's the man's opinion of his new supervisor? （這位男士對他的新上司有什麼看法？） 3. How has the man's opinion changed over time? （這位男士的看法是如何隨著時間改變了呢？）
未來的動作	1. What will probably happen next? （接下來可能會發生什麼事？） 2. What will the woman likely say next? （這位女士接下來會說什麼？） 3. What will the woman likely do later? （這位女士等一下可能會做什麼？）

題型實戰演練

作答說明：每題請聽光碟放音機播出一段對話及一個相關的問題後，從試題冊上A、B、
C、D 四個選項中選出一個最適合者作答。每段對話及問題只播出一遍。

1
A. Dark.
B. Worried.
C. Frustrated.
D. Cheerful.

2
A. They're talking about where to go.
B. They are at a shopping mall.
C. It's down the alley on the left.
D. They're at a night market.

3
A. She's a construction worker.
B. She's occupied at the moment.
C. She needs to see his license and registration.
D. She is a police officer.

4
A. This is their son's first game.
B. They feel helpless.
C. They're having a great time.
D. They are probably embarrassed.

5
A. She's a little disappointed.
B. She is very frustrated.
C. She is happy to help.
D. She's enthralled.

6
A. They'll resolve their problems peacefully.
B. They'll talk with their psychologist again.
C. They'll most likely get divorced.
D. They want to keep the children together.

7
A. Boss and employee.
B. It's not a cordial relationship.
C. No, they're not likely related.
D. Landlord and tenant.

8
A. Here's our menu, sir.
B. You should have bought a nicer suit.
C. Oh, that's today's special.
D. Let me get you another bowl.

9
A. Her friend will come and visit her.
B. She was accepted into university.
C. Her aunt and uncle live in Tainan.
D. She has finally become a nurse.

10
A. He wants to stop drinking beer.
B. Running on a treadmill is as good as riding a stationary bike.
C. He should start to exercise more.
D. He'll start swimming at a local health club.

3-5 聽出問題與解決方式

基本觀念

在日常生活中，人們幾乎每天都會遇到大大小小的不同問題，像是找不到鑰匙或者是在街道上來回繞了五圈才找到停車位之類的。考試有時候也會考到有關問題與問題解決方法的對話。面對這類題型，請仔細聆聽說話者所提出的建議、觀點和面對問題的態度，推論出說話者可能會如何處理這個問題。

範 例

M: It's getting worse and worse.	真是每況愈下。
W: I think it looks just fine.	我認為它看起來還好。
M: Come on. My receding hairline looks awful.	少來了，我逐漸後移的髮線看起來很可怕。
W: Maybe you should try a short hairstyle.	也許你應該嘗試短髮造型。
M: Do you think any oils will help?	妳覺得抹點油會有幫助嗎？
W: I doubt it.	我懷疑。

Q: What does the woman suggest the man do?	這位女士建議男士做什麼？
A. Try some different oils.	試試一些不同的髮油。
B. Have his hair cut shorter.	將他的頭髮剪短一點。
C. Accept the fact that he's going bald.	接受即將禿頭的事實。
D. She suggested that he keep his short hairstyle.	她建議他繼續維持他的短髮造型。

解析 1. 本題情境是美髮師和男顧客或是兩位熟識朋友的對話，對話內容主要是談論男士髮線的問題。

2. 答題線索是在 Maybe you should try a short hairstyle. 由此我們得知她建議嘗試短髮造型。

3. 關鍵字彙：receding hairline「逐漸後移的髮線」。 **答案** B

▶ **常見問題**

1. What's the problem?（問題是什麼？）

2. What seems to be the problem?（看起來是什麼問題？）

3. What solution does the man suggest?（這位男士建議什麼解決方式？）

4. How will the man handle this problem?（這位男士將如何處理這個問題？）

5. What problem does the city have?（這個城市有什麼問題？）

6. Why are the speakers in such a dilemma?（為何說話者會陷入這困境當中？）

7. Why is the man disappointed?（為何這位男士會失望？）

8. Why the long face?（為何臭著一張臉？）

▶ **和疑難問題相關的慣用語**

1. I'm **in a bind**.（我左右為難。）

2. My cousin is **in a pickle**.（我的表弟陷入困境。）

3. We need to **get to the bottom of** this.（我們需要找出這件事情的真相。）

4. If we don't fix this problem, it could **spiral out of control**.
   （如果我們不解決這個問題，情況可能會失控。）

5. This scandal is only the **tip of the iceberg**.（這一件醜聞只是冰山一角。）

6. We ran into another **stumbling block** trying to finalize this deal.
   （在試圖完成這筆交易的同時，我們碰到了另一個絆腳石。）

7. If you quit studying English, you'll be **digging your own grave**.
   （如果你放棄學習英語，等於是自掘墳墓。）

8. When troubles come, politicians often find a way to **pass the buck**.
   （遇到麻煩時，政客們時常想辦法推卸責任。）

作答技巧

▶ 不放棄，堅持下去

考試時，你可能會遇到聽不懂的單字或慣用語，這時不要慌張，請繼續聽下去，也不要告訴自己：「完蛋了」。在某些情況下，對話中充滿了不相關的小細節，當你專注於要聽懂每一個細節，並且用力推敲每句話的含意時，你可能會沒聽清楚整段對話，因而錯過了解題的關鍵字或線索。有時候最後一句話才是關鍵的線索。所以不要陷入你聽不懂的細節，千萬不要放棄，要堅持下去——繼續聽。

範　例

W: Is this your first time camping?	這是你第一次露營嗎？
M: No, I've been camping many times. Just last month some friends and I went up to Ali Mountain.	不，我已經露營過好多次了。上個月，我才和幾個朋友去阿里山。
W: How was that?	怎麼樣呢？

M: It was great. The weather was nice, but someone stole some of our camping supplies, like our mini camping stove, a compass, and some coolers.

很棒。天氣很不錯,但是有人偷走了我們一些露營用品,像是我們的露營小火爐、一個指南針和一些冷藏箱。

W: We'll be careful this time. I just hope Typhoon Tiffany doesn't hit Taiwan.

這一次我們會小心一點。我只希望蒂芬妮颱風不會侵襲台灣。

M: That would definitely put a damper on things.

那肯定是令人掃興的事情。

Q: **What problem might the campers encounter on their trip?**

露營者可能會在這趟旅行中遇到什麼問題?

A. Someone stole their camping supplies.

有人偷了他們的露營用品。

B. There might be too much traffic near Ali Mountain.

在阿里山附近可能會交通堵塞。

C. A typhoon might hit Taiwan.

颱風可能會侵襲台灣。

D. They'll likely encounter some beautiful wildlife.

他們可能會遇到一些美麗的野生動物。

 1. 本題情境是兩位要去露營的朋友在討論露營的計畫,題目是問這一次他們可能會遇上什麼問題。

2. 答題線索是在 I just hope Typhoon Tiffany doesn't hit Taiwan. 所以我們得知他們擔心颱風可能會侵襲台灣。

3. 關鍵字彙:camping supplies「露營用品」、compass「指南針」、coolers「冷藏箱」、put a damper on things「令人掃興」。

答案 C

題型實戰演練　　　　▶▶ 2-10

作答說明：每題請聽光碟放音機播出一段對話及一個相關的問題後，從試題冊上A、B、
C、D 四個選項中選出一個最適合者作答。每段對話及問題只播出一遍。

1. A. She's in a real pickle.
   B. She's too punctual.
   C. She took a left and got lost.
   D. She's late for a meeting.

2. A. He'll have his finger cut off.
   B. He'll go see his daughter.
   C. He'll see a doctor.
   D. He cut his finger, and now it's infected.

3. A. There aren't enough parks.
   B. There aren't many parking lots.
   C. It's not safe at night.
   D. The city needs to reduce the air pollution.

4. A. On the kitchen table.
   B. Under his coat.
   C. They couldn't find them, so they'll walk.
   D. In his coat pocket.

5. A. The mayor was cheating on his wife.
   B. Nothing was broken.
   C. A private investigator helped break the scandal.
   D. It's fabulous news.

6. A. A dishwasher.
   B. An air conditioner.
   C. A heater.
   D. A fan.

7. A. She wants to go shopping instead.
   B. She's petrified of heights.
   C. She's not feeling too well.
   D. She said she'll go later after shopping.

8. A. Alex is lost.
   B. The market is enormous.
   C. They can't find any second-hand DVDs.
   D. They can't find their daughter.

9. A. She's checking his phone messages.
   B. She suspects he won't call her at night.
   C. She believes her boyfriend is playing the field.
   D. She's a little insecure about herself.

10. A. The couple's flight is delayed.
    B. There's a long line at customs.
    C. They have to check their carry-on items.
    D. They can't decide whether to cut in line.

第三部分答題技巧複習

學習完第三部分，你是否已經學會了在「簡短對話」這個部分的所有答題技巧呢？請在你已經學會的方格中打勾。

簡短對話的答題技巧	✔
1. 在參加聽力測驗之前，我已經熟悉各種日常生活中的對話主題和相關字彙與慣用語。	
2. 聆聽對話之前，我會快速瀏覽四個選項，找出相同之處，並且預測題目的主題和內容。	
3. 聆聽對話時，我懂得運用「由上而下」與「由下而上」的思考模式來掌握對話中的主旨與細節。	
4. 聆聽對話時，我熟悉英語口語中的弱音、連音、消音與變音。	
5. 聆聽對話時，我已經學會邊聽邊做筆記的技巧，來幫助自己快速地記下細節。	
6. 聆聽對話時，我懂得利用上下文的大意、例子、對比與反義字來推論出生字的意思。	
7. 聆聽對話時，我已經學會利用說話者的身分、關係和說話的態度，來推論出對話的情境與結論，也可以聽出弦外之音或是暗喻之意。	
8. 聆聽對話時，不管是否有生字，我會不慌不忙、不放棄地堅持聽完整段對話，找出正確答案。	

筆記欄

TEST 聽力測驗總複習

本測驗分三部分，全為四選一之選擇題，共 45 題，作答時間約 30 分鐘。

第一部分　看圖辨義

 2-11

共 15 題，試題冊上有數幅圖畫，每一圖畫有 1~3 個描述該圖的題目，每題請聽光碟放音機播出題目以及四個英語敘述之後，選出與所看到的圖畫最相符的答案，每題只播出一遍。

A Question 1

C Question 4

B Questions 2-3

D Questions 5-6

E Question 7

F Question 8

G Questions 9-10

H Questions 11-12

I Question 13

J Question 14

K Question 15

第二部分　問答

共 15 題。每題請聽光碟放音機播出一英語問句或直述句之後，從試題冊上 A、B、C、D 四個回答或回應中，選出一個最適合者作答。每題只播出一遍。

16
A. No, thanks. I like the color it is now.
B. Yes, just a little off the back.
C. Sounds good.
D. I shampoo it every day.

17
A. Sorry, that's not my chair.
B. Can I borrow your pen?
C. I don't think it would look good there.
D. I really don't want to disturb her.

18
A. I can't recall when.
B. It's a phenomenon.
C. It's not hard to change the dates.
D. Yeah, maybe it's time to buy a new computer.

19
A. It's under Wang.
B. Party of four, thanks.
C. It's under the clipboard.
D. I think her name is Lucy.

20
A. We won't accept any excuses.
B. Well, I think it's fair.
C. Oh, it's delicious.
D. No, it's just around the corner.

21
A. How often does he go?
B. Does he make a lot of money?
C. That's an odd game to play.
D. Mine doesn't, either.

22
A. I'm sick of school.
B. The city built this bridge a year ago.
C. It never ends.
D. I feel sorry for the instructors.

23
A. Yes, I've done it several times now.
B. It's been six months.
C. I have, but I miss my family a lot.
D. No, I don't have one.

24
A. She just asked me for my phone number.
B. It's good for me.
C. I'm in a hurry.
D. Because we need to warn them of a landslide.

25
A. I'm driving to work.
B. I'm picking my friends up at school.
C. My fault. Sorry.
D. I watch mostly cartoons.

A. Well, the delicate items are handled with care.
B. I don't think we're on the right page.
C. It wasn't that hard.
D. My mother encouraged me to be optimistic.

 A. You were a big help.
B. What are friends for?
C. You said it.
D. Not too much.

 A. I didn't know he could ride a horse.
B. That's a good assumption.
C. When the cat's away, the mice will play.
D. That's too bad.

 A. What possessed her to buy one?
B. That's bad news for Cindy.
C. She must download all her music.
D. She shouldn't regret it.

 A. I don't think they're home.
B. They're still engaged in online gambling.
C. They lost the number.
D. Yeah, they haven't been getting along very well recently.

共 15 題。每題請聽光碟放音機播出一段對話及一個相關的問題後，從試題冊上 A、B、C、D 四個選項中選出一個最適合者作答。每段對話及問題只播出一遍。

31
A. The boy is in high school.
B. The woman is taller than the boy.
C. The boy is taller than the woman.
D. The boy is 116 centimeters tall.

32
A. The interview went well.
B. The man wants the woman to stay.
C. The woman works in business.
D. The woman's parents are overbearing.

33
A. At a harbor.
B. At a restaurant.
C. On a street corner.
D. At a fish market.

34
A. They'll visit Lugang and stay in a bed and breakfast.
B. They probably won't spend too much money.
C. They'll spend the entire weekend there.
D. They want to go down to Kenting.

35
A. She wants to pray that her daughter gets into a good university.
B. She wanted to meet Henry there to discuss business.
C. She lost one of her contacts at the temple.
D. She wants her company to have better luck in the future.

36
A. In November.
B. They want to get married in November.
C. During Chinese New Year.
D. After his parents give their approval.

37
A. Nancy and Paul will help their grandma.
B. Grandma is cooking the dumplings by herself.
C. Nancy is helping her father.
D. Paul is helping his grandma cook the dumplings.

38
A. The woman is paying her phone bill.
B. The woman is checking out a video recorder.
C. The woman is looking at a cell phone.
D. The sales clerk is showing the woman an MP3.

39. A. It's Christmas.
    B. It's Chinese New Year.
    C. It's Double Ten Day.
    D. It's Halloween.

40. A. He'll spend a total of NT$2,400.
    B. No more than NT$1,000.
    C. He's spent time shopping for Mandy.
    D. He'll spend NT$1,200.

41. A. The electric bill isn't included in the rent.
    B. The man won't let her rent the apartment for only one month.
    C. She wants to look at a few others first.
    D. She can't afford the deposit.

42. A. He feels depressed.
    B. He feels disappointed.
    C. He's a little confused.
    D. He's pretty excited.

43. A. She'll go shopping.
    B. She'll notify her husband of the delay.
    C. She'll get something to eat.
    D. She'll stay in the boarding area and do some shopping.

44. A. They seem to agree about what should be done.
    B. They're talking about where to take a hike.
    C. They're discussing the woman's roommate.
    D. They're not happy living together.

45. A. A week after he graduates.
    B. On the 16th.
    C. He'll leave before he visits his relatives.
    D. On the 27th.

答案與解析

1-1 辨別人物圖片

▶▶ 1-02

⊙ 答案

① B **②** B **③** C **④** C **⑤** C **⑥** C **⑦** D **⑧** B **⑨** A **⑩** A
⑪ C **⑫** D **⑬** A **⑭** C **⑮** B

⊙ 解析

For Question Number 1, please look at Picture A.

① **What are Sam and his classmates doing at school?**
山姆和他的同學在學校做什麼？

A. They were studying.
他們那時正在讀書。

B. **They're studying in the library. 他們正在圖書館讀書。**

C. He's talking with his classmates. 他正在和同學說話。

D. They're looking for salmon. 他們正在找鮭魚。

1. 題目是問「動作」。
2. 問句是現在進行式時態，所以過去進行式的選項 A 不可選。
3. 注意 salmon「鮭魚」是發音混淆字，所以不選。 ⊙答案 B

For Questions Number 2 and 3, please look at Picture B.

② **What is Ed's occupation?**
愛德的職業是什麼？

A. He worked at a bank. 他以前在銀行工作。

B. **He's a banker. 他是位銀行員。**

C. He's paying his bills. 他正在付他的帳單。

D. He's occupied with a customer. 他正忙著接待一位顧客。

1. 題目是問 occupation「職業」。
2. 問句是用現在簡單式，所以過去時態的選項 A 不可選。
3. 選項 D 的 occupied「忙於…」是發音混淆字，不可選。
答案 B

❸ **Please look at Picture B again.**

What is the relationship between these two people?
這兩個人是什麼關係？

A. They are relatives. 他們是親戚。

B. They are planning a trip. 他們正在計畫一趟旅行。

C. **One is a clerk, and the other is a customer.** 一位是辦事員而另一位是顧客。

D. They have a good relationship. 他們的關係很好。

題目是問 relationship「關係」，所以答案是 C。
答案 C

For Question Number 4, please look at Picture C.

❹ **Where will the girls likely go?**
女孩們可能要去哪裡？

A. To a shopping mall. 去購物中心。

B. They like to go swimming. 她們喜歡去游泳。

C. **To a beach.** 去海邊。

D. They're going to have a great time. 她們將會玩得很開心。

1. 由疑問詞 where 可知本題考的是場所的名稱。
2. 由她們身上的泳衣可知，她們將要去海邊游泳。
答案 C

For Question Number 5, please look at Picture D.

❺ **What did the boy on the left do?**
左邊的那位男孩做了什麼？

A. He spilled his popcorn. 他弄灑了爆米花。

B. They went to a baseball game. 他們去看了棒球賽。

C. **He caught a fly ball.** 他接到了高飛球。

D. He left by himself. 他獨自離開了。

1. 題目是問動作,問句是用過去時態。

2. 焦點是放在左手邊的那位男孩子,所以選 C。

3. 選項 D 是取同音不同義 left 來混淆考生的答案,left 當動詞是「離開」的過去式,當形容詞則是「左邊」的意思。 ➡答案 C

For Questions Number 6 and 7, please look at Picture E.

6 **What do you think Amy is going to do?**
你認為愛咪將要做什麼事情?

A. Light fireworks. 點燃煙火。

B. Call for help. 打電話求救。

C. Take a picture. 拍照。

D. Buy more fireworks. 買更多煙火。

1. 題目是問推論性的動作,由 is going to 得知這個動作是將要做,但尚未發生,從圖中 Amy 手上的相機,我們可推論出她將要拍照。

2. 寫出主角的名字時,要特別留意題目是問哪一位。 ➡答案 C

7 **Please look at Picture E again.**

Who seems to be more at ease? 誰看起來比較輕鬆自在?

A. Amy thinks the fireworks are easy to set off.
愛咪覺得放煙火很容易。

B. Kelly feels more at ease. 凱莉感覺比較輕鬆自在。

C. Kelly seems to be having the time of her life. 凱莉似乎正樂在其中。

D. Amy is more relaxed. 愛咪比較放鬆。

1. 題目是問細節。要聽懂關鍵片語 at ease「輕鬆自在」。

2. 選項 A 的 easy「容易的」是混淆選項,要小心。 ➡答案 D

For Question Number 8, please look at Picture F.

8 **What happened to the woman while she was exercising?**
當這位女士運動時,發生了什麼事?

A. Her heart was broken. 她的心碎了。

B. She hurt her ankle. 她傷到腳踝了。

C. She felt tired and had to sit down. 她很累,必須坐下來。

D. She hurt her leg. 她傷到腿了。

解題關鍵

1. 題目是問推論，圖片中她摸著腳踝，所以應該是那裡受傷了。
2. 此題必須聽出關鍵字 ankle「腳踝」，也要知道身體其他部位的說法。
3. 選項 A 的 heart「心臟」和選項 hurt「受傷」是混淆字。

➡ 答案 B

For Question Number 9, please look at Picture G.

9 Vincent is in a restaurant. What is the waitress doing?
文生正在餐廳裡。而女服務生正在做什麼事？

A. **She's refilling his drink. 她正在幫他續杯。**

B. He often comes to this restaurant. 他經常來這家餐廳。

C. He's waiting for a drink. 他正在等一杯飲料。

D. She's apologizing to him. 她正在向他道歉。

解題關鍵

1. 本題考的是在餐廳裡常見的動作，問句的時態是現在進行式。
2. refill 是「免費續杯」的意思，美式餐廳的某些飲料都可以續杯。

➡ 答案 A

For Questions Number 10 and 11, please look at Picture H.

⑩ These three moviegoers are watching a horror film.
How do they feel?
這三位常看電影的人正在看恐怖片。他們感覺如何？

A. **They feel scared. 他們感覺很害怕。**

B. They feel excited. 他們覺得很刺激。

C. They felt like crying. 他們覺得想要哭。

D. They want to go home. 他們想要回家。

解題關鍵

1. 本題考的是圖片中的細節，此題時態用的是現在簡單式，選項 C 中 felt 是過去式動詞，所以不可選。
2. 過去分詞當形容詞用時，多半用來形容人的感覺情緒。常見的有：interested「感到有興趣的」、surprised「驚訝的」、confused「困惑的」、frightened「驚嚇的」、satisfied「滿意的」、bored「無聊的」、tired「疲倦的」。

➡ 答案 A

⑪ **Please look at Picture H again.**

What do these boys have in common?

這幾位男孩有什麼共同點？

A.　Their eyes are closed. 他們的眼睛都閉起來。

B.　Yes, they all have an income. 對的，他們都有薪水。

C.　**They look scared to death. 他們看起來都嚇得半死。**

D.　They went to see a comedy. 他們去看喜劇片。

1.　問句的關鍵片語是 in common，表示「共同」的意思。

2.　本題考圖片細節中關於感覺與臉部表情的單字，必須仔細聆聽選項，找出正確的描述。

3.　疑問詞是 what，所以答案不須回答 Yes 或是 No，加上 income「收入」和 in common「共同」是相似音，故選項 B 不可選。　　　►答案 C

For Questions Number 12 and 13, please look at Picture I.

⑫ **Sarah and Frank are spending the afternoon together.**

What is Frank carrying?

莎拉和法蘭克一起共度一個下午。法蘭克手上拿著什麼東西？

A.　He's caring for Sarah. 他喜歡莎拉。

B.　He wants to teach Sarah how to surf. 他想要教莎拉如何衝浪。

C.　He's going to spend time with Sarah. 他要與莎拉共度時光。

D.　**He's carrying a surfboard. 他手上正拿著衝浪板。**

1.　本題是考與海邊水上活動有關的字彙與動作。關鍵字 surfboard 是「衝浪板」的意思。

2.　spend time with someone 是表示「和某人共度時光」的意思。

3.　caring for「喜歡」和 carrying「帶著；拿著」是混淆字。　　　►答案 D

⑬ **Please look at Picture I again.**

Why is Frank so nervous? 為什麼法蘭克如此緊張呢？

A.　**This is probably his first time surfing.**

　　這也許是他第一次衝浪。

B.　He has to hit the can. 他必須去上廁所。

C.　He enjoys being near us. 他喜愛和我們在一起。

D.　Because he's wearing a bikini. 因為他正穿著比基尼泳裝。

PART 1

看圖辨義

1. 本題考的是推論，所以要根據圖片推論出正確的答案。

2. 選項 B 中 hit the can 是「上廁所」的俚語，為男生用語，女生不能這樣說。

3. nervous「緊張的」和 near us「接近我們」是混淆字，所以不能選。 ➡ 答案 A

For Questions Number 14 and 15, please look at Picture J.

⑭ **Who is overweight? 誰過胖？**

A. The mother will wait in the car. 媽媽將會在車上等。

B. The daughter is. 是女兒。

C. The father could go on a diet. 爸爸可以減肥。

D. The boy isn't over eight. 男孩還不滿八歲。

1. 問句是問細節，關鍵字是 overweight「過胖」。

2. 選項 A 的 will wait 和選項 D 的 over eight 都和 overweight 聽起來相似，所以要小心。 ➡ 答案 C

⑮ **Please look at Picture J again.**

Who doesn't want to go home? 誰不想要回家？

A. The girl wants to go home. 小女孩想要回家。

B. The boy doesn't want to go home. 小男孩不想要回家。

C. They are going home together. 他們正要一起回家。

D. Because they had a wonderful time at the park.
因為他們在公園玩得很愉快。

1. 由疑問詞 who 可知要問細節，要找出符合圖片的選項。

2. 關鍵字就是 doesn't want to go home，從圖片中人物的表情可知，小男孩不想回家。 ➡ 答案 B

144

1-2　辨別地方圖片

▶▶ 1-03

◉ 答案

❶ D　❷ B　❸ D　❹ A　❺ C　❻ B　❼ D　❽ B　❾ C　❿ C

⓫ A　⓬ D　⓭ B　⓮ C　⓯ D

◉ 解析

For Question Number 1, please look at Picture A.

❶ **Why might someone go to this place?**

為什麼人們會去這個地方？

A. To get away and be alone. 要離開人群，自己一個人。

B. To buy something for Hank. 買東西給漢克。

C. To mail a letter. 去寄信。

D. To get a loan. 去申請貸款。

1. 題目是問到這個地方的理由。圖中的地方是銀行，所以選項 D 是最好的答案。
2. 關鍵字彙：get a loan「申請貸款」。
3. 選項 B 中 Hank 是混淆字，語意不對。

▶答案 D

For Question Number 2, please look at Picture B.

❷ **What might someone say at this kind of event?**

在這種活動當中，人們可能會說什麼？

A. We should call the fire department.

我們應該打電話給消防局。

B. Do you think the sweet potatoes are ready? 你覺得地瓜可以吃了嗎？

C. Grandma was kind to send you a gift. 奶奶人真好，寄給你一個禮物。

D. Sometimes I enjoy being a couch potato.

有時我喜歡當一個整天躺在沙發上看電視的人。

1. 問題的關鍵字是 what might someone say，由圖片可看出此事件是在炕窯或是烤東西，所以和燒烤相關的選項只有 B。

2. 選項 D 中 couch potato 是「整天躺在沙發上看電視的人」，和食物不相關。

▶ 答案 B

For Question Number 3, please look at Picture C.

❸ **What has happened in the picture? 圖片中發生了什麼事？**

A. Traffic is moving very slowly. 交通流動的速度非常緩慢。

B. The road is closed for repairs today.
今天道路封閉進行維修。

C. Streets are closed because of a parade. 道路因為遊行而封閉。

D. **There's been an accident. 這裡發生了交通事故。**

1. 由問題的現在完成式可知是問已經發生的事，所以答案選 D。

2. 關鍵字彙：road is closed「道路封閉」、repairs「維修」、parade「遊行」。

▶ 答案 D

For Questions Number 4 and 5, please look at Picture D.

❹ **Which statement does not match the picture?**
下列哪種說法和圖片不符？

A. **Many people are supporting their political candidate.**
許多人都支持他們的政黨候選人。

B. There's a concert in town this weekend.
這個週末在城裡有一個演唱會。

C. The band is pretty impressive. 這個樂團令人印象非常深刻。

D. Many people are attending the concert. 很多人參加演唱會。

1. 關鍵字是 does not match the picture，所以只要找出不符合圖片的說法。

2. 選項 A 中是有關政黨活動，和圖片主題完全不相關，所以是最適合的答案。

3. 關鍵字彙：support「支持」、political candidate「政黨候選人」、concert「演唱會」、impressive「令人印象深刻的」。

▶ 答案 A

5 **Please look at Picture D again.**

Which announcement would you most likely hear at this place?

你會在這個地方聽到哪一種宣布？

A. They announced their decision last night.
他們昨晚宣布了他們的決定。

B. Today's dessert is half-price. 今天的甜點半價。

C. **We're going to play one of our new songs. 我們將要演奏其中一首新歌。**

D. Thank you for shopping at Rockin' Music. 謝謝你在搖滾音樂行購物。

1. 由演唱會這個表演場所可得知要宣布的事和音樂相關，所以選項 C 是正確的答案。選項 D 是和音樂相關，但和宣布無關。

2. 關鍵字彙：announce「宣布」、decision「決定」。 答案 C

For Question Number 6, please look at Picture E.

6 **What would people likely do at a place like this?**
人們可能會在這樣的地方做什麼？

A. They like to go hiking in the mountains.
他們喜歡去山區健行。

B. **They would enjoy the scenery and take pictures.**
他們將會欣賞風景和拍照。

C. It's a peaceful place to relax. 這是一個可以放鬆的安靜地方。

D. Find a nice bed and breakfast. 找個不錯的民宿。

1. 問題的關鍵字是 people likely do at a place like this，重點要回答出在這個地方會做的「動作」。

2. 問題是用假設語氣 would 來問，所以正確答案也要用 would 來回答，所以 B 是對的。

3. 選項 A 中 like to「喜歡」和問句的 likely「可能」聽起來相似，但是意思不同。

4. 關鍵字彙：bed and breakfast「提供床和早餐的民宿，簡稱 B&B」。 答案 B

For Questions Number 7 and 8, please look at Picture F.

7 **Where can you buy a pair of running shoes?**

在哪裡可以買到一雙慢跑鞋？

A. You can't run in the department store.

你不能在百貨公司裡面跑步。

B. The restaurant sells pears. 這家餐廳有賣梨子。

C. Yes, you can find them on sale. 是的，你可以發現它們在特價。

D. Try the third floor. 請試試三樓。

1. 疑問詞 where 是問地方，問題的關鍵字是 buy a pair of running shoes，所以回答三樓是正確答案。

2. 選項 A 和 B 的語意不對，其中 pears「梨子」和 pair「雙」發音相近，是混淆字；此問題不能用 Yes 或 No 來回答，所以選項 C 不對。

3. 關鍵字彙：on sale「特價」。　　　　　　　　　　　　　　　　　答案 D

8 **Please look at Picture F again.**

Which statement isn't true about the picture?

關於圖片下列哪一種敘述不正確？

A. You can buy CDs at this department store.

你可以在這家百貨公司買到 CD。

B. They aren't having a sale this weekend. 這個週末沒有特價。

C. They probably sell swimming suits on the third floor. 三樓可能有賣泳衣。

D. The restaurant is on the fourth floor. 餐廳在四樓 。

一聽到 which statement isn't true 的時候，就要先留意圖片中各樓層所賣的物品，與重要的標誌 sale，明顯地選項 B 是錯誤的。　　　　　　　　　答案 B

For Questions Number 9 and 10, please look at Picture G.

9 **What do people do at a place like this?**

人們都在這樣的地方做什麼？

A. They hit a ball with a bat. 他們用球棒打球。

B. Most people enjoy hiking. 大部分的人喜愛登山健行。

C. **They play golf.** 他們打高爾夫球。

D. They do aerobic exercise. 他們做有氧運動。

1. 問題的關鍵字是 what do people do，所以是問「動作」，高爾夫球場中會做的動作就是 play golf。

2. 選項 A、B、D 都沒有回答正確的動作，所以不對。

3. 關鍵字彙：play golf「打高爾夫」。　　　　

---

❿ **Please look at Picture G again.**

How's the weather in the picture? 圖中的天氣如何？

A. It looks like a windy day. 看起來像是個刮風的日子。

B. Heather must be having a pleasant time.
海瑟一定玩得很愉快。

C. **It's a clear, sunny day.** 這是一個晴朗的天氣。

D. It's dangerous for her to play in a thunderstorm. 她在大雷雨中玩很危險。

1. 圖中是個無風、無雲且天氣晴朗的天氣，所以不選 A；選項 B 中的 Heather「（人名）海瑟」和 weather「天氣」是相近音，所以是混淆字，不可選。選項 D 語意不對。選項 C 是正確的。

2. 關鍵字彙：pleasant「令人愉快的」、thunderstorm「暴風雨」。　

For Question Number 11, please look at Picture H.

⓫ **What's happening in the picture?** 圖中發生什麼事情？

A. **Someone's car is being towed.** 有人的車被拖走了。

B. The police found a stolen car. 警方發現被偷的汽車。

C. They are cleaning up after an accident.
事故之後他們正在清理。

D. They are going to repair the road. 他們將要維修道路。

1. 一聽到 what's happening 時就要辨別出圖中的事件，此圖中的車子正被拖走了。

2. 明顯地選項 B、C 與 D 的敘述都不對，選項 A 的語意最適合。

3. 關鍵字彙：towed「被拖走的」、stolen「被偷的」、clean up「清理」、repair「修理」。

For Questions Number 12 and 13, please look at Picture I.

⑫ **Why is the pool closed today? 為什麼游泳池今天關閉？**

    A. The pool is in good repair. 游泳池維修得很好。

    B. The boy thinks it's unfair. 男孩認為這不公平。

    C. Because they spotted a bear. 因為他們看見一隻熊。

    D. The pool is under repair. 游泳池正在修理中。

    1. 問句是問此場所關閉的原因，而門上面的招牌寫著「維修中」。

    2. 選項 A 和 C 的敘述不合理；選項 B 沒有回答原因，選項 C 中 a bear「一隻熊」和 repair「修理」聽起來相近，是混淆字，選項 D 的答案最合理。

    3. 關鍵字彙：in good repair「維修良好的」、unfair「不公平」、under repair「維修中」。   **➜ 答案 D**

⑬ **Please look at Picture I again.**

What is true about the picture? 關於圖片的敘述何者正確？

    A. The pool will open tomorrow. 游泳池明天會開放。

    B. The boy looks disappointed. 這男孩看起來很失望。

    C. It's a clean pool. 它是個乾淨的游泳池。

    D. Many people thought the pool would be open.
　　很多人以為游泳池會開放。

    1. 問題是問圖片中的細節。

    2. 圖片中無法得知選項 A、C 或 D 是否正確。小男孩臉上失望的表情是肯定的，所以選項 B 是正確的。

    3. 關鍵字彙：disappointed「失望的」。   **➜ 答案 B**

For Questions Number 14 and 15, please look at Picture J.

⑭ **The mother is looking for the dog. Where is it?**
這位母親正在尋找她的狗。牠在哪裡？

    A. It's in the living room watching TV. 牠正在客廳看電視。

    B. It's in the bedroom. 牠在臥室裡。

    C. It's in the bathroom. 牠在浴室裡。

    D. Hiding under the couch. 躲在沙發底下。

問句是問小狗在哪裡。由圖可看出小狗在馬桶旁。選項 A、B 和 D 都不對。答案是 C。

▶答案 C

⑮ **Please look at Picture J again.**

Which of the following statements is true?

下列哪項敘述是對的？

A. The children are busy working on a project.
孩子忙著做作業。

B. The father is writing a book. 父親正在寫一本書。

C. The mother is cleaning the house. 媽媽正在打掃房子。

D. The dog is drinking out of the toilet. 這隻小狗正在喝馬桶裡的水。

1. 此問句是問圖片中的細節。

2. 選項 A、B、C 所描述的細節和圖片都不符合，正確答案是 D。

▶答案 D

1-3 辨別物件圖片

◉ 答案

1 D **2** C **3** C **4** D **5** C **6** D **7** A **8** C **9** B **10** D
11 A **12** C **13** B **14** D **15** C

◉ 解析

For Question Number 1, please look at Picture A.

1 What might someone say about this kind of weather?
關於這種天氣人們可能會說什麼？

A. What a pleasant afternoon. 真是一個愉快的下午。

B. You don't need your umbrella. 你不用帶雨傘。

C. Trash is flying across the street. 垃圾正飛過街道。

D. It's best to stay inside. 最好待在室內。

1. 圖中看得出這是颱風天，問題的關鍵字為 what might someone say。

2. 選項 C 是圖片的描述，但是並沒有回答問題，所以不選。

3. 人們最可能會説的話是 D。 ➡ 答案 D

For Questions Number 2 and 3, please look at Picture B.

2 Can I make an appointment for this week?
我可以預約這個星期的門診嗎？

A. Anytime on Friday is open. 星期五每個時間都是開放的。

B. How about Monday? 約星期一好嗎？

C. Friday from 1:00–2:00 is available. 星期五 1 點到 2 點有空。

D. I'm sorry. There are no openings this week.
對不起，這個星期沒有時段開放。

1. 問題是問「預約門診的時間」，要留意圖片中門診開始和結束的時間，要找出牙醫師的空檔時間。

2. 可預約的時間只有三個，所以答案是 C。 ➡ 答案 C

❸ **Please look at Picture B again.**

Why is Tuesday evening not a good time to make an appointment?

為什麼星期二晚上不是預約的好時機？

A. The dentist will surely be there. 牙醫師確定將會在那裡。

B. It's a good time to schedule an operation.
那是個安排手術的好時機。

C. **The dentist has scheduled an operation at that time.**
在那個時候，牙醫師已經排了一個手術。

D. Because he enjoys seeing Gary then. 因為他喜歡看到蓋瑞。

1. 問題是問「星期二晚上不能預約的理由」。
2. 圖片顯示當時已經安排手術了，所以要選 C。
3. 注意 surgery「手術」和 seeing Gary「看到蓋瑞」聽起來很相似，但是意思差很多。
4. 關鍵字彙：schedule「排定時間」、operation「開刀手術」。　➡答案 C

For Question Number 4, please look at Picture C.

❹ **When is a good day to go hiking?**

何時是登山健行的好日子？

A. It's going to rain a lot this week. 這星期會下很多雨。

B. Any day would be good to visit the king.
任何一天都是拜訪國王的好時機。

C. Tuesday or Wednesday would be good.
星期二或星期三會是好時機。

D. **Wednesday or Thursday would be perfect.**
星期三或星期四最好。

1. 題目是問「何時去登山健行」，所以要選晴天。
2. 天氣預報顯示只有星期三和四是晴天，所以要選 D。
3. 選項 B 中的 king「國王」和 hiking「健行」是發音相近的混淆字。　➡答案 D

For Question Number 5, please look at Picture D.

5 **How does Danny spend most of his money?**
丹尼大部分的錢都是怎麼花的？

A. He spends it wisely. 他花錢很聰明。

B. He spends the least amount of money on books.
他花最少錢在書籍上。

C. **He spends most of his money on food and beverages.**
他花最多錢在食物和飲料上。

D. He loves spending money on entertainment.
他喜愛將錢花在娛樂上。

1. 只要是圓餅圖題，一定要先看清楚上面的標題，了解占最大比率與最小比率的項目為何。

2. 一定要聽出的關鍵字為 spend most of，題目是問「佔最大比率的項目」，所以答案是 C。

3. 選項 B 的敘述是正確的，但是並沒有回答問題。 ➲ 答案 C

For Question Number 6, please look at Picture E.

6 **When will Hannah go on vacation? 漢娜何時會去渡假？**

A. She'll visit Kay on the 14th. 她會在 14 日時去看凱。

B. She'll leave on the 14th. 她會在 14 日離開。

C. She'll be gone from the 4th to the 11th.
她 4 日到 11 日都不在。

D. **She'll leave on the 4th. 她會在 4 日離開。**

1. 該聽出的關鍵字為 go on vacation「渡假」，題目問「何時去渡假」。

2. leave on 是「在什麼時候離開」的意思，而 leave for 是「前往」的意思，不要弄錯了。 ➲ 答案 D

For Questions Number 7 and 8, please look at Picture F.

7 **Where is the library located? 圖書館的位置在哪裡？**

A. **It's across from the bakery. 它在麵包店的對面。**

B. Barrie is crossing the street. 裴里正在過馬路。

C. It's next to the police station. 它在警察局的隔壁。

D. Yes, it's a local library. 是的，它是個當地的圖書館。

1. 一看到城市街道圖，馬上就要看出圖上主要的建築物和商店，也要找出相對的位置。
2. 選項 B 中 Barrie「裴里」和 library「圖書館」是發音混淆字，不要上當了。
3. 題目是問圖書館的「位置」，所以答案是 A。　●答案 A

8 **Please look at Picture F again.**

If you're at the library, which directions to the park are correct?

如果你正在圖書館，哪個前往公園的指示是正確的？

A. It's best to take a taxi. 最好的方式是搭計程車。

B. As you exit the library, turn right. Walk two blocks. The park is on the left.
出圖書館後就右轉。往下走兩個街口，公園就在左手邊。

C. **Go north on First Street. Then take a left at the first intersection. You'll see the park on your left.**
在第一街上朝北走，然後在第一個十字路口左轉。你會看到公園就在左手邊。

D. As you exit the library, turn left. At the first traffic light, turn right. You'll see the park on the right.
出圖書館後左轉。在第一個紅綠燈右轉。你會看到公園在右手邊。

1. 該聽出的關鍵字是 If you're at the library「如果你在圖書館」和 to the park「去公園」。
2. 一聽到這種題型時，要馬上將焦點移到圖書館，然後仔細聆聽選項，沿著地圖找出答案，正確答案是 C。　●答案 C

For Question Number 9, please look at Picture G.

9 **Which statement is true about the picture?**
關於圖片的敘述何者正確？

A. The shirt is more expensive than the skirt.
襯衫比裙子貴。

B. **The socks are the least expensive item. 襪子是最便宜的東西。**

C. The skirt costs NT$615. 這件裙子要新台幣 615 元。

D. The shirt costs NT$650. 這件襯衫要新台幣 650 元。

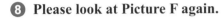

1-3

辨別物件圖片

155

1. 一看到東西上面有價錢,而且至少有三樣東西時,就是要「比較價格」。

2. 要聽清楚 the least expensive「最便宜的」和價錢的數字。

3. shirt「襯衫」和 skirt「裙子」的發音相近,要聽清楚。

答案 B

For Questions Number 10 and 11, please look at Picture H.

⑩ **Which statement best describes this picture?**

哪一個敘述最適合描寫這張圖?

A. Roller coaster B is not as big as the other roller coaster.

B 雲霄飛車比另一個雲霄飛車小。

B. Roller coaster B is designed for children.

B 雲霄飛車是專為兒童設計的。

C. Roller coaster A is faster than roller coaster B.

A 雲霄飛車比 B 雲霄飛車的速度快。

D. **Roller coaster B is scarier than roller coaster A.**

B 雲霄飛車比 A 雲霄飛車可怕。

1. 題目是問圖中的細節,所以請快速地比較兩座雲霄飛車,找出相似和差異之處。

2. 雲霄飛車 A 是設計給孩子坐的,所以答案是 D。

答案 D

⑪ **Please look at Picture H again.**

What would someone on roller coaster B likely say?

在 B 雲霄飛車上的人可能會說什麼?

A. **I think I'm going to barf. 我想我快吐了。**

B. I don't want to ride that roller coaster.

我不想要坐那個雲霄飛車。

C. This is a great place to relax. 這是一個放鬆的好地方。

D. Can we stop at the next rest stop? 我們可以在下一個休息站停嗎?

題目是要推論圖中的人可能會說的話,所以答案是 A。

答案 A

For Question Number 12, please look at Picture I.

⑫ **On what date will Jasmine be in Bangkok?**
潔思敏哪一天會在曼谷？

A. It will be her third date this month.
這是她這個月的第三次約會。

B. She'll be there on July 30th. 7 月 30 日時她會在那裡。

C. June 13th. 6 月 13 日。

D. Bangkok is the third place on her schedule to visit.
在她的參觀行程中，曼谷是第三個地方。

1. 要聽出的關鍵字是 what date「哪一天」和 in Bangkok「在曼谷」。

2. 選項 A 中的 date 是「約會」，和「日期」是同字不同義，不要選錯。 答案 C

For Question Number 13, please look at Picture J.

⑬ **Which statement is true about this picture?**
關於這張圖片的敘述何者正確？

A. Willy and Andrew are cousins. 威利和安德魯是表兄弟。

B. Sandy is Judy's aunt. 珊蒂是茱蒂的舅媽。

C. Cindy has two grandchildren. 辛蒂有兩個孫子。

D. Angela and Heather are sisters. 安琪拉和海瑟是姐妹。

一看到家族樹的題型，一定要馬上分辨一共有幾代，並且注意家庭成員的名字與相互的關係。 答案 B

For Question Number 14, please look at Picture K.

⑭ **What is happening? 現在發生什麼事？**

A. There's a forest fire. 有森林大火。

B. People are going to watch the fireworks.
人們正要去看煙火。

C. People are going to watch the volcano erupt.
人們即將去看火山爆發。

D. A volcano is erupting. 火山正在爆發。

PART 1

看圖辨義

1. 題目是問圖片中的狀況。

2. 關鍵字彙：volcano「火山」、erupt「爆發」。

答案 D

For Question Number 15, please look at Picture L.

⑮ **Which statement is not true about the picture?**
關於圖片的敘述何者不正確？

A. Henry graduated from high school in 2006.
亨利在 2006 年時從高中畢業。

B. Henry has a baby girl. 亨利有一個女娃娃。

C. Henry enjoys pies a lot. 亨利非常喜愛派。

D. Henry is a pilot. 亨利是位飛行員。

1. 一看到有兩張照片，就要留意上面的日期、主角、場景、拍照的目的和相似與差異之處。

2. 題目是問不正確的敘述，所以答案是 C。

3. pies a lot 和 pilot 的發音相似，不要上當。

答案 C

2-1 建議的回應

▶▶ 1-09

⊙ 答案

❶ A ❷ B ❸ D ❹ A ❺ C ❻ A ❼ C ❽ A ❾ C ❿ A

⊙ 解析

❶ **You should take a picture of the seagull.** 你應該拍一張海鷗的照片。

  A. Where is it? 牠在哪裡？

  B. Which girl are you talking about? 你在說哪一位女孩？

  C. I don't have any paper. 我沒有紙。

  D. I'm too shy. 我太害羞了。

  1. 這題是單字題，看你是否聽懂 seagull「海鷗」這個字，選項 B 的 girl 和 seagull 的字尾發音相似，但是意思不對，所以不可選。

  2. 按照語意應該選 A，選項 C 和 D 意思不對。　　　　⊖ 答案 A

❷ **You ought to go visit him in the hospital.** 你應該去醫院探望他的。

  A. Is she okay? 她還好嗎？

  B. I know. I should go. 我知道。我應該去的。

  C. I heard he loves it there. 我聽說他非常喜歡那裡。

  D. He works 40 hours a week. 他每週工作 40 個小時。

  1. ought to 是「應該；必須要」的意思，所以選 B。

  2. 選項 A 是 she，但是住院的是 he，所以不可選。

  3. 選項 C 與現實生活不符合所以不可選。選項 D 和題目無關。　　⊖ 答案 B

❸ Why don't you try on the red shirt? 你為什麼不試穿看看這件紅色的 T 恤？

A. Oh, I like this skirt. 哦，我喜歡這條裙子。

B. I'm not in the mood. 我沒有心情。

C. Sure, I'll read it. 當然，我會讀的。

D. I prefer the black one. 我比較喜歡黑色那件。

1. shirt「襯衫」和 skirt「裙子」是相似音，所以不選 A。

2. 選項 B 和 C 的意思不對。選項 D 說明了原因，所以是正確的。　　答案 D

❹ How about going to Bali for vacation? 去峇里島渡假好不好？

A. That's a great idea! 這是一個很棒的主意！

B. Yes, I went there last summer. 是的，我去年夏天去過了。

C. My parents have been there. 我的父母親曾經去過那裡。

D. I can take a vacation in July. 我可以七月的時候去渡假。

1. 這題考意見和想法，選項 A 正面回應了說話者的意見，所以是正確答案。

2. 選項 B 用 Yes 回答是錯誤的，選項 C 和 D 語意不對。　　答案 A

❺ I suggest you exercise more. 我建議你多運動。

A. I don't have much extra money. 我沒有多餘的錢。

B. I want to learn how to speak French. 我想要學習如何說法語。

C. Yes, I should swim more. 是的，我應該要多游泳。

D. The XL size T-shirts are too big. 這些加大尺碼的 T 恤太大了。

1. 與運動主題有關的選項是 C。

2. 選項 A 中的 extra 和選項 D 中的 XL size (extra-large) 和 exercise 聽起來有點相近，不要被誤導。　　答案 C

❻ What about making dumplings for dinner? 晚餐包水餃吃好不好？

A. We had dumplings last night. 昨天晚上我們已經吃過水餃了。

B. I'll set the table. 我將會擺好碗筷。

C. I'm glad you could make it for dinner. 我很高興你可以來吃晚餐。

D. Yes, her room is a dump. 沒錯，她的房間是個垃圾場。

1. what about 通常是問別人的意見，回應的問句有時候沒有直接回答好或是不好，可以先用刪去法刪去不相關的選項 D。
2. 雖然選項 B 和 C 都和晚餐有關，但和問題的語意不符，所以不可選。 ➡️ 答案 A

❼ **If I were you, I wouldn't take the job. 如果我是你，我就不會接受這份工作。**

A. Okay, I'll start work on Monday. 好吧，我會在星期一開始工作。

B. Yes, you're a lot like me. 是的，你有很多地方像我。

C. I agree. I can find a better job. 我同意。我可以找到更好的工作。

D. Sure, I'll take it home. 當然，我將會把它帶回家。

1. 這題是與事實相反的假設語氣，表達出說話者對這份工作不認同。
2. 關鍵字是 wouldn't take the job，所以最適當的回應是選項 C。 ➡️ 答案 C

❽ **You'd better put it in a locker. 你最好把它放在置物櫃裡。**

A. You're right. It'll be safe there. 你說的對。放在那裡會很安全。

B. I don't think it's better. 我不認為這樣比較好。

C. We should be safe inside. 我們在裡面應該是安全的。

D. But I don't love her. 但是我不愛她。

1. 關鍵字是 had better 和 locker，選項 B 出現 better，但不是最好的答案。
2. 選項 C 的語意不對。選項 D 中的 love her 和 locker 聽起來相似，但語意不符合。
3. 最好的回應是選項 A。 ➡️ 答案 A

❾ **Let's go to the night market. 我們去逛夜市吧。**

A. Yeah, I went yesterday. 好呀，我昨天去過了。

B. I hate having nightmares. 我討厭做噩夢。

C. We can eat some stinky tofu! 我們可以吃一些臭豆腐！

D. I often go to the night market. 我經常去逛夜市。

1. Let's...，是一種常見的提議句型，表示對接下來或未來的事情做出提議。
2. 選項 A 是提到過去的經驗，不可選。選項 B 中 nightmares「噩夢」和 night market「夜市」聽起來相似，但是意思差很多。
3. 選項 C 中的 stinky tofu「臭豆腐」是在夜市中常見的食物，也是最恰當的答案。選項 D 是說平時的經驗，所以不對。 ➡️ 答案 C

❿ You could buy her a diamond necklace. 你可以買給她一條鑽石項鍊。

A. **Are you crazy?** 你瘋了嗎？

B. It's difficult to say good-bye. 要說再見很難。

C. I've never been there. 我從來沒有去過那裡。

D. No, her neck feels fine. 不，她的脖子感覺還好。

1. 關鍵字是 buy her a diamond necklace，當別人建議你做某事，但你不認同時，可以像選項 A 一樣來做回應。

2. 選項 B 的 difficult「困難的」和 diamond「鑽石」是相似音，但意思不對。

3. 選項 D 的 neck「脖子」和 necklace「項鍊」發音相似，但不符合文意，所以不可選。

➡️ 答案 A

2-2　情境的回應

▶▶ 1-10

◉ 答案

❶ B　❷ C　❸ B　❹ A　❺ A　❻ C　❼ D　❽ C　❾ D　❿ A

◉ 解析

❶ **Do you enjoy going to the health club? 你喜愛去健身中心嗎？**

A. I might join one near my house. 我可能會加入我家附近的。

B. Yes, I love the aerobics classes they offer. 是的，我喜愛他們提供的有氧課程。

C. It's open only on the weekends. 它只在週末開放。

D. No, I often get caught in traffic. 不，我常常遇到塞車。

1. 要聽懂的關鍵字是 health club「健身中心」。
2. 疑問詞是 do 所以應該要回答 Yes/No，最合乎情境的回答是選項 B，因為說明了喜愛去的原因。選項 A、C、D 都不合理。　　➡ 答案 B

❷ **My date last night was so boring. 我昨晚約會的對象太無聊。**

A. Was it the 10th of July? 它是在 7 月 10 日嗎？

B. You can still change the date. 你仍然可以更改日期。

C. Maybe she felt the same way. 也許她也這樣覺得。

D. Dates are quite nutritious. 棗子很有營養。

1. 關鍵字是 date「約會的對象」，最合乎情境的回答是選項 C。
2. 選項 A、B 中 date 指的是「日期」，而選項 D 中指的是「棗子」。　　➡ 答案 C

❸ **Kyle knows that buying pirated CDs is illegal, doesn't he?**
凱爾知道購買盜版光碟是非法的，不是嗎？

A. Yes, a pirate hit him in the nose. 是呀，有一位海盜打他的鼻子。

B. Yes, but he can't afford new ones. 是呀，可是他負擔不起新的。

C. No, he never saw a pirate. 不，他從來沒有見過海盜。

D. The quality is often very poor. 品質通常都很差。

1. 關鍵字是 pirated「盜版的」而不是「海盜」。
2. 選項 B 說明了凱爾購買盜版光碟的原因,所以最恰當。
⊙答案 B

❹ **I think my hairdresser is gay. 我想我的美髮造型師是同性戀。**

　　A. No way! 不可能吧!

　　B. He should try working in finance. 他應該試著在金融界工作。

　　C. That's a cool name. 這是個很酷的名字。

　　D. You should try a different shampoo. 你應該嘗試用不同的洗髮精。

1. 關鍵字是 gay「同性戀」,題目是對別人行為舉止的推測,所以最佳的回應方式是表達聽到這個消息的感覺,選項 A 的答案最合理。
2. 選項 D 則是和頭髮相關的混淆字。
⊙答案 A

❺ **We offer many scholarships at our university.**
我們的大學提供了很多獎學金。

　　A. I think I qualify for some of them. 我想我有資格可以申請其中一些。

　　B. How much are they? 多少錢?

　　C. Yes, but I'm not interested in designing ships. 對呀,但我對設計船沒興趣。

　　D. I prefer living in an apartment. 我比較喜歡住在公寓。

1. 關鍵字是 scholarship「獎學金」和 university「大學」。
2. 可以推測出這是在談論學校獎學金的問題,最合理的答案是選項 A。
3. 金錢是不可數的,一定不用複數,故選項 B 錯誤,選項 C 中 designing ships 和 scholarships 相似,是陷阱題,不要上當。選項 D 也不合理。
⊙答案 A

❻ **Why are you whispering? 你為什麼要輕聲細語?**

　　A. It's good for your skin. 它對你的皮膚很好。

　　B. Because I'm a rebel. 因為我是一個反叛者。

　　C. I don't want the boss to hear me. 我不想讓我的老闆聽到。

　　D. My doctor says it's good for me. 我的醫生說這對我有好處。

1. 關鍵字是 whispering「輕聲細語」。
2. 本題考輕聲細語的合理原因,其中四個選項都提出了理由,但是選項 C 是最合理的答案。
⊙答案 C

❼ Was headquarters impressed with your presentation?
總公司對你的簡報留下了深刻的印象嗎？

A. I think they wanted a different present. 我想他們想要不一樣的禮物。

B. Yes, I hope hc'll likc it. 是的，我希望他會喜歡。

C. It's about how to increase consumer spending. 它是關於如何提高消費者的消費。

D. I couldn't tell. 我看不出來。

1. 關鍵字是 headquarters「總公司」、impressed with「對…印象深刻」、presentation「簡報；口頭報告」。

2. 問句的時態是過去式，可知這個簡報已經結束，所以不能選 B。 答案 D

❽ You look like you've had a rough week. 你看起來好像過了辛苦的一週。

A. Yeah, I need to take a leak. 是啊，我需要去尿尿。

B. I do. 我是呀。

C. My employer is giving me a lot of pressure. 我的老闆給我很多壓力。

D. Yes, it's been an easy week. 對呀，它真是個輕鬆的一週。

1. 關鍵字是 you've had「你已經過了」和 rough「艱苦」。

2. 留意句子是用現在完成式，所以 I do 是錯誤的，I have 才是對的。

3. 注意 take a leak 是俚語「撒尿」的意思，是男生用語，女生不能這樣說。

4. 選項 C 是正確合理的答案。 答案 C

❾ When we met, I knew it was fate. 當我們相遇時，我知道這是命運的安排。

A. How did you know it was Fay? 你怎麼知道那就是菲菲？

B. I fainted, too. 我也暈倒了。

C. I can't remember where we met. 我不記得我們相遇的地方。

D. I had the same feeling. 我也有相同的感覺。

1. 本題該聽懂的關鍵字是 fate「命運」，選項 A 的 Fay「（人名）菲菲」和選項 B 的 fainted「暈倒」都是和 fate 發音相似的字，要小心。

2. 注意句子是用過去式，所以回答也要用相同的時態。 答案 D

⑩ Do you have any idea what he's saying? 你聽得懂他在說什麼嗎？

A. No, it's all nonsense to me. 不，對我而言都是廢話。

B. Yes, I have some. 是的，我有一些。

C. I think it's a great idea. 我想這真是一個好主意。

D. Sorry, I didn't. 對不起，我沒有。

1. 關鍵字是 have any idea「聽得懂」，所以不要只聽到 idea 就選 C。

2. 此問句是對某人的説法提出意見或表示懷疑，所以正確的答案是 A。

3. 留意句子是用現在式，所以回答要用相同的時態。　　　　　　　　　⟶ 答案 A

2-3　地點的回應

▶▶ 1-11 🎧

◉ 答案

1 A　**2** C　**3** A　**4** D　**5** B　**6** B　**7** C　**8** D　**9** B　**10** C

◉ 解析

1 **Are there any good restaurants in town? 城裡有什麼好餐廳嗎？**

A. **Yes, there's one close to our house. 有的，有一個離我們的房子很近。**

B. No, there aren't many places to rest in town.
沒有，在城裡沒有很多地方可以休息。

C. We should take a taxi downtown. 我們應該搭計程車去鬧區。

D. Perhaps we should make a reservation. 也許我們應該先訂位。

解題關鍵

1. 因為是 Yes / No 問句，所以要回答 Yes 或 No，很明顯地答案是 A。

2. 選項 B 中的 rest「休息」是發音混淆字要當心。　➡️ 答案 A

2 **Anne's not from Taichung, is she? 安妮不是來自台中，是嗎？**

A. No, she's from Taichung. 不是，她從台中來的。

B. Yes, she works there. 是的，她在那裡工作。

C. **Yeah, she was born and raised there. 是啊，她是在那裡出生和長大的。**

D. She enjoys living there a lot. 她非常喜愛居住在那裡。

解題關鍵

1. 要聽懂的是 Anne's not ..., is she?，附加問句不會影響回答的方式，而是要根據事實狀況來回答。

2. 選項 A 中的 no 要和 not 連用才可以，所以不正確。　➡️ 答案 C

3 **Do you know where Becky is today? 你知道蓓姬今天在哪裡嗎？**

A. **She's meeting new students at the airport. 她去機場迎接新的學生。**

B. She'll be back late tonight. 她今晚會很晚回來。

C. She drove her own car. 她開她自己的車。

D. I'll see her tomorrow at the game. 明天我會在比賽的地方看到她。

1. 要聽懂的部分是 where Becky is today，所以正確答案要說出她今天在哪裡，選項 A 是最合理的答案。

2. 選項 C 和 D 的時態不對。　　　　　　　　　　　　　　　　　　　　　　⏩答案 A

❹ **Where does your family like to vacation? 你的家人喜歡去哪裡渡假？**

A. The scenery there is magnificent. 那裡的風景很壯麗。

B. We usually vacation in July. 我們通常會在 7 月時去渡假。

C. We went to Green Island. 我們去了綠島。

D. We enjoy spending time in Kenting. 我們喜愛花時間在墾丁。

1. 此問句的疑問詞是 where，所以要直接說出地點，或是說明還不知道的原因，而問句的時態是用現在式，所以選項 C 的答案是錯的。

2. 選項 B 只說明時間沒說地點，也不對。

3. 選項 A 並沒有回答問題。　　　　　　　　　　　　　　　　　　　　　　⏩答案 D

❺ **Is there a lifeguard on duty? 這裡是否有救生員值班？**

A. No, this is a safe town. 沒有，這是一個安全的小鎮。

B. Yes, he's the sexy man sitting over there. 有的，他就是坐在那裡的性感男人。

C. It's due to arrive next week. 下週應該就會抵達。

D. Yes, I enjoy my life very much. 是的，我很享受我的生活。

1. 要聽懂的關鍵字是 lifeguard on duty「值班救生員」，因問句的疑問詞是 is there，而主詞是 a lifeguard，那麼選項 A 和 C 中的主詞 this 和 it 都是錯誤的。

2. 選項 D 中出現相似字，但是和文意不合。　　　　　　　　　　　　　　　⏩答案 B

❻ **How far is it to the canyon? 到峽谷有多遠？**

A. The offer will not last long. 供應將不會持續太久。

B. It's about another kilometer. 大約還要再一公里。

C. Only three more kilograms. 只有多三公斤。

D. We can stay there until dark. 我們可以在那裡待到天黑。

此問句的疑問詞是 how far，是問「距離有多遠」，很明顯地選項 A、C、D 都和距離無關，所以 B 才是正確答案。　　　　　　　　　　　　　　　　　　　　　　⏩答案 B

❼ **The bride is nowhere to be found. 到處都找不到新娘。**

A. Check the boxes. 檢查箱子。

B. I'm glad you found it. 我很高興你找到了它。

C. Try calling her mother. 試試看打電話給她的母親。

D. She lost her love handles. 她擺脫了她肚子上的游泳圈。

1. 要聽懂的是 bride「新娘子」，我們可以得知說話者對這件事感到很震驚，最恰當的回答應該是提出解決問題，所以 C 是最佳的答案。

2. 關鍵字彙：love handles 是「肚子上的游泳圈」。 答案 C

❽ **What's on your collar? 你的衣領上是什麼？**

A. It beats me what the caller said. 我被打電話來的人所說的事給問倒了。

B. I don't foresee any problems. 我預見不到任何問題。

C. I'm not sure what's on his mind. 我不確定他在想什麼。

D. It's lipstick. 它是口紅印。

1. 該聽懂的字是 collar「衣領」，選項 A、B 和 C 的說法和問句無關，所以選項 D 的回答最適當。

2. 注意混淆字 collar「衣領」和 caller「打電話的人」。

3. 關鍵字彙：it beats me 是「考倒我了」，foresee 是「預見」的意思。 答案 D

❾ **Can you tell me where the vitamins are? 你能告訴我維他命在哪裡嗎？**

A. They're living in Italy now. 他們現在住在義大利。

B. Aisle 12. 走道 12。

C. They're driving me nuts. 他們快把我弄瘋了。

D. They're hiding in the bushes. 他們躲藏在樹叢下。

1. 要聽懂的關鍵字是 vitamins「維他命」，問句是用間接問句 Can you tell me 開始的，但是主要問句是 where the vitamins are 。所以最有可能找到維他命的地方就是選項 B 。

2. 關鍵字彙：drive someone nuts 是「把某人弄瘋了」。 答案 B

⑩ I want to buy a cozy cottage on the lake. 我想在湖上買一個舒適的小木屋。

A. You have many fond memories of that place. 在那個地方你有許多美好的回憶。

B. Where are you going to put it? 你準備把它放在哪裡？

C. That's a splendid idea. 這是一個很棒的主意。

D. I don't think Jake wants one. 我不認為傑克會想要一個。

1. 題目是用現在簡單式，表示是說話者現階段的想法，按照常理接話者會給予正面贊成或是反對的理由，所以答案是 C 。

2. 注意相似字 lake「湖」和 Jake「（人名）傑克」。

3. 關鍵字彙：cottage 是「小木屋」、fond 是「美好的」、memory 是「回憶」、splendid 是「極好的」。　　　　　　　　　　　　⊙ 答案 C

2-4　態度的回應

▶▶ 1-12

⊙ 答案

❶ B　**❷** A　**❸** B　**❹** D　**❺** B　**❻** A　**❼** D　**❽** C　**❾** A　**❿** C

⊙ 解析

❶ I enjoy new challenges. 我喜愛新的挑戰。

A. You ought to visit them this weekend. 這個週末你應該要去拜訪他們。

B. So do I. 我也是。

C. Don't eat too many. 不要吃太多。

D. Let's challenge them to a game of beach volleyball.
　 讓我們和他們挑戰一場沙灘排球賽。

1. 關鍵字是 challenges「挑戰」，說話者清楚表達了積極冒險的態度，應答的方向可以是正面或是負面的回應。選項 B 才是正確的。

2. 注意選項 D 中有出現 challenge 的字眼，但是可不是正確的答案喔。　 答案 B

❷ Are you worried about the exam? 你是否擔心考試？

A. It should be a piece of cake. 它應該是很容易的。

B. Sam should be okay by himself. 山姆自己應該會好起來。

C. Yes, I prepared a lot for it. 是的，我為它做了很多準備。

D. I'm taking the exam next week. 我下個禮拜要參加考試。

1. 關鍵字是 worried about「擔心」，選項 B 出現 Sam 和題目的 exam 讀音相似，但意思不對。

2. 選項 C 中的 Yes 表示擔心，可是後面又表現出正面的態度，前後矛盾。選項 D 不合理。正確答案是 A。

3. 關鍵字 a piece of cake 是形容事情很簡單。　 答案 A

❸ **Dad says it might rain tomorrow. 爸爸說明天可能會下雨。**

A. No, my train comes today. 不，我的火車今天會來。

B. Maybe you should cancel the barbecue. 也許你應該取消烤肉。

C. I don't think it did. 我認為它不是這樣的。

D. You enjoy dancing in the rain, don't you? 你喜愛在雨中跳舞，不是嗎？

1. 關鍵句是 it might rain「可能會下雨」，只要是下雨就不能做的事就是負面的回應，反之則是正面的。
2. 選項 B 是正確的答案。注意選項 A 的 my train 和 might rain 聽起來相似，千萬不要被騙了。
3. 選項 C 中用過去式所以不可選，選項 D 不合理。　　　　　　　➡ 答案 B

❹ **We can make a difference if we recycle. 如果我們做資源回收就會讓世界變得不一樣。**

A. Yes, cycling can make a difference. 是，騎自行車可以變得不一樣。

B. They're easy to make. 它們很容易做。

C. I don't think we should call now. 我認為我們現在不應該打電話。

D. I believe you're right. 我相信你是對的。

1. 關鍵句是 make a difference if we recycle，題目表達出對資源回收有自信的態度，接話者可能會給正面的回應或是不贊同的態度。
2. 選項 A 的 cycling「騎自行車」是混淆字，一定要仔細聽。
3. 最合理的答案是 D。　　　　　　　　　　　　　　　　　　　➡ 答案 D

❺ **You should be more optimistic. 你應該要更加樂觀。**

A. You're right. I shouldn't be. 你是對的。我不應該那樣。

B. You're right. 你是對的。

C. We're totally different. 我們兩個完全不一樣。

D. Think more positively. 要更正面思考。

1. 關鍵字是 optimistic「樂觀」，題目表達出對某人的建議，所以答案應該要選表示贊成或反對的看法。正確答案是 B。
2. 關鍵字彙：positively「積極；正面」。　　　　　　　　　　　➡ 答案 B

❻ Sandy's writing a new book. 珊蒂正在寫一本新書。

A. I'm so proud of her. 我真為她感到驕傲。

B. I told you she was a good cook. 我告訴過你，她是一個好廚師。

C. When will she write it? 她什麼時候會寫呢？

D. She always wanted to move there. 她總是想要搬到那裡。

1. 題目是用現在進行式，表示手邊在進行的動作，此動作尚未完成。

2. book「書」和選項 B 的 cook「廚師」是混淆字。

3. 選項 C 用未來式問，時態不對。最合理的答案是 A。 ▶ 答案 A

❼ You should relax when you're on vacation. 當你在渡假時，你應該要放輕鬆。

A. I already sent the fax. 我已經傳真了。

B. I know. I need a vacation. 我知道。我需要一個假期。

C. I might vacation there this summer. 今年夏天我可能會去那裡渡假。

D. You're right. I should relax. 你說得對。我應該要放鬆。

1. 關鍵字為 relax「放輕鬆」、on vacation「渡假」。說話者的目的是建議別人，所以最合理的答案是選項 D。

2. 選項 A 的 fax「傳真」和 relax「放鬆」讀音相近，不要被騙了。 ▶ 答案 D

❽ The situation looks grave. 情況看起來很嚴重。

A. The weather should clear up. 天氣應該會放晴。

B. That's great news. 這真是個好消息。

C. What are we going to do? 我們該怎麼辦？

D. You're right. I'm sitting too much. 你說得對。我坐太久了。

1. 關鍵字是 grave「重大的」意思。

2. 注意 situation「情況」和 sitting「坐」聽起來相似。

3. 當面臨危險的情況或是難題，大部分的人會不知所措，所以選項 C 的答案是合理的。 ▶ 答案 C

問答

9 **How was your honeymoon?** 你的蜜月過得怎麼樣呢？

    A. I wish we could have stayed another week. 我希望我們可以再住一個星期。

    B. They were too sweet. 它們太甜了。

    C. Don't call me Honey! 不要叫我親愛的！

    D. We'll be going to Japan for a week. 我們將會去日本一個星期。

  1. 問句是用過去式，表示已經度完蜜月了，明顯地不能選 D。

  2. 選項 A 是最好的答案。   答案 A

10 **I'm still hopeful that we can resolve our differences.**
我仍然希望我們能夠解決我們的歧見。

    A. I do, too. 我也是這樣做。

    B. There's a significant difference in quality. 在品質上有明顯的差別。

    C. I am, too. 我也是。

    D. I'm glad we resolved the differences. 我很高興我們解決了歧見。

  1. 關鍵句是 resolve our differences「解決不同的意見或是紛爭」。

  2. 題目用的是 I'm，所以表示附和的用法也要用 be 動詞，選項 A 是錯誤的，選項 C
才是正確的。   答案 C

2-5　意見的回應

▶▶ 1-13

答案

1 B　**2** A　**3** C　**4** B　**5** C　**6** B　**7** B　**8** D　**9** D　**10** A

解析

1 **I think she likes this brand of perfume. 我想她喜歡這個牌子的香水。**

A. Yes, she loves that band. 是的，她喜歡那個樂團。

B. Are you sure? 你確定嗎？

C. It costs NT$1,200 a bottle. 它一瓶要台幣 1,200 元。

D. It was a nice birthday gift. 它是一個不錯的生日禮物。

1. 題目是考你如何回應別人的想法，所以選項 B 的答案最合理。
2. 選項 A 的 band「樂團」和 brand「牌子」是相似字，意思差很多，所以不可選。
3. 選項 D 是過去式，所以和題目不符。　　　　**答案 B**

2 **I want to learn how to play the guitar. 我想學習如何彈吉他。**

A. So do I. 我也是。

B. Don't kick it too hard. 不要太用力踢。

C. I'm sorry I don't know how to play. 對不起，我不知道怎麼彈。

D. How are your classes? 你的課上得如何？

1. 題目是考你如何回應別人的想法，選項 A 是表示贊同的反應。
2. 此直述句是現在簡單式，表示尚未學習，所以選項 D 不可選。　　**答案 A**

3 **What did you think of the movie? 你覺得這個電影如何？**

A. It didn't take too long to move everything.
把所有的東西搬走並沒有花很久時間。

B. I think we'll see it soon. 我想我們很快就會看到它了。

C. It's one of the best I've seen in a while. 這是最近我看過最好看的。

D. Let's go to the seven o'clock show. 我們去看 7 點的表演吧。

175

1. 選項 A 中的 move「移動」和 movie「電影」是相似字，不要聽錯了。
2. 題目是用過去式，表示已經看過電影了，表示未來狀態的選項 B 和 D 都不可選。
3. 關鍵字彙：in a while 是「近來」的意思。　　答案 C

❹ **How about we adopt a stray dog? 我們來認養一隻流浪狗怎麼樣？**

A. I'm not sure why it strays from home. 我不確定牠為什麼要離家出走。

B. That's a great idea. 這是一個很棒的想法。

C. We can't afford another child. 我們負擔不起另一個孩子。

D. Maybe someone at the animal shelter can pick it up.
也許有人在動物收容所可以撿到牠。

1. 題目是提出一個想法，尚未進行，所以選項 A 和 D 都不可選。
2. 選項 C 的意思不對。
3. 關鍵字彙：adopt「認養」、stray dog「流浪狗」、afford「負擔得起」、animal shelter「動物收容所」。　　答案 B

❺ **Do you think she'll lose her temper? 你認為她會發脾氣嗎？**

A. No, she didn't lose it. 不，她沒有失去它。

B. I haven't met her. 我還沒有見過她。

C. There's a good chance she will. 她很有可能會發脾氣。

D. Yes, I don't think she'll win. 是的，我不認為她會獲勝。

1. 題目是問看法，所以只有選項 C 表達出肯定的想法。
2. 題目雖然是用疑問詞 Do 開頭，但是主要問句是在後面，不用回答 Yes 或 No。
3. 選項 B 的 met her「見過她」和 temper「脾氣」聽起來相似，但意思不對。
4. 關鍵字彙：lose temper 是「發脾氣」、a good chance「機會很大」。　　答案 C

❻ **What did you think of that horror movie? 你覺得那部恐怖電影如何？**

A. I love horror movies. 我喜歡恐怖電影。

B. It was out of this world. 它真是太精彩了。

C. I prefer to watch movies at home. 我喜歡待在家裡看電影。

D. Her movie theater used to be a pub. 她的電影院曾經是一個酒吧。

1. 題目是用過去式問的，表示已經看完電影了，所以回應的句子也應該要用過去式，所以選項 B 最合理。

2. 選項 A、C、D 中雖然有提到電影，但是意思都不對。

3. 關鍵字彙：out of this world 是表示「太棒了；很精彩」的意思。　　●答案 B

❼ **Do you think Gary will be jealous? 你認為蓋瑞會吃醋嗎？**

A. No, I don't think Gary will tell us. 不，我不認為蓋瑞會告訴我們。

B. I'm sure he'll be jealous. 我確定他一定會吃醋。

C. No, he always gets jealous. 不，他總是吃醋。

D. Yes, I think he should remain in jail. 是，我認為他應該留在監獄。

1. 題目是問對他人行為的預測，所以選項 B 的答案最好。

2. 選項 A 的 tell us「告訴我們」和 jealous「吃醋」聽起來相似，意思差很多。

3. 關鍵字彙：jealous「吃醋的；嫉妒的」、jail「監獄」。　　●答案 B

❽ **Where should we spend our next vacation? 下一次我們應該去哪裡渡假？**

A. I won't spend much money. 我將不會花很多錢。

B. Probably for about five days. 大概 5 天左右。

C. We went to Holland. 我們去了荷蘭。

D. Let's try a week in Kenting. 讓我們試試去墾丁一個星期。

1. 題目是問去哪裡渡假，所以應該回答「地點」。選項 D 最正確。

2. 句中的 spend 是指花在時間上，千萬不要和花錢搞混了。　　●答案 D

❾ **What did you think of the survey? 你對這份調查有什麼看法？**

A. That's not my responsibility. 這不是我的責任。

B. It was delicious. 它真是美味。

C. It's a beautiful place to visit. 它是一個美麗的參觀地點。

D. I thought it helped us collect the data we needed.
我認為它對我們需要收集的資料有幫助。

1. 題目是問看法，所以應該提出意見，選項 D 是正確的。

2. 關鍵字彙：survey「調查」、data「資料」。　　●答案 D

❿ I can't believe he was drunk. 我真不敢相信他喝醉了。

　A. **I can't, either. 我也不敢相信。**

　B. So do I. 我也是。

　C. He should have ducked sooner. 他應該更早躲開的。

　D. He's on a diet now. 他現在正在節食中。

1. 題目表達出對別人行為的意見，回應的方式可以贊成，也可以反對。

2. 選項 C 中的 ducked「避免」和 drunk「喝醉」聽起來相似，不要選錯。

3. 關鍵字彙：diet「節食」。　　　　　　　　　　　　　　　　　➜ 答案 A

簡短對話

3-1 聽出主旨

▶▶ **2-01** 🎧

⊙ 答案

① C **②** D **③** C **④** B **⑤** A **⑥** B **⑦** B **⑧** A **⑨** C **⑩** D

⊙ 解析

① W: How can I help you today? 今天我可以為你服務什麼？

M: I've lost my passport. 我的護照丟了。

W: Do you have any ID with you? 你有任何的身分證明文件嗎？

M: I have my driver's license. 我有駕駛執照。

W: That'll do. No need to worry. We'll get you a new one in a couple of days.
那可以。沒有必要擔心。我們會在幾天內給你一個新的。

M: I appreciate your help. 我很感謝妳的幫助。

Q: Where are the speakers now? 說話者在哪裡？

A. They're in a coffee shop. 他們在一家咖啡廳裡。

B. They're at a grocery store. 他們在一家雜貨店裡。

C. They're in an embassy. 他們在大使館裡。

D. They're in a license bureau. 他們在證照局裡。

1. 本題是問對話發生的地點，所以要從說話者談論的細節來推論出情境。
2. 答案的線索是在於 I've lost my passport. 和 We'll get you a new one in a couple of days. 這兩句話，我們可以知道護照只有在大使館或是領事局這樣的地方才可以申請補發，所以正確答案是 C。
3. 關鍵字彙：passport「護照」、ID「身分證明文件」、embassy「大使館」、license bureau「證照局」。

➡ 答案 C

② M: How about some dessert? 來一些甜點怎麼樣？

W: I'd love some apple pie. 我想要一些蘋果派。

M: And with a scoop of vanilla ice cream. 再加上一球香草冰淇淋。

W: Actually, I really shouldn't. I'm trying to watch my figure.
事實上，我真的不應該吃。我正試著注意我的身材。

M: You look great! 妳看起來很棒！

W: Well, my love handles aren't getting any smaller.
嗯，我肚子上的游泳圈並沒有變小。

Q: What is the woman trying to do? 這位女士想做什麼？

A. She's trying to find a new love. 她正嘗試尋找新的愛情。

B. She wants the man to get some dessert. 她想要這男士點一些甜點。

C. She's trying to order some apple pie without ice cream.
她正試著點一些蘋果派，但不加冰淇淋。

D. She's trying not to gain any more weight. 她努力不再增加體重。

1. 本題是問女方的意圖，所以要聽清楚關鍵字來推測她想做什麼。

2. 答案的線索是在於 I'm trying to watch my figure. 和 my love handles aren't getting any smaller 這兩句話，我們可以知道她正在節食中，並不想吃甜點。

3. 關鍵字彙：a scoop of「一球」、figure「身材」、love handles「肚子上的游泳圈」、gain weight「變胖」。　　　　　　　　　　　　　⊙答案 D

③ W: Who wants a red envelope? 誰想要紅包呀？

M: I do! 我要！

W: Have you studied hard at school? 你在學校有努力學習嗎？

M: Uh... I think so. 嗯…我想有的。

W: Here you go. 給你。

M: Thanks Aunt Fay. 謝謝菲菲阿姨。

W: How about some New Year cake? 來吃一點年糕怎麼樣？

M: Yeah! 好啊！

Q: Which occasion is this? 這是什麼時機場合？

A. It's the boy's birthday party. 這是小男孩的生日會。

B. It's a barbecue. 這是烤肉活動。

C. It's Chinese New Year. 這是農曆新年。

D. It's the boy's graduation ceremony. 這是男孩的畢業典禮。

解題關鍵

1. 本題是問對話發生的時機，要仔細聽清楚細節來判斷。
2. 答案的線索是在於 Who wants a red envelope? 和 How about some New Year cake? 我們只有在婚宴喜慶或是逢年過節時送紅包，題目是長輩送給孩子的，所以就是在過年時期。
3. 關鍵字彙：red envelope「紅包」、New Year cake「年糕」。　　➔答案 C

❹ W: Thank you so much for helping. 謝謝你大力協助。

M: It's what we're trained to do, ma'am. 我們就是受訓來做這些的，女士。

W: This quake was just devastating. 這是個破壞性很強的地震。

M: Yes, it took some time to restore electricity and water.
　　對呀，花了一些時間才恢復電力和水。

W: You've done a wonderful job. 你表現得非常出色。

Q: Why is the woman so grateful? 為什麼這位女士如此地感激？

A. She got her electricity and water bills reduced. 她的電費和水費帳單減少了。

**B. People helped restore things back to normal after an earthquake.
在地震後人們幫忙恢復原狀。**

C. She received useful training. 她接受了很有用的訓練。

D. Now she can watch her favorite TV show. 現在她可以看她最喜歡的電視節目。

 解題關鍵

1. 本題是問女士感激的原因，所以要聽懂男方所做的事。
2. 答案的線索是在 this quake was just devastating、it took some time to restore electricity and water，所以這位男士協助女方地震後的復原。
3. 關鍵字彙：devastating「嚴重的；具破壞性的」、restore「恢復」、electricity「電力」、reduce「減低」。　　➔答案 B

❺ M: Please sit back and relax. 請往後坐好，並且放輕鬆。

W: Is it going to hurt? 會痛嗎？

M: The needle might, but just for a second. 打針可能會，但是只有一下子。

W: I wish I had brushed my teeth more regularly. 我真希望之前更常刷牙。

M: That would have helped for sure. 那樣肯定有幫助。

Q: What is the man's occupation? 這位男士的職業是什麼？

A. He's a dentist. 他是一位牙醫。

B. He's a nurse. 他是一位護士。

C. He's a cosmetic surgeon. 他是一位整型外科醫生。

D. He's a salesman. 他是一位推銷員。

PART3

簡短對話

1. 本題是問男士的職業，所以我們需要由情境來推論答案。

2. 答案的線索是在 The needle might, but just for a second. 和 I wish I had brushed my teeth more regularly. 由這位男士提到要打針，和女方後悔沒有更規律地刷牙得知，他就是牙醫。

3. 關鍵字彙：regularly「規律地」、cosmetic surgeon「整型外科醫生」。 ➔ 答案 A

6 M: Could you get your dog to quit barking? 可以請你叫你的狗不要再叫了嗎？

W: Mind your own business. 關你什麼事。

M: How can I take a nap with that mutt barking?
那隻雜種狗一直叫，我怎麼有辦法睡午覺呢？

W: He's not a mutt. 牠不是雜種狗。

M: It looks like a mutt. 牠看起來就像雜種狗。

W: My husband is going to have a word with you. 我的丈夫很快就會去找你談談。

M: Good. Maybe I can talk some sense into him. 好呀。也許我可以和他理性溝通。

Q: What is the relationship between these two speakers?
這兩位談話者是什麼關係？

A. They're old friends. 他們是老朋友。

B. They're neighbors. 他們是鄰居。

C. They're doctor and patient. 他們是醫生和病人。

D. They're dog trainers. 他們是狗的訓練員。

解題關鍵

1. 本題內容是兩位鄰居在吵架，題目問他們的關係。

2. 答題的線索是在 How can I take a nap with that mutt barking? 會吵到別人睡午覺就是隔壁的鄰居。

3. 關鍵字彙：Mind your own business.「不要管別人的事」、mutt「雜種狗」、have a word with someone「和某人談談」、talk some sense into someone「使某人理解一下；和某人溝通」。 ➔ 答案 B

7 M: Ma'am, I'm sorry you can't return this bowl. 小姐，對不起，妳不能退回這個碗。

W: What do you mean I can't return it? 我不能退回是什麼意思？

M: When I sold it to you, nothing was wrong with it.
我把它賣給妳的時候是完好無缺的。

W: Look, when I got home, I took it out of the box, and it was already broken.
聽好，我回家把它從盒子裡拿出來時，它已經是破的了。

M: Let me talk to my manager, okay? 讓我和我的經理談談，好嗎？

W: Thank you. 謝謝你。

Q: Why is the customer a little upset? 為什麼顧客有點不高興？

A. The ball she bought broke. 她買的球破了。

B. The man said she can't return the merchandise.
這位男士說，她不能把商品退回。

C. The clerk won't buy the lady a new bowl. 店員不會買一個新碗給這位女士。

D. She wants to speak to the manager. 她想要和經理談談。

1. 本題內容是顧客和店員的對話，題目是問顧客不高興的原因。

2. 答題的線索是在 you can't return this bowl 和 When I got home, I took it out of the box, and it was already broken. 這兩句話，雖然她不高興她的碗竟然破了，但是令她沮喪的是店員不讓她退換商品。

3. 關鍵字彙：manager「經理」、merchandise「商品」。　　　　　　答案 B

❽ M: You deserve it, Caroline. 這是妳應得的，卡羅琳。

W: I've waited so long for this. 這一刻我已經等很久了。

M: The work you've done this year has been remarkable.
今年你表現得相當卓越。

W: Do you think I'll get a raise? 你想我會加薪嗎？

M: I'm sure you will – along with more responsibilities, too.
我敢肯定妳一定會，也會有更多的責任。

Q: What are the speakers discussing? 說話者在討論什麼？

A. They're discussing the woman's promotion. 他們在討論女士的升遷。

B. They're talking about their weekend plans. 他們在談論週末計畫。

C. They want to improve their work conditions. 他們希望改善工作條件。

D. They're talking about their responsibilities at work. 他們在談論他們的工作職責。

1. 由對話的細節內容得知，這是同事之間或是上司對屬下的對話，題目是問對話的主題。

2. 答題的線索是在 The work you've done this year has been remarkable. 和關鍵詞 get a raise 和 responsibilities，由此可知內容是在討論升遷加薪的事。

3. 關鍵字彙：You deserve it.「你應得的；實至名歸」、remarkable「卓越；優異的」、get a raise「加薪」、responsibilities「責任」。　　　　答案 A

❾ W: I need a break. My legs are killing me. 我需要休息一下,我的腿痛死了。

M: Hey, where's my bag? 耶,我的袋子呢?

W: Don't worry. I think Dad took yours. 不要擔心,我想爸爸幫你拿了。

M: Are we going to ride that roller coaster again?

我們還要再坐一次雲霄飛車嗎?

W: Yeah, but I need a drink and some shade first.

好啊,但是我需要先找個陰涼的地方喝點飲料。

M: I want to go on that water ride, too. 我也想去玩那個水上設施。

Q: Where are the speakers likely having this conversation?

在這一段對話中,說話者可能在哪裡?

A. They're in Tokyo. 他們在東京。

B. They're in the shade, probably under a tree. 他們在陰涼處,很可能在樹蔭下。

C. They're at an amusement park. 他們在遊樂園裡。

D. They're at a shopping mall. 他們在購物商場裡。

1. 這是手足之間的對話,內容是有關家庭旅遊,題目是問對話發生的場景或地點。

2. 答題的線索是在 Are we going to ride that roller coaster again? 和 I want to go on that water ride, too. 這兩句話,我們可以知道他們一定是在遊樂園裡。

3. 關鍵字彙:roller coaster「雲霄飛車」、shade「樹蔭;蔭涼處」、water ride「水上遊樂器材」。

4. took yours「拿你的東西」聽起來和 Tokyo「東京」很像,不要上當。　　➡ 答案 C

❿ M: Their music just blew me away. 他們的音樂真是讓我震憾不已。

W: I know. And their dancing was even more impressive.

對呀,而且他們的舞蹈更是令人印象深刻。

M: I'm glad I bought their newest album. 我很高興買了他們的最新專輯。

W: You definitely have to lend it to me. 你一定要借給我。

M: Yeah, no problem. 好啊,沒問題。

W: Hey, let's go get a drink. 嘿,我們去喝一杯吧。

M: Sounds good. 聽起來不錯。

Q: What kind of event are the speakers talking about?

說話者正在談論什麼事?

A. They're talking about an impressive tornado that hit town.

他們正在談論一個襲擊鎮上、令人印象深刻的龍捲風。

B. They're talking about their newest album.

他們正在談論他們的最新專輯。

C. They're deciding where to get a drink.

他們正在決定要到哪裡去喝一杯。

D. They're talking about the concert they just attended.

他們正在談論剛剛參加的演唱會。

1. 本題內容是兩位朋友之間的對話，題目是問他們談論的主題。

2. 答題的線索是在 their music、their dancing 和 I'm glad I bought their newest album。
所以我們可以知道他們正在討論剛才的表演。

3. 關鍵字彙：blow someone away 是「令某人震驚」、impressive「令人印象深刻的」、newest album「最新專輯」。 ▶ 答案 D

3-2 聽出意圖

◎ 答案

Exercise 1 🎧 2-04

1. The children seemed a little re<u>stl</u>ess.
2. When does the ne<u>xt m</u>ovie start?
3. I to<u>ld t</u>hem to sta<u>nd t</u>he chairs against the wall.
4. I need to wi<u>nd d</u>own after a long day.
5. We shou<u>ld d</u>o our be<u>st t</u>o assist the police.
6. The touri<u>st s</u>tayed with us for two days.
7. We'll have the party in the vaca<u>nt l</u>ot beside the school.
8. She spoke to us about her bli<u>ndn</u>ess.
9. Le<u>nd D</u>anny your car tonight.
10. Did<u>n't F</u>rank tell you?

Exercise 2 🎧 2-05

1. I (can / can't) prove who stole the parcel.
2. Why (can / can't) they go?
3. You (can / can't) call me anytime you want.
4. We (can / can't) wait outside.
5. (Can / Can't) they hear us from the back?
6. I (can / can't) help you this afternoon.
7. She (can / can't) finish before she goes home.
8. Hank (can / can't) compete in the race.
9. We (can / can't) perform without them.
10. (Can / Can't) they ask for a temporary extension?

1 B   **2** D   **3** C   **4** C   **5** A   **6** C   **7** D   **8** A   **9** B   **10** C

⊙ 解析 ▶▶ 2-07

❶ M: I was pretty disappointed in Jerry and Diane's wedding ceremony.
對於傑瑞和黛安娜的結婚典禮，我真是相當失望。

W: I felt the same way. 我也這樣覺得。

M: Should we try and find a different wedding planner?
我們是否應該試著去找不同的婚禮策劃師？

W: I'm calling a new one tomorrow. 明天我會打電話找一個新的。

Q: What will the woman likely do? 這位女士可能會做什麼？

A. Plan a wedding. 計畫婚禮。

B. Call a wedding planner. 打電話給一位婚禮策劃師。

C. Call and change the appointment. 打電話更改約談時間。

D. She likes to plan weddings. 她喜歡策劃婚禮。

1. 本題情境為兩人在討論一場婚禮，題目是問女方接下來可能會做的事。

2. 答題線索在最後兩句 Should we try and find a different wedding planner? 和 I'm calling a new one tomorrow. 可知他們想找其他的婚禮策劃師。

3. 關鍵字彙：disappointed「令人失望的」、ceremony「典禮」、wedding planner「婚禮策劃師；婚禮顧問」。　　　　　　　　　　　　　⊙答案 B

❷ W: This movie is so boring. 這部電影真無聊。

M: I know. I almost fell asleep. 我知道。我差點睡著了。

W: Do you want to go buy some ice cream? 你想要去買冰淇淋嗎？

M: Sure, but I'm broke. 當然，但是我沒錢了。

W: That's funny. So am I. 那很好笑，我也是。

M: How about another dip in the pool. 要不要再來泡一次游泳池呀。

W: I'll race you! 和你比賽看誰先到那裡！

Q: What will the children likely do next? 小朋友接下來可能會做什麼？

A. They'll go buy some ice cream. 他們將會去買冰淇淋。

B. They'll fix what's broken. 他們將會修理破掉的東西。

C. They'll finish watching the movie. 他們將會看完這部電影。

D. They'll go swimming. 他們將會去游泳。

1. 本題情境為兩位熟識的小朋友對話，題目是問他們的意圖。
2. 答題線索為 How about another dip in the pool. 和 I'll race you! 雖然他們本來想去買冰淇淋，但是兩人都沒有錢，所以我們可確認他們會去游泳。
3. 關鍵字彙：I'm broke.「我沒錢了」。 ➡ 答案 D

❸ M: Why don't we stay in a villa like we did last year?
　　我們為什麼不住在像去年那樣的渡假別墅？

W: I don't know. I didn't enjoy all the mosquitoes.
　　我不知道。我不喜歡蚊子。

M: That's right. I forgot about that. 沒錯。我忘記那件事了。

W: How about a five-star hotel? 住五星級飯店怎麼樣？

M: You did get a nice bonus this year. 妳今年的確領了不少獎金。

W: Actually, they cancelled the bonus. 事實上，他們取消了獎金。

M: Well, scratch the five-star hotel. How about a beach hut?
　　嗯，那五星級飯店就算了，海邊小木屋好嗎？

W: That sounds good to me. Why not? 聽起來不錯。有何不可？

Q: What kind of place will the couple likely stay in?
這對夫婦可能會住在什麼樣的地方？

A. A five-star hotel. 五星級飯店。

B. A hotel by the beach. 一個飯店的海灘。

C. A beach hut. 一間海邊小屋。

D. A villa just like last year. 一個像去年一樣的渡假別墅。

1. 本題情境為夫妻在討論渡假的細節，題目是問他們可能選擇渡假的飯店型式。
2. 答題的線索為 Well, scratch the five-star hotel. How about a beach hut? 和 That sounds good to me. Why not? 由這兩句話可以得知，這對夫妻最後決定要住在海邊小木屋。
3. 關鍵字彙：bonus「紅利；獎金」、cancel「取消」、scratch「取消」。 ➡ 答案 C

❹ W: I love hiking in the early morning. 我喜愛在清晨爬山。

M: Is that a dog over there? 那邊是一隻狗嗎？

W: Oh, I think it's hurt. 哦，我覺得牠受傷了。

M: Let's go check it out. 我們去看看牠。

W: It's bleeding. 牠正在流血。

M: Yeah, we should take it somewhere. 是的，我們應該把牠帶到別的地方。

Q: What will the man and woman probably do?
這位男士和女士接下來可能會做什麼？

A. Stop the dog's bleeding. 幫小狗止血。

B. Go somewhere else to hike. 到別的地方去爬山。

C. Take the dog to a veterinarian. 帶小狗去看獸醫。

D. Look for the dog's owner. 尋找狗的主人。

1. 本題情境為夫妻兩個人去登山所遇到的事，題目是問接下來他們會怎麼處理。

2. 答題的線索為 It's bleeding. 和 Yeah, we should take it somewhere. 由這兩句話我們知道，他們很心疼這隻狗，所以會馬上帶牠去看獸醫。

3. 關鍵字彙：check it out「看一下」、veterinarian「獸醫（簡稱是 vet）」。 ➡答案 C

❺ M: I think you'll like this perfume. 我想妳會喜歡這個香水。

W: It smells fabulous. 味道聞起來好極了。

M: That'll be $1,700, ma'am. 這樣是 1,700 元，女士。

W: Let me check my wallet. Oops! I'm out of cash.
我看看我的錢包。糟糕！我的現金用完了。

M: That's okay. We take credit cards. 沒關係，我們收信用卡。

W: Well, here you go. 嗯，給你。

Q: How will the woman probably pay? 這位女士可能會如何付錢？

A. She'll pay with her credit card. 她將會用信用卡付錢。

B. She'll leave without the purchase. 她將會沒有購買就離開。

C. She'll borrow some cash. 她將會去借一些現金。

D. She'll write a check for the perfume. 她會開支票來付香水。

1. 本題是顧客和店員的對話，題目是問顧客付款的方式。

2. 答題的線索為 Oops! I'm out of cash. 和 That's okay. We take credit cards. 這兩句話告訴我們，她會用信用卡付款。

3. 關鍵字彙：fabulous「好極了」、out of「用完了」。 答案 A

❻ W: Excuse me. 對不起。

M: Are you ready to order? 妳準備好要點菜了嗎？

W: Yes, we'll have the fried chicken and some stir-fried vegetables.
是的，我們要炸雞和一些炒青菜。

M: I'm sorry. We're sold out of the fried chicken. 很抱歉。我們的炸雞賣完了。

W: That's a bummer. 真是掃興呀。

M: How about a chicken casserole? 燉雞怎麼樣？

W: No, thanks. How are the beef and noodles? 不，謝謝。牛肉麵的味道如何？

M: One of our specialties. 是我們的招牌菜之一。

W: We'll have two bowls then. 那麼我們要兩碗。

Q: What will the girl probably have? 這位女孩可能會吃什麼？

A. Beef and noodles and some chicken butts. 牛肉麵和一些雞屁股。

B. Fried chicken and some stir-fried vegetables. 炸雞和一些炒青菜。

C. Some noodles and stir-fried vegetables. 有些麵條和炒青菜。

D. Two bowls of today's special. 兩碗今日特餐。

1. 本題是餐廳服務生和顧客之間的對話，題目是問顧客可能會點的菜。

2. 答題的線索為最後三句話 How are the beef and noodles?、One of our specialties. 和 We'll have two bowls then. 所以我們知道這位女士最後要吃牛肉麵。

3. 關鍵字彙：stir-fried vegetables「炒青菜」、bummer「掃興；可惜」、specialties「特色；招牌菜」。

⊙答案 C

❼ M: Excuse me. How much is this skirt? 對不起。這條裙子多少錢？

W: Let's see. It's NT$2,300. 我看看。要台幣 2,300 元。

M: That's a little over my budget. 有一點超過我的預算。

W: How much do you want to spend? 你想要花多少錢？

M: I was thinking around NT$1,000. 我想大概台幣 1,000 元左右。

W: How about this shirt? 這件襯衫怎麼樣？

M: I don't really care for the design. Oh, I like this bracelet, though.
我不喜歡這個設計。噢，但是我喜歡這個手鐲。

W: It's on sale. 這個在特價。

M: Can you wrap it for me? 你能幫我包起來嗎？

W: No problem. 沒問題。

**Q: What will the man likely buy for his girlfriend?
這位男士可能會為他的女朋友買什麼東西？**

A. A skirt. 一條裙子。

B. A sandwich wrap. 一個三明治餅。

C. A shirt with a scary design. 一件設計可怕的襯衫。

D. A bracelet. 一個手鐲。

1. 本題是顧客和店員的對話，這位女店員在幫男顧客挑選禮物。題目是問他要買什麼禮物，所以前面所提到的細節就不那麼重要。

2. 答題線索為 Oh, I like this bracelet 和 Can you wrap it for me?，所以可得知男顧客最後要買手鐲。

3. 關鍵字彙：budget「預算」、care for「喜歡」、bracelet「手鐲」。 答案 D

❽ M: Do you have any time this Saturday? 妳這個星期六有沒有空？

W: Yeah, I think so. Why? 有啊，我想應該是有。為什麼問？

M: I'm going home to help my parents redecorate their kitchen.
我要回家幫我父母重新裝修他們的廚房。

W: Sounds like fun, but don't we have an exam on Monday?
聽起來很有趣，但我們星期一不是要考試嗎？

M: That's right! I totally forgot. 對啊！我完全忘記了。

W: Maybe we can help them next Saturday.
也許我們可以下週六再幫他們。

Q: What do the speakers plan to do this Saturday?
說話者計畫在這個星期六做什麼？

A. **They'll study for an exam.** 他們將唸書準備考試。

B. They'll redecorate a kitchen. 他們將重新裝修廚房。

C. They'll visit the man's parents. 他們將去拜訪男孩子的父母。

D. They'll likely help the man's parents next Saturday.
下週六他們可能會去幫這位男孩子的父母。

1. 本題是朋友之間的對話，內容在討論星期六的計畫，題目是問他們星期六決定要做的事。

2. 答題線索為 but don't we have an exam on Monday? 和 Maybe we can help them next Saturday，所以我們知道他們這個星期六要準備考試。

3. 關鍵字彙：redecorate「重新整修」。 答案 A

❾ W: Honey, I want to get engaged. 親愛的，我想要訂婚。

M: I know, but my parents won't agree with it. 我知道，但我父母不會同意的。

W: Why? 為什麼？

M: They think I should work for a few years before we get married.
他們認為我應該在結婚前先工作幾年。

W: I said engaged, not married. 我是說訂婚，不是結婚。

M: You're right. Why wait any longer? 妳說得對，為什麼還要再等呢？

Q: What will the man likely do next? 這位男士接下來可能會做什麼？

A. Find a job. 找工作。

B. Ask his girlfriend to marry him. 請他的女友嫁給他。

C. Tell his girlfriend to wait a little longer. 告訴他的女朋友再等一會兒。

D. Call his parents and tell them that they're right.
   打電話給他的父母，告訴他們，他們是對的。

1. 本題是男女朋友的對話，內容是討論訂婚的事，題目是問男士接下來會做的事。

2. 答題線索在於 I said engaged, not married. 和 Why wait any longer? 這兩句話，男子很明顯同意要訂婚，所以他會向他的女友求婚。

3. 關鍵字彙：get engaged「訂婚」。　　　　　　　　　　　　　　　　➡ 答案 B

🔟 M: Are we taking a taxi to the concert? 我們要坐計程車去聽演唱會嗎？

W: Why don't we take a bus? 我們為什麼不坐公車？

M: I don't want to walk all the way to the bus stop, though.
   但是我不想要一路走去公車站。

W: How about we take my scooter? 我們騎我的機車去好不好？

M: You don't have your license yet. 妳還沒有駕照。

W: Surprise! 驚訝吧！

M: Awesome! Is it safe, though? 真棒！但是安全嗎？

W: That was so funny I forgot to laugh. 這個笑話真有趣，我都忘了要笑。

Q: How will the man and woman get to the concert?
   這名男子和女子要如何去演唱會？

A. They'll take a taxi. 他們將會坐計程車去。

B. They'll take a bus. 他們將搭公車去。

C. The woman will ride her scooter. 這名女子將會騎她的機車去。

D. It'll probably take them twenty minutes to get there. 到那裡可能會花他們二十分鐘。

1. 本題是朋友之間的對話，內容是討論要如何去演唱會，題目是問要怎麼去。

2. 答題線索在 I don't want to walk all the way to the bus stop, though. 和 How about we take my scooter? 而女方表示已經有駕照了，即使男方嘲笑她，他們還是會騎機車去。　　　　　　　　　　　　　　　　➡ 答案 C

3-3　聽出細節

▶▶ 2-08

⊙ 答案

① B　**②** B　**③** D　**④** D　**⑤** D　**⑥** B　**⑦** C　**⑧** A　**⑨** A　**⑩** D

⊙ 解析

① M: Well, I'd better run. 嗯，我要走了！

W: Where are you going? 你要去哪裡？

M: I'm just heading off to the library. 我只是要去圖書館。

W: Don't you have a class later tonight? 今晚晚一點你不是有課嗎？

M: No, but I have to study for a biology test tomorrow.
沒有，但是我必須要唸書，準備明天的生物考試。

W: Good luck. 祝你好運。

M: Thanks. I'll need it. 謝謝，我會需要的。

Q: What will the man do tonight? 這位男生今晚將會做什麼？

A. Go see Gary. 去見蓋瑞。

B. Study at the library. 在圖書館唸書。

C. Take a biology test. 考生物。

D. Have dinner with a friend. 和一位朋友吃晚餐。

1. 本題是兩位熟識的朋友或家人之間的對話，內容是說男方晚上活動的安排，題目是問男士今晚將要做什麼事。

2. 答案的線索在 I'm just heading off to the library. 和 I have to study for a biology test tomorrow. 這兩句話，所以我們知道他要去圖書館唸書，準備明天的考試。

3. 關鍵字彙：head off「前往」、biology「生物」。　　⊖答案 B

② W: I think it's going to rain tomorrow. 我覺得明天會下雨。

M: So are we still going to Sun Moon Lake? 那麼，我們是否還要去日月潭？

W: Sure. If it rains, we can relax in a pagoda.
當然。如果下雨，大家可以在涼亭裡休息。

M: Maybe it'll be sunny like today. 也許天氣會像今天一樣晴朗。

W: Hope so! 希望如此！

Q: What's the weather like? 今天的天氣怎麼樣？

A. It will rain tomorrow. 明天會下雨。

B. It's sunny. 天氣晴朗。

C. It's raining. 正在下雨。

D. They prefer sunny days. 他們偏愛陽光普照的日子。

1. 本題內容是在討論天氣與出遊的計畫，題目是問今天的天氣如何。
2. 答題的線索是在 Maybe it'll be sunny like today. 可得知今天的天氣晴朗。
3. 關鍵字彙：pagoda「涼亭」。

➡ 答案 B

❸ W: Mike, are you picking me up for the movie? 邁克，你會來接我去看電影嗎？

M: I'd love to, but my car is being repaired. 我很樂意，但是我的車子還在修理當中。

W: That's too bad. 那太糟糕了。

M: Why don't we take a bus? 我們為什麼不坐公車去？

W: I'd rather take a taxi. I hate waiting for a bus. 我寧願坐計程車，我討厭等公車。

M: Yeah. So you'll grab a taxi and then pick me up?
對啊。那麼妳招一輛計程車後來接我好嗎？

W: How's 7 o'clock? 七點如何？

M: I'll be waiting. 我會等妳。

Q: How will the woman get to the movie? 這位女孩將如何去看電影？

A. She'll go with Mike. 她會和邁克一起去。

B. Mike will drive. 邁克會開車去。

C. She'll take a bus with Mike. 她將和邁克一起搭公車去。

D. She'll take a taxi with Mike. 她將和邁克一起坐計程車去。

1. 本題內容是討論要搭哪一種交通工具去看電影，題目是問這位女孩會如何去。
2. 答題線索在 I'd rather take a taxi. I hate waiting for a bus. 和 So you'll grab a taxi and then pick me up? 這兩句話，所以我們知道她會坐計程車去。
3. 關鍵字彙：pick someone up「去接某人」、grab「攔截」。

➡ 答案 D

❹ M: What happened to you, Caroline? 卡洛琳，妳發生了什麼事？

W: I sprained my ankle. 我扭傷了腳踝。

M: Playing basketball again, yeah? 又是因為打籃球，是嗎？

W: Well, I did play basketball, but I hurt it walking down the stairs.
嗯，我是打了籃球，但我是下樓梯時受傷的。

M: Do you think you can play tomorrow? 妳認為妳明天可以打球嗎？

W: I doubt it. 我懷疑。

Q: How did Caroline hurt herself? 卡洛琳是怎麼受傷的？

A. She heard them walking down the stairs. 她聽到他們走下樓梯。

B. She hurt her ankle. 她傷了她的腳踝。

C. She probably won't play tomorrow. 她可能明天不會打了。

D. She hurt herself walking down the stairs. 她下樓梯時受傷的。

1. 本題是朋友之間的對話，內容是討論女方的問題，題目是問女方是如何受傷的。

2. 答題線索在於 I hurt it walking down the stairs. 這句話上，所以我們知道她是下樓梯時受傷的。選項 A 中 heard「聽到」和 hurt「受傷」是相似音，要小心。

3. 關鍵字彙：sprain「扭傷」、I doubt it「我懷疑；我想不會」。 答案 D

❺ W: Excuse me. How much are these shirts? 請問這些襯衫要多少錢？

M: They are on sale for NT$290 each. 每件特價台幣 290 元

W: That's a good price. 這個價錢很好。

M: You can get three for only NT$750. 任選三件台幣 750 元。

W: In that case, I'll take three. 那樣子的話，我要三件。

Q: How much will the woman pay? 這個女士要付多少錢？

A. She'll pay for three shirts. 她將會付三件襯衫的錢。

B. She'll pay only NT$715. 她將只會付台幣 715 元。

C. She'll pay NT$290 each. 她將付每件台幣 290 元。

D. She'll pay NT$750. 她將會付台幣 750 元。

1. 本題是賣衣服的店員和顧客之間的對話，題目是問這位女士要付多少錢。

2. 答題線索為 You can get three for only NT$750.、In that case, I'll take three. 這兩句話，我們知道她要買三件。

3. 關鍵字彙：on sale「特價」、in that case「那樣的話」。 答案 D

❻ M: I can't take it anymore. 我再也受不了了。

W: What's wrong? 怎麼了？

M: Well, my boss is a total nut. If it weren't for my salary, I would have quit a long time ago.

嗯，我的老闆是一個笨蛋。如果不是為了薪水，我很久以前就辭職了。

W: How about your colleagues? 你的同事怎麼樣？

M: They're awesome. I'm going to miss them when I leave.

他們真棒。當我離開時，我會想念他們的。

Q: Why does the man want to change jobs? 為什麼這位男士想要換工作？

A. His salary isn't very good. 他的薪水不是很好。

B. He doesn't like his boss. 他不喜歡他的老闆。

C. Because he wants more benefits. 因為他希望有更多福利。

D. His colleagues are awful. 他的同事們都非常糟糕。

1. 本題是朋友之間的對話，內容是男士在抱怨對上司的不滿，題目是問男方想離職的原因。

2. 答題線索為 I can't take it anymore. 表示無法忍受這份工作，而 my boss is a total nut 和 If it weren't for my salary, I would have quit a long time ago. 這句話透露出想離職的意願和原因。

3. 關鍵字彙：I can't take it anymore「我受不了」、nut「笨蛋」、quit「辭職」、colleague「同事」。　　　　　　　　　　　　　　　　　　　⇒答案 B

❼ W: Hi, can you tell me where I can find the closest MRT station?

嗨，你能告訴我在哪裡可以找到最近的捷運站嗎？

M: Let's see. Okay, go down this street and take a right at the second traffic light. You'll see the MRT station on the left.

我看看。好的，沿著這條街走下去，在第二個紅綠燈右轉，你會看到捷運站就在左邊。

W: Thanks. I can't wait to see Taipei 101. 謝謝。我等不及要看到台北 101 了。

M: Taipei 101? 台北 101？

W: Yes, have you been there? 是的，你去過那裡嗎？

M: That's it right behind you. 在妳背後的就是。

Q: Which statement is incorrect? 下列哪種說法是不正確的？

A. The woman wanted to find an MRT station. 這位女士想要找捷運站。

B. The woman wants to see Taipei 101. 這位女士希望看到台北 101。

C. The woman will take the MRT. 這位女士將會搭乘捷運。

D. The woman is very close to Taipei 101. 這位女士非常接近台北 101。

1. 本題的內容是問路和指示，題目問不正確的敘述，本題的細節比較多，此時運用做重點筆記的技巧就很實用。

2. 答題線索為 I can't wait to see Taipei 101. 這句話表示她找捷運站的原因，由 That's it right behind you. 這句話可以得知，不需要搭地鐵就可以看到台北 101 大樓。

3. 關鍵字彙：go down「走下去」。

❽ M: Is this your first time in Taiwan? 這是妳第一次來台灣？

W: Yes, it is. 是的。

M: Well, I hope you enjoy your stay. 嗯，我希望妳在這裡過得愉快。

W: Thank you. Taiwan is such a beautiful country.
謝謝你。台灣是非常美麗的國家。

M: Are you from Canada? 妳從加拿大來的嗎？

W: No, I'm from America, but I'm actually living in Ireland now.
不，我從美國來的，但我現在住在愛爾蘭。

Q: Where is the woman from? 這位女士來自何處？

A. She's from America. 她從美國來。

B. She's from Canada. 她從加拿大來。

C. She's vacationing in Taiwan. 她正在台灣渡假。

D. She's living in Ireland. 她現在住在愛爾蘭。

1. 本題是陌生人之間的對話，內容在談論這位異鄉來的女士背景資料，題目是問她來自何處。

2. 答題線索是 I'm from America. 雖然她補充說明她現在的居住地，但是選項 D 的敘述並沒有回答問題。

❾ W: Do you have the time? 你知道現在的時間嗎？

M: Yeah, it's 1 o'clock. 知道，現在是一點鐘。

W: Well, the schedule says the next bus to Yuanlin leaves in 10 minutes.
嗯，時刻表上說，下一班到員林的公車 10 分鐘後離開。

M: What time will we arrive? 我們什麼時候會到達？

W: Around 2 p.m. 下午 2 點左右。

M: Perfect. Let's get our tickets. 好極了。我們去買車票。

Q: What time will the bus leave for Yuanlin? 往員林的公車什麼時候離開？

A. At ten after one. 一點十分。

B. It's 1 o'clock. 一點鐘。

C. At ten to ten. 九點五十分。

D. At 2 p.m. 在下午兩點鐘。

1. 本題內容是談論要坐公車去員林的細節，題目是問公車的時間。

2. 答題線索是在 it's 1 o'clock 和 the next bus to Yuanlin leaves in 10 minutes，由這兩句話可得知公車一點十分會出發。

3. 關鍵字彙：schedule「時刻表」。 **答案 A**

⑩ M: What can I get you? 我能為妳服務嗎？

W: I'll have a pearl green tea, please. 請給我一個珍珠綠茶。

M: I'm sorry. We're out of pearls. 我很抱歉，我們的珍珠沒有了。

W: Then I'll have a passion fruit tea. 那我要一個百香果茶。

M: Sugar? 多少糖？

W: Just a little, please. 請給我微糖。

M: That's NT$50. 台幣五十元。

W: Oops! I can't believe I forgot my purse. 糟糕！真不敢相信我忘記帶錢包了。

Q: What kind of tea will the woman buy? 這位女士會買什麼茶？

A. She likes fruit tea. 她喜歡水果茶。

B. She'll buy a passion fruit tea. 她將會買一個百香果茶。

C. She usually buys pearl green tea. 她經常買珍珠綠茶。

D. She won't buy any tea. 她什麼茶也不會買。

1. 本題是顧客和紅茶店員的對話，題目是問女士接下來會買什麼茶。

2. 答題線索是在最後一句 Oops! I can't believe I forgot my purse. 因為我們知道沒有錢就無法買茶了，答案是 D。

3. 關鍵字彙：pearl green tea「珍珠綠茶」、passion fruit tea「百香果茶」、purse「錢包」。 **答案 D**

3-4 聽出推論

⊙ 答案

① B ② D ③ D ④ C ⑤ A ⑥ C ⑦ D ⑧ D ⑨ B ⑩ C

⊙ 解析

① M: I think we ought to head back. 我想我們應該往回走。

W: Let's keep hiking. It's so beautiful up here. 我們再繼續爬山。上面非常美。

M: But it's going to get dark soon. It'll be difficult walking down if we can't see well.
但是天很快就會暗下來。如果我們看不清楚的話，下山將會很困難。

W: Yeah, you're right. 是啊，你說得對。

Q: Which word best describes the man's feelings?
哪個字最能形容這位男士的感受？

A. Dark. 黑暗的

B. Worried. 擔心的

C. Frustrated. 挫折的

D. Cheerful. 興高采烈的

1. 本題情況為兩人去登山，對話內容是討論是否該返回下山了，題目是問男士的感覺。

2. 答題線索在 I think we ought to head back. 和 It'll be difficult walking down if we can't see well. 由這兩句話我們可以推論出他擔心天快黑了，下山會危險。

3. 關鍵字彙：head back「往回走」。 ⊙ 答案 B

② W: I can't believe I got that shirt for only NT$200.
真不敢相信！我只花了台幣 200 元就買到了這件襯衫。

M: It really looks good on you. 在妳身上看起來真的很好看。

W: Hey, are you hungry? 耶，你會餓嗎？

M: A little bit. 有一點。

W: How about some stinky tofu? 來吃點臭豆腐怎麼樣？

M: I know a great place. It's just down this alley on the left.
　　我知道一個好地方。就在這條小巷走到底的左手邊。

Q: Where is this conversation likely taking place?
　　這段對話最有可能發生在哪裡？

A. They're talking about where to go. 他們正在談論去哪裡玩。

B. They are at a shopping mall. 他們在一個購物商場。

C. It's down the alley on the left. 它在這條小巷走到底的左手邊。

D. They're at a night market. 他們在夜市。

1. 本題情境為兩人在逛街購物，對話內容是談論要去附近吃點東西，題目是問對話發生的地點。

2. 答題線索為 I know a great place. It's just down this alley on the left. 這兩句話透露出他們並不是在百貨公司或是購物中心，有便宜的東西和美味臭豆腐，最可能的地方就是在夜市。

3. 關鍵字彙：something looks good on someone「某物在某人身上很好看」、stinky tofu「臭豆腐」、alley「巷子」。　　⊙答案 D

❸ W: I need to see your license and registration, please.
　　我需要看你的駕照和行照，麻煩你了。

M: Why did you pull me over? 妳為什麼攔我下來？

W: You just turned right on a red light. 你剛剛紅燈右轉。

M: I'm sorry. I didn't notice. 很抱歉。我沒有注意到。

W: I'll give you a warning this time. 這一次我給你口頭警告。

M: I appreciate that. 我非常地感激。

W: Be more careful next time. 下次要小心一點。

Q: What is the woman's occupation? 這位女士的職業是什麼？

A. She's a construction worker. 她是一個建築工人。

B. She's occupied at the moment. 她此刻正在忙。

C. She needs to see his license and registration. 她需要看他的駕照和行照。

D. She is a police officer. 她是位警察。

1. 本題情境為正在執行公務的警察和駕駛者的對話,題目是問女方的職業。

2. 答題線索在 I need to see your license and registration, please. 和 I'll give you a warning this time. 這兩句話透露出女方是具有權威性的,所以我們可以推論出她是警察。

3. 關鍵字彙:license and registration「駕照和行照」、pull someone over「把某人的車子攔下」。

 答案 D

④ M: Go Johnny! 強尼,加油!

W: Be quiet! You'll embarrass him. 安靜!你會讓他丟臉的。

M: This is his first baseball game. I can't help it.
這是他第一次的棒球比賽。我忍不住。

W: Wow! 哇!

M: He just hit a home run! 他剛剛打了全壘打!

W: That's my son! 那是我的兒子耶!

M: Honey, sit down. 親愛的,坐下。

Q: How do you think the couple feels? 你覺得這對夫婦感覺如何?

A. This is their son's first game. 這是他們兒子的第一場比賽。

B. They feel helpless. 他們感到無助。

C. They're having a great time. 他們非常愉快。

D. They are probably embarrassed. 他們可能會尷尬。

1. 本題情境為夫妻兩人去看兒子的球賽,題目是問這對夫妻的感覺。

2. 答題線索是在 He just hit a home run! 和 That's my son! 由這兩句話可以推論出他們很融入這場球賽,也以他們的兒子為榮。

3. 關鍵字彙:hit a home run「擊出全壘打」。 答案 C

⑤ W: This doesn't look very good. 這看起來不是很好。

M: It's just my math grade that's terrible. 只有我的數學成績很糟而已。

W: Why didn't you ask for help? 你為什麼不請求幫助呢?

M: I was too busy studying for my other tests. 我太忙於準備別科的考試。

W: Maybe we should enroll you in a cram school.
也許我們應該讓你報名一家補習班。

M: My math does stink. 我的數學真的很爛。

Q: Which statement best describes how the woman feels?
哪一項描述最能描寫出這位女士的感覺？

A. She's a little disappointed. 她有一點失望。

B. She is very frustrated. 她非常挫折。

C. She is happy to help. 她很樂意提供協助。

D. She's enthralled. 她被迷住了。

1. 本題的情境為媽媽和兒子的對話，內容是在談論兒子的成績，題目是問媽媽的感覺。

2. 答題線索是在 This doesn't look very good. 和 Why didn't you ask for help? 由這兩句的語氣可以推論出這位媽媽有一點失望。

3. 關鍵字彙：ask for help「請求幫忙」、enroll「報名；註冊」、cram school「補習班」、stink「爛；糟糕」。　　　　　　　　　　　　　⇨ 答案 A

❻ M: I think we can resolve this peacefully. 我認為我們可以和平地解決這件事。

W: Not in a million years. 絕對不可能的。

M: Maybe we could talk to our... 也許我們可以諮詢我們的…

W: To our psychologist? 找我們的心理醫生嗎？

M: Why not? 為什麼不呢？

W: We've tried that before, and nothing's changed. I can't stand living with you any more. 我們已經試過了，什麼也沒有改變。我再也不能忍受和你一起生活了。

M: Well, what about the kids? 好，那孩子們怎麼辦？

W: Our lawyers will work that out. 我們的律師會解決。

Q: What can you infer from this conversation? 從這段對話中你可以推論出什麼？

A. They'll resolve their problems peacefully. 他們會和平地解決他們的問題。

B. They'll talk with their psychologist again. 他們將會再和心理醫生談談。

C. They'll most likely get divorced. 他們最有可能會離婚。

D. They want to keep the children together. 他們希望和孩子在一起。

1. 本題的情境是夫妻兩人正在討論離婚的事情，題目是要我們推論對話的主旨大意。

2. 答題線索是在 I can't stand living with you anymore. 和 Our lawyers will work that out. 由這兩句話聽出女方的心意已決，所以我們可以推論出他們應該會離婚。

3. 關鍵字彙：Not in a million years.「絕對不可能的。」、psychologist「心理醫生」、work... out「解決；弄清楚」　　　　　　　　　　　　　⇨ 答案 C

❼ W: I know you're at home. (Knock, Knock, Knock) 我知道你在家。（叩。叩。叩。）

M: How does she know I'm home? 她怎麼知道我在家裡？

W: Your rent is overdue, and if I don't get it before five o'clock, I'm going to evict you in a heartbeat.

你的房租過期了，如果我在五點之前沒有收到錢的話，我要馬上把你趕走。

M: I wish she'd just go away. 我真希望她走開。

W: I'll be in the office waiting. 我會在辦公室裡等候。

M: What am I going to do? 那我該怎麼辦？

Q: What is the relationship between these two people?
他們兩個人之間是什麼關係？

A. Boss and employee. 老闆和員工。

B. It's not a cordial relationship. 不是友好的關係。

C. No, they're not likely related. 不，他們不太可能有關係。

D. Landlord and tenant. 房東與房客。

1. 對話內容是女方來要房租，而男方躲起來不見面。題目是要我們推論出他們之間的關係。

2. 答題線索是在 Your rent is overdue. 和 I'm going to evict you in a heartbeat. 由女方提到房租和趕他走的部分可以推論出兩人是房東和房客的關係。

3. 關鍵字彙：overdue「過期」、evict「逐出」、in a heartbeat「立刻；馬上」、cordial「真誠的」、landlord「房東」、tenant「房客」。　　➡ 答案 D

❽ M: Excuse me, miss. 小姐，不好意思。

W: Yes, may I help you? 我能為你服務嗎？

M: Yeah, there's a cockroach in my soup. 嗯，我的湯裡有一隻蟑螂。

W: Oh, my! 哦，我的媽呀！

M: I don't think that was on the menu. 我想在菜單上並沒有這個吧。

Q: What will the woman likely say next? 這位女士接下來會說什麼？

A. Here's our menu, sir. 這是我們的菜單，先生。

B. You should have bought a nicer suit. 你應該要買更好的西裝。

C. Oh, that's today's special. 喔，這就是今日特餐。

D. Let me get you another bowl. 讓我給你換一碗新的。

1. 本題情境為客人和女服務生的對話，題目是要我們推測女服務生接下來會説的話。

2. 答題線索是在 there's a cockroach in my soup 和 Oh, my! 這兩句話，女服務生的語氣透露出抱歉的口吻，所以我們可推論她會做補償的動作。選項 B 中 suit「西裝」和 soup「湯」發音相近，要小心。

3. 關鍵字彙：cockroach「蟑螂」。

 答案 D

❾ W: I got an acceptance letter in the mail today. 我今天收到一封學校的入學許可函。

M: And? 然後呢？

W: Looks like I'll be a nurse after all. 看來我終究會成為一名護士。

M: Congratulations. Do you think you'll stay in a dorm your freshman year?
恭喜妳。妳想妳大一會住在宿舍裡嗎？

W: No. My aunt and uncle live in Tainan, so I'll be staying with them.
不會。我的姑姑和姑丈住在台南，所以我會住在他們家。

M: I hope I can visit you. 真希望我可以去拜訪妳。

W: Anytime. 隨時歡迎。

Q: Why is the woman so excited? 為什麼這位女子如此興奮？

A. Her friend will come and visit her. 她的朋友會來探望她。

B. She was accepted into university. 她被一所大學接受入學了。

C. Her aunt and uncle live in Tainan. 她的姑姑和姑丈住在台南。

D. She has finally become a nurse. 她終於成為一名護士了。

1. 本題為朋友之間的對話，內容是談論女方即將離家去上學的事情，題目要我們推論女子興奮的理由。

2. 答題線索是在 I got an acceptance letter in the mail today. 整個對話的主題就是繞著這件事，我們可以推論出興奮的理由是收到大學入學許可信。

3. 關鍵字彙：acceptance「接受」、after all「終究」、dorm「宿舍（dormitory 的簡稱）」、freshman「大一新生」。

答案 B

❿ M: I need to get rid of my beer belly. 我需要甩掉我的啤酒肚。

W: I think swimming is the best way to lose weight. 我想減肥最好的辦法就是游泳。

M: You're probably right. 也許妳是對的。

W: Why don't you get a membership at a local health club?
你為什麼不成為當地的健身房會員？

M: I think I will, but I prefer riding a stationary bike or running on a treadmill.
　 我想我會的，但是我比較喜歡騎健身腳踏車，或是在跑步機上跑步。

W: Running can be bad for your knees. 跑步對你的膝蓋不好。

M: Then I'll stick to the stationary bike. 那我就只用健身腳踏車。

Q: Which statement best describes the man's opinion?
哪一樣敘述最能描述這位男士的意見？

A. He wants to stop drinking beer. 他想停止喝啤酒。

B. Running on a treadmill is as good as riding a stationary bike.
　 在跑步機上跑步和騎健身腳踏車一樣好。

C. He should start to exercise more. 他應該開始多運動。

D. He'll start swimming at a local health club. 他將開始在當地的健身房游泳。

1. 本題對話內容是談論這位男生的運動新計畫，題目是要我們推論出男方的意圖與
　 計畫。

2. 答題線索是在 I prefer riding a stationary bike or running on a treadmill 和 Then I'll
　 stick to the stationary bike. 最後一句說出了男方要開始運動的結論。

3. 關鍵字彙：get rid of「甩掉」、beer belly「啤酒肚」、stationary bike「健身腳踏
　 車」、treadmill「跑步機」。　　　　　　　　　　　　　　　　　　 ➔ 答案 C

3-5 聽出問題與解決方式

 ▶▶ 2-10

⊙ 答案

❶ D **❷** C **❸** B **❹** D **❺** A **❻** B **❼** B **❽** D **❾** C **❿** B

⊙ 解析

❶ M: Why is Sandy late for the meeting? 為什麼珊蒂開會遲到了？

W: I'm not sure. She's never on time. 我不太確定。她從來沒有準時過。

M: Should I try and call her? 我應該試著打電話給她嗎？

W: Yeah, see if she's left home. 好啊，看看她是否離開家了。

M: I don't think the boss will tolerate this behavior much longer.
我認為老闆再也不會容忍她這種行為。

W: I'm afraid her number might be up. 我擔心她可能快要遭殃了。

Q: What's Sandy's problem? 珊蒂的問題是什麼？

A. She's in a real pickle. 她慘了。

B. She's too punctual. 她太準時了。

C. She took a left and got lost. 她左轉，然後迷路了。

D. She's late for a meeting. 她開會遲到了。

1. 本題情境是兩位同事之間的對話，內容是在談論另一位同事 Sandy 的情形。題目是問 Sandy 出了什麼問題。

2. 答題線索是在 Why is Sandy late for the meeting? 和 She's never on time. 這兩句話透露出說話者對 Sandy 工作態度的評論，所以可得知 Sandy 的問題在於遲到這件事。

3. 關鍵詞彙：on time「準時的」、tolerate「容忍」、in a real pickle「陷入困境」、punctual「準時的」。

➔答案 D

❷ W: What's wrong with your finger? 你的手指頭怎麼了？

M: I cut it preparing dinner, and when I woke up this morning, it looked like this.
我準備晚飯時切到了，我今天早上醒來時，它看起來就像這樣子。

W: It looks infected. 看起來好像發炎了。

M: Do you think they'll have to cut it off? 妳覺得他們會將它切掉嗎？

W: Yeah, right. 是呀，才怪。

M: Maybe I should go see my doctor. 也許我應該去看醫生。

W: Duh. 當然囉。

Q: How will the man handle this problem? 這位男士將如何處理這個問題？

A. He'll have his finger cut off. 他將會把他的手指頭切斷。

B. He'll go see his daughter. 他會去看他的女兒。

C. He'll see a doctor. 他會去看醫生。

D. He cut his finger, and now it's infected. 他切到手指頭，現在感染發炎了。

1. 本題是兩位朋友在談論男方的問題，題目是要我們推測這位男士將會如何處理他的問題。

2. 答題線索是 It looks infected. 由這句話可知手指頭有發炎的情形，而男方說 Maybe I should go see my doctor. 可知他接下來會去看醫生。

3. 關鍵詞彙：infected「感染發炎的」、Duh「廢話；當然囉」。 答案 C

❸ M: Do you enjoy working in Taichung? 妳喜愛在台中工作嗎？

W: Yeah, it's not bad. The night-life is great, but sometimes it takes me forever to find a place to park.
是啊，不錯。這裡的夜生活很棒，但是有時候找個地方停車要很久。

M: Why don't you buy a scooter? 妳為什麼不買部機車？

W: I thought about it, but after my sister had her accident, my parents don't want me riding one. 我想過，但我的姐姐出車禍之後，我的父母親就不讓我騎了。

M: I understand. So are we gonna paint the town red tonight?
我明白。那麼，我們今晚要出去狂歡作樂嗎？

Q: What problem does the city have? 這個城市有什麼問題呢？

A. There aren't enough parks. 這裡沒有足夠的公園。

B. There aren't many parking lots. 這裡沒有很多停車場。

C. It's not safe at night. 晚上不安全。

D. The city needs to reduce the air pollution. 這個城市需要減少空氣污染。

1. 本題情境是兩位朋友之間的對話,內容是在聊女方在台中的新生活,題目是問住在台中市有什麼問題。

2. 答題線索是在 Sometimes it takes me forever to find a place to park. 由這句話可得知這個城市停車不易。

3. 關鍵詞彙:it took me forever「花了我很多時間」、paint the town red「狂歡作樂」。

⊕ 答案 B

❹ W: Honey, I'll be waiting in the car. 親愛的,我會在車上等你。

M: Hold on. I just have to find my keys. 等一下。我只需要找到我的鑰匙。

W: Are they on the kitchen table? 它們在廚房的桌上嗎?

M: Oh, there they are. No, these are Laura's keys.

哦,在這裡。不,這是蘿拉的鑰匙。

W: Did you check your coat pockets? 你檢查過大衣的口袋嗎?

M: Oops. 糟糕。

W: Let's hit the road, genius. 我們上路吧,天才。

Q: Where did the man find his keys? 這位男士是在哪裡找到他的鑰匙?

A. On the kitchen table. 在廚房的桌子上。

B. Under his coat. 在他的外套下。

C. They couldn't find them, so they'll walk. 他們找不到,所以他們會走路去。

D. In his coat pocket. 在他的外套口袋裡。

1. 本題情境是夫妻之間的對話,內容是在幫這位男士尋找鑰匙,題目是問鑰匙在哪裡找到的。

2. 答題線索是在 Did you check your coat pockets? 和 Oops. 由此可知他在外套的口袋中找到鑰匙。

3. 關鍵慣用語:hit the road「上路;出發了」。

⊕ 答案 D

❺ M: Did you hear about our mayor? 妳有沒有聽到有關市長的事?

W: No. What happened? 沒有,發生了什麼事?

M: He was caught having an affair with an intern.

他和實習生有外遇被抓到了。

W: No way! 怎麼可能!

M: I guess his wife saw the messages on his phone and hired a private investigator.

我猜他的妻子看到他的手機簡訊,就雇了私家偵探。

W: This is great news. I never did like him. 這真是個好消息。我一點也不喜歡他。

Q: What new scandal broke in the news? 新聞揭發什麼醜聞？

A. **The mayor was cheating on his wife. 市長背叛他的妻子。**

B. Nothing was broken. 沒有東西破掉。

C. A private investigator helped break the scandal. 一名私家偵探幫忙揭發醜聞。

D. It's fabulous news. 是個極好的消息。

1. 本題情境是兩位朋友之間的對話，內容是在聊市長的醜聞，題目是問醜聞的內容是什麼。

2. 答題的線索在 He was caught having an affair with an intern. 和 hired a private investigator，這兩句話告訴我們醜聞的細節。

3. 關鍵詞彙：have an affair「有外遇」、intern「實習生」、investigator「偵探」、break the scandal「揭發醜聞」。　　　　　　　　　　　　➜答案 A

❻ W: Something must be out of whack with this thing. 這個東西一定是壞掉了。

M: You're right. It feels like a sauna in here. 妳說得對。這裡感覺好像三溫暖。

W: I turned the temperature all the way down to 22 degrees.
我已經將溫度調降到 22 度了。

M: Why don't we take it to the repair shop? 我們為什麼不將它送到修理廠？

W: Let's see if my uncle can fix it first. He's a real handyman.
我們先看看我的叔叔可不可以修理好。他的手很巧。

Q: What are the speakers having problems with? 說話者的什麼東西出了問題？

A. A dishwasher. 洗碗機。

B. **An air conditioner. 冷氣機。**

C. A heater. 暖氣。

D. A fan. 電風扇。

1. 本題的對話內容是兩位朋友在談論家中空調出了問題，題目要我們推論是什麼東西壞掉了。

2. 答題線索是在 It feels like a sauna in here. 和 I turned the temperature all the way down to 22 degrees. 我們知道室內溫度很高，所以一定是冷氣機出問題了。

3. 關鍵詞彙：out of whack「感覺不對勁；壞掉了」、sauna「蒸氣浴；三溫暖」、repair shop「維修廠」、handyman「手巧的人；萬能的人」。　　➜答案 B

7 M: Look! There's Taipei 101. 看！是台北 101 大樓。

W: It's so amazing. 這真是令人驚豔。

M: Are we going up to the observation deck? 我們是否要上到觀景台？

W: Why don't we go shopping first? 我們為什麼不先去逛街買東西？

M: You're not afraid of heights, are you? 妳不怕高，是嗎？

W: Let's just say my hands get sweaty when I'm on a ladder.
這樣說好了，只要我站在梯子上，我的手就會出汗。

M: Oh, then it should be no problem. 喔，那麼應該是沒有問題的。【諷刺的說法】

Q: Why doesn't the woman want to go up to the observation deck?
為什麼這位女士不想要上去觀景台？

A. She wants to go shopping instead. 她反而想要去購物。

B. She's petrified of heights. 她怕高。

C. She's not feeling too well. 她感覺不太舒服。

D. She said she'll go later after shopping. 她說逛街購物之後再去。

1. 本題內容在談論是否要去觀景台看看，題目是問這位女士不想去的原因。

2. 答題線索是在 Let's just say my hands get sweaty when I'm on a ladder. 流汗就是代表擔心或害怕。請聽清楚 ladder「樓梯」和 later「等一下」，不要混淆了。

3. 關鍵詞彙：observation deck「觀景台」、petrified「嚇呆的」。　　　◆答案 B

8 W: Look at all these shops. It'll take us all day to explore this market.
看看所有的商店。我們需要花一整天來逛這個市場。

M: I bet I can find some second-hand DVDs here.
我打賭，我可以在這裡找到一些二手 DVD。

W: Where's Alice? 愛麗絲在哪裡？

M: I thought she was holding your hand. 我以為她牽著妳的手。

W: Let's split up and look around. 我們分頭去找找看。

M: I'll meet you back here in five minutes. 5 分鐘後我在這裡和妳碰面。

Q: Why are the speakers in such a dilemma?
為什麼說話者會陷入這樣的困境中？

A. Alex is lost. 艾力克走丟了。

B. The market is enormous. 市場超級大。

C. They can't find any second-hand DVDs. 他們找不到任何二手 DVD。

D. They can't find their daughter. 他們找不到他們的女兒。

1. 本題的情境是夫妻兩人在市場裡的對話，題目是問他們遇到了什麼困難。
2. 答題線索在 Where's Alice? 和 I thought she was holding your hand. 由這兩句話可知他們的女兒 Alice 不見了，注意 Alice 和 Alex 聽起來相近，不要搞錯了。
3. 關鍵詞彙：split up「分開」、look around「四處看看」、in a dilemma「陷入進退兩難的困境」。 ➡答案 D

⑨ M: My girlfriend has been acting a little strange lately.
我的女朋友最近表現得怪怪的。

W: How's that? 怎麼樣怪呢？

M: She's checking the messages on my cell phone and always calling me late at night.
她檢查我的手機簡訊，而且總是很晚時打電話給我。

W: Do you think she knows about us? 你覺得她知道我們的事嗎？

M: I think she does. 我想她知道。

Q: Why is the man's girlfriend suspicious? 為什麼這位男士的女朋友疑神疑鬼的？

A. She's checking his phone messages. 她檢查他手機的簡訊。

B. She suspects he won't call her at night. 她懷疑他晚上不會打電話給她。

C. She believes her boyfriend is playing the field. 她相信她的男朋友劈腿。

D. She's a little insecure about herself. 她自己有點沒安全感。

1. 本題內容是男方懷疑他的女朋友已經知道他劈腿的事，題目是問他的女朋友為什麼疑神疑鬼。
2. 答題線索是在 checking the messages on my cell phone 和 calling me late at night，由此可知他女朋友懷疑他劈腿，而 Do you think she knows about us? 這句話證實他劈腿了。
3. 關鍵詞彙：suspicious「懷疑的」、play the field「劈腿；腳踏兩條船」。 ➡答案 C

⑩ W: Look at these lines. 看看這些隊伍。

M: We need to get through customs quickly; otherwise, we're gonna miss our flight.
我們要盡快過海關，否則我們將會錯過班機。

W: We still have to check our carry-on items, too.
我們隨身攜帶的物品仍然要通關檢查。

M: Should we cut in line? 我們應該要插隊嗎？

W: Well, let's ask this man for help. 好吧，我們請這位男士幫忙好了。

211

M: I hope our flight's delayed. 我真希望我們的班機延誤了。

Q: What seems to be the problem? 看起來有什麼問題？

A. The couple's flight is delayed. 這對情侶的班機延誤了。

B. There's a long line at customs. 過海關的隊伍很長。

C. They have to check their carry-on items. 他們必須檢查隨身攜帶的物品。

D. They can't decide whether to cut in line. 他們不能決定是否要插隊。

1. 本題的情境是一對情侶在機場的對話，對話內容是在談論通關的人很多，而他們的飛機快要起飛了，題目是問他們面臨了什麼問題。

2. 答題線索是在 Look at these lines. 和 We need to get through customs quickly; otherwise, we're gonna miss our flight. 所以可得知過海關的人太多了，他們即將錯過班機。

3. 關鍵詞彙：get through customs「過海關」、carry-on items「隨身行李」、cut in line「插隊」、delayed「延誤的」。

⊙ 答案 B

TEST 聽力測驗總複習

 2-11

◎ 答案

1 A　**2** D　**3** D　**4** C　**5** B　**6** A　**7** D　**8** C　**9** D　**10** A
11 C　**12** B　**13** C　**14** D　**15** D

◎ 解析

For Question Number 1, please look at Picture A.

1 **Where can I buy some cosmetics? 我可以在哪裡買到化妝品？**

　A. On the first floor. 在一樓。

　B. On the second floor. 在二樓。

　C. On the third floor. 在三樓。

　D. On the fourth floor. 在四樓。

 本題考的是「場所」，由圖片可知化妝品在一樓。　　　　　▶ 答案 A

For Questions Number 2 and 3, please look at Picture B.

2 **What type of transportation does the man usually take?**
這位男士通常搭乘哪一種交通工具？

　A. He took a train. 他坐火車。

　B. He usually takes the bus. 他通常搭公車。

　C. He often takes a taxi. 他時常搭計程車。

　D. He usually takes the train. 他通常搭火車。

1. 本題考「交通工具名稱」，圖片很清楚是在火車上。
2. 選項 A 不可選，因為時態不對。
3. 選項 B 和 C 不可選，因為交通工具名稱不對。　　　▶ 答案 D

③ Please look at Picture B again.

What might the man say to the woman?

這位男子可能對女子說什麼？

A. So, where are you heading? 那妳要去哪裡呢？

B. May I have a refill? 我可以續杯嗎？

C. Enjoy your meal. 請享用妳的餐點。

D. May I have some chopsticks, please? 請給我筷子好嗎？

解題關鍵　本題考的是推論這位男子可能會「說什麼」。因為他正要吃便當，所以選項 D 是正確的。

答案 D

For Question Number 4, please look at Picture C.

④ How many days will Cathy go for a walk this week?

凱西這一週去散步幾天呢？

A. She'll work three days this week. 這週她將工作三天。

B. She works in the mornings and afternoons.
她在早上和下午工作。

C. Just one day. 只有一天。

D. This is her first week at work. 這是她工作的第一個星期。

解題關鍵　本題考的是有關「時間」，由凱西的行事曆可知她只有一天去散步。

答案 C

For Questions Number 5 and 6, please look at Picture D.

⑤ What is the couple doing? 這對夫妻正在做什麼？

A. They're saying grace before dinner.
他們在晚餐前禱告。

B. They're worshipping. 他們正在拜拜。

C. They feel quite thankful. 他們感到非常感激。

D. They're at a temple. 他們是在一個寺廟裡。

解題關鍵　本題考「動作」，由圖片可得知他們正在廟裡拜拜。

答案 B

6 Please look at Picture D again.

What's true about the picture? 關於這張圖片何者為真？

A. Incense is burning in the temple. 香火正在寺廟裡燃燒著。

B. The couple is very generous. 這對夫妻非常慷慨。

C. Not everyone worships in a temple.
不是每個人都去廟裡拜拜。

D. The couple is likely attending a funeral. 這對夫妻很可能正在參加葬禮。

本題考的是圖片中的「細節」，只有選項 A 的敘述是對的，聽得懂拜拜的相關字彙是很重要的。 ➡ 答案 A

For Question Number 7, please look at Picture E.

7 Can you tell me where I can find a bank?

你能告訴我，在那裡可以找到銀行嗎？

A. Try the department store. 試試百貨公司

B. It's across from the hair salon. 它在美髮店的對面。

C. It's between the post office and the high school. 它在郵局和中學之間。

D. It's next to the hair salon. 它就在美髮店的旁邊。

題目是問銀行的「方位」，這時聽清楚正確的介系詞就很重要，在圖片中很快就可以找到銀行就在美髮店的隔壁。 ➡ 答案 D

For Question Number 8, please look at Picture F.

8 How do I get to the video store from the police station?

我要如何從警察局到錄影帶出租店？

A. Go up 2nd Street and turn left on Mott Avenue.
You'll see it on the left.
沿著第二街往上走，然後在莫特大道左轉，你會看到它就在左邊。

B. It's on the corner of Mott Avenue and 1st Street.
它就在莫特大道和第一街的轉角。

C. Go up 2nd Street and turn right on Mott Avenue. You'll see the video store on your left.
沿著第二街往上走，然後在莫特大道右轉。你會看到錄影帶出租店就在你的左邊。

D. You should take a train. It's pretty far. 你應該搭火車去。那裡很遠。

本題考的是「方向指示」，聽的時候要用手指著地圖來辨別位置與方向，記得要聽清楚左或右、幾個街口和路名。 ➡答案 C

For Questions Number 9 and 10, please look at Picture G.

⑨ How do these girls feel about the party?

這些女孩子覺得派對如何？

A. They're having a great time. 她們玩得開心極了。

B. They're probably waiting for their dates to show up.
她們可能正在等待她們的對象出現。

C. They wish they had taken dance lessons. 她們希望以前有修過舞蹈課。

D. **They think the party is dull. 她們覺得這個派對很無趣。**

本題是問她們的「感覺」，從臉上的表情可知答案是 D。

⑩ Please look at Picture G again.

Why are the girls bored? 為什麼這些女孩子覺得無聊？

A. **It seems no one wants to dance with them.**
似乎沒有人想要跟她們跳舞。

B. They'll be glad when the party is over.
當派對結束時她們會很開心。

C. It's obvious that they aren't having fun. 很顯然的她們玩得不開心。

D. The girl on the left is sleeping. 左邊的那位女孩正在睡覺。

題目是問她們覺得無聊的「原因」，選項 B、C、D 都沒有說明原因，只有選項 A 回答問題。 ➡答案 A

For Questions Number 11 and 12, please look at Picture H.

⑪ What is the man likely saying to the woman?

這位男士可能會對這位女士說什麼？

A. Could I have my bill, please? 可以把帳單給我嗎？

B. You look handsome tonight. 今晚妳看起來很帥。

C. **You eat like a horse. 妳吃很多喔。**

D. Yes, it's obvious he likes her. 沒錯，很顯然他喜歡她。

1. 本題是推測圖片中人物「可能會說的話」，很明顯的他們正在吃飯，所以應該是說有關吃飯的事，選項 C 最合理。

2. 關鍵詞彙：You eat like a horse.「你吃得很多。」

➔ 答案 C

For Question Number 12, please look at Picture H.

⑫ **What isn't true about this picture?**
關於這張圖片何者不正確？

A. The couple seems to be having a pleasant time.
這對夫妻似乎渡過一個愉快的時光。

B. **They seem to be vegetarians. 他們似乎是素食者。**

C. They're using chopsticks. 他們正使用著筷子。

D. The restaurant doesn't look very busy. 餐廳看起來不忙。

本題是問不符合圖片「細節」的問題，我們可以看到桌上有魚和肉，所以他們一定不是吃素的。

➔ 答案 B

For Question Number 13, please look at Picture I.

⑬ **What does this picture tell you? 這張圖片告訴你什麼？**

A. The parking lot is full. 停車場是滿的。

B. You can fill up on gas here. 你可以在這裡加滿油。

C. **This rest stop is busy. 這個休息站很忙。**

D. It's the weekend. 這是週末。

本題考的是有關這個「地點」的正確描述，由旁邊的高速公路和停車場上的車子可以判斷，這是一個休息站。因為停車場上的車子很多，可以得知此休息站生意很好，但是停車場尚有空位，所以選項 A 不可選。

➔ 答案 C

For Question Number 14, please look at Picture J.

⑭ **On which channel can I watch a soap opera?**
我可以在哪個頻道看連續劇？

A. There's no opera on TV tonight. 今晚電視沒有連續劇。

B. Try channel 14. 試試 14 頻道。

C. You can watch the news on channel 51. 你可以在 51 頻道看新聞。

D. **Try channel 40. 試試 40 頻道。**

圖片是一張電視節目表，本題是考你是否聽懂了 soap operas「連續劇」，答案很明顯是 40 頻道。

➡️ 答案 D

For Question Number 15, please look at Picture K.

⑮ **Where are these passengers waiting?** 旅客們正在哪裡等候？

　A. In a lobby. 在大廳。

　B. On a bench. 在長椅上。

　C. At a rest stop. 在休息站。

　D. At a train station. 在火車站。

 本題考的是「場所」，由圖可知是在火車站，圖上有一個人站著，所以不選 B，最佳的答案是 D。

➡️ 答案 D

第二部分　問答

▶▶ 2-12 🎧

◉ **答案**

⑯ C　**⑰** B　**⑱** D　**⑲** A　**⑳** D　**㉑** B　**㉒** C　**㉓** C　**㉔** A　**㉕** C

㉖ D　**㉗** B　**㉘** B　**㉙** C　**㉚** D

◉ **解析**

⑯ Would you like me to shampoo your hair? 請問你要我幫你洗頭嗎？

A. No, thanks. I like the color it is now. 不，謝謝。我喜歡現在這個顏色。

B. Yes, just a little off the back. 好，只要後面剪一點。

C. Sounds good. 聽起來不錯。

D. I shampoo it every day. 我每天都洗頭。

> **解題關鍵**
> 這題是考 shampoo 這個字，當動詞時是「洗頭髮」的意思，本題是問對方要不要洗頭髮，所以選項 C 的回應最恰當。雖然其他選項和頭髮都有關係，但都不是最好的答案。
> ➡ **答案 C**

⑰ I need your signature here, please. 我需要你在這裡簽名。

A. Sorry, that's not my chair. 對不起，那不是我的椅子。

B. Can I borrow your pen? 我可以借用你的筆嗎？

C. I don't think it would look good there. 我不認為放在那裡會好看。

D. I really don't want to disturb her. 我真的不想打擾她。

> **解題關鍵**
> 這題是考 signature「簽名」這個字，當別人要求你簽名時，大多數人的反應都是要借筆。選項 A 和 D 都出現發音混淆字：chair「椅子」、disturb「打擾」，小心不要上當了。
> ➡ **答案 B**

⑱ Much of your hardware is outdated. 你大部分的電腦硬體都過時了。

A. I can't recall when. 我不記得什麼時候。

B. It's a phenomenon. 它是一個稀有的事情。

C. It's not hard to change the dates. 要改變日期並不難。

D. Yeah, maybe it's time to buy a new computer.
　　對啊，也許是該買台新電腦的時候了。

hardware「電腦硬體」、outdated「老舊的；過時的」。選項 A 和 C 是用和時間相關的 when 和 date 來混淆。　　　　　　　　　　　　　　　　⊙ **答案 D**

⑲ **Whose name is the reservation under? 是用誰的名字訂位的？**

　A. **It's under Wang.** 是用王先生。

　B. Party of four, thanks. 我們有四個人，謝謝。

　C. It's under the clipboard. 在寫字夾板下面。

　D. I think her name is Lucy. 我想她的名字是露西。

本題考句子 Whose name is the reservation under?，意思是「用誰的名字訂位」，所以最合理的答案應該是 A。　　　　　　　　　　　　　　　　⊙ **答案 A**

⑳ **Is it very far? 它很遠嗎？**

　A. We won't accept any excuses. 我們不接受任何藉口。

　B. Well, I think it's fair. 好吧，我認為這是公平的。

　C. Oh, it's delicious. 哦，它很美味。

　D. **No, it's just around the corner.** 不，就在轉角。

題目是詢問某個地方的距離，所以最佳的回應是 D。選項 B 中的 fair「公平的」是發音混淆字，要小心。　　　　　　　　　　　　　　　　⊙ **答案 D**

㉑ **My grandfather loves to play the stock market. 我的爺爺喜歡炒股票。**

　A. How often does he go? 他多久去一次？

　B. **Does he make a lot of money? 他賺很多錢嗎？**

　C. That's an odd game to play. 這是一個奇怪的遊戲。

　D. Mine doesn't, either. 我的也沒有。

題目是陳述爺爺喜歡炒股票，所以最適當的回應就是有關炒股票的事。　　⊙ **答案 B**

㉒ **Great! More construction. 真是好呀！更多施工工程。**

　A. I'm sick of school. 我很厭倦學校了。

　B. The city built this bridge a year ago. 這個城市一年前蓋了這座橋。

　C. **It never ends. 真是沒完沒了。**

　D. I feel sorry for the instructors. 我對教練感到很抱歉。

由說話者的語氣聽來，可知是用反諷的語氣來表達對新建工程的厭倦，所以只有選項 C 回應了題目的說法。 答案 C

㉓ Have you adapted well to college life? 你已經適應大學生活了嗎？

A. Yes, I've done it several times now. 是的，我至今已經做了好幾遍了。

B. It's been six months. 已經 6 個月了。

C. I have, but I miss my family a lot. 是呀，但是我很想念我的家人。

D. No, I don't have one. 不，我一個也沒有。

本題是詢問別人的大學生活近況，所以應該回應感覺或是想法。 答案 C

㉔ Why are you blushing? 你為什麼臉紅？

A. She just asked me for my phone number. 她剛才跟我要電話號碼。

B. It's good for me. 這對我有好處。

C. I'm in a hurry. 我正在趕時間。

D. Because we need to warn them of a landslide.
因為我們必須去警告他們有關土石崩塌的事。

1. 本題是問對方臉紅的原因，所以只有選項 A 的答案最合理。

2. 關鍵字彙：blush「臉紅」、landslide「土石崩塌」。 答案 A

㉕ Watch where you're driving, idiot! 笨蛋，開車要看路！

A. I'm driving to work. 我開車去上班。

B. I'm picking my friends up at school. 我要去學校接我的朋友。

C. My fault. Sorry. 抱歉，是我的錯。

D. I watch mostly cartoons. 大部分的卡通我都看。

由 idiot 這個字可以得知說話者很生氣，可見對方開車不小心。選項 A 和 B 都和開車有關，但都不是合理的回應。 答案 C

㉖ How do you handle difficulties so well? 你怎麼這麼會處理困難呢？

A. Well, the delicate items are handled with care. 嗯，易碎的物品要小心處理。

B. I don't think we're on the right page. 我想我們在雞同鴨講。

C. It wasn't that hard. 它不是那麼困難。

D. My mother encouraged me to be optimistic. 我的母親鼓勵我要樂觀。

1. 本題是問對方擅長處理困境的原因，所以說明原因的只有選項 D。
2. 關鍵詞彙：delicate「易碎的」、on the wrong page「雞同鴨講」、optimistic「樂觀的」。

➡️ 答案 D

㉗ Thanks for helping me out this afternoon. 感謝你今天下午幫我的忙。

A. You were a big help. 你幫了很大的忙。

B. What are friends for? 朋友是用來做什麼的呀？

C. You said it. 你說對了。

D. Not too much. 還好。

當別人表達致謝之意時，我們應該用謙虛的方式來回應。

➡️ 答案 B

㉘ I assume he's out horsing around with his friends.
我猜想他出去和朋友鬼混了。

A. I didn't know he could ride a horse. 我不知道他會騎馬。

B. That's a good assumption. 那真是一個很好的假設。

C. When the cat's away, the mice will play.
當貓不在時，老鼠玩得自在。【家裡沒大人管！】

D. That's too bad. 真糟糕。

1. 本題是對別人的行為做推測，因為無法得知他是否出去了，所以選項 B 比較合理。
2. 關鍵詞彙：assume「假設；猜想」、horse around「鬼混胡鬧」、assumption「假設」。

➡️ 答案 B

㉙ Margaret doesn't possess a single CD. 瑪格麗特一張 CD 也沒有。

A. What possessed her to buy one? 什麼原因讓她去買一個？

B. That's bad news for Cindy. 對莘蒂而言是個壞消息。

C. She must download all her music. 她一定是下載所有的音樂。

D. She shouldn't regret it. 她不應該後悔。

本題描述瑪格麗特的狀況，所以她一定是下載所有的音樂。選項 B 中的 Cindy 和 CD 是發音混淆字，所以不可選。

➡️ 答案 C

㉚ Why don't they call off the engagement? 他們為什麼不取消婚約？

A. I don't think they're home. 我想他們不在家。

B. They're still engaged in online gambling. 他們還在從事線上賭博。

C. They lost the number. 他們遺失了電話號碼。

D. Yeah, they haven't been getting along very well recently.
對啊，他們最近相處得不好。

1. 本題是表達不認同其他人行為的意見，所以應該用贊成或反對來回應，選項 D 是正確答案。

2. 關鍵詞彙：call off「取消」、engage in「從事」、gambling「賭博」。　　　➡ 答案 D

第三部分　簡短對話

 ▶▶ 2-13

⊙ 答案

31 B　**32** C　**33** A　**34** D　**35** D　**36** D　**37** D　**38** C　**39** D　**40** D

41 D　**42** D　**43** B　**44** C　**45** D

⊙ 解析

31 W: How tall are you now? 你現在有多高？

M: I'm about 160 centimeters. 我大約 160 公分。

W: You're much taller than I was in junior high school.
你比我在國中的時候高太多了。

M: Yeah, but you're still taller than I am. 是啊，但妳還是比我高。

W: By a hair. 只差一點點。

Q: What is true about this conversation? 關於這段對話何者是正確的？

A. The boy is in high school. 這位男孩在讀高中。

B. The woman is taller than the boy. 這位女士比這位男孩高。

C. The boy is taller than the woman. 這位男孩比這位女士高。

D. The boy is 116 centimeters tall. 這位男孩 116 公分高。

 解題關鍵

1. 本題內容是兩個人在討論身高，題目是問對話的「細節」。

2. 答題線索是在 Yeah, but you're still taller than I am. 由這句話我們得知這位女士還是比男孩高。

3. 關鍵詞彙：by a hair「只差一點點」。　　　　　　　　　　　⊙ 答案 B

32 W: I might have a new job. 我可能會有一份新工作。

M: Are you kidding me? 妳在開玩笑吧？

W: I'm serious. A marketing company in Tainan wants to interview me this week.
我是認真的。一家在台南的行銷公司，這個星期想要和我面談。

M: That's awesome. What do your parents think?
太棒了。妳的父母覺得如何？

W: They're happy for me, but they prefer I live closer to home.
他們為我感到高興，但他們比較喜歡我住得離家近一點。

M: Well, good luck with the interview. 那麼祝妳面談順利。

Q: **What can you infer from this conversation? 從這個談話你可以推測出什麼？**

A. The interview went well. 面試進行得很順利。

B. The man wants the woman to stay. 這位男士希望這名女士留下來。

C. **The woman works in business. 這位女士從商。**

D. The woman's parents are overbearing. 這名女子的父母都很霸道。

1. 本題是朋友之間的對話，內容是談論女方的新工作，題目是要我們做出「推論」。

2. 答題的關鍵是在 A marketing company in Tainan wants to interview me this week. 因為她將去行銷公司面談，所以可推論這名女子是從事和商業有關的工作。

3. 關鍵詞彙：Are you kidding me?「你在開玩笑吧？」、marketing company「行銷公司」。

➡️ 答案 C

㉝ W: Good catch today, Mr. Lu? 盧先生，今天漁獲不錯吧？

M: Not too bad. Caught quite a few crabs. 還不錯啦，抓了不少螃蟹。

W: Any tuna? 有鮪魚嗎？

M: No, I wasn't that lucky. 沒有，我沒有那麼幸運。

W: Well, let's unload your boat and get those crabs to the market.
嗯，我們把你的船卸貨，並且送這些螃蟹去市場。

M: Then it's time for lunch. I'm so hungry I could eat a horse.
那麼現在正是吃午飯的時候。我快餓死了。

Q: **Where is this conversation likely taking place? 這段對話可能是在哪裡發生的？**

A. **At a harbor. 在港口。**

B. At a restaurant. 在餐廳。

C. On a street corner. 在街角。

D. At a fish market. 在魚市場。

1. 本題是兩個朋友之間的對話，內容是在談論漁獲量和接下來要做的事，題目是問對話發生的「地點」。

2. 答題線索是在 let's unload your boat and get those crabs to the market 我們知道他們正要將船上的漁獲卸下，所以他們一定是在港口。

3. 關鍵詞彙：unload「卸貨」、I could eat a horse.「我快餓死了。（形容一個人很餓，餓到可以吃下一匹馬。）」

➡️ 答案 A

34 W: I need to get out of the city and relax. 我需要離開城市放鬆一下。

M: That's a great idea. What do you have in mind?

這是一個好主意。妳有什麼想法？

W: Let's go to Lugang. 我們去鹿港吧。

M: I've never been there, but isn't that a little far away?

我從來沒有去過那裡，但是那裡不是有一點遠嗎？

M: We could find a bed and breakfast in Kenting.

那我們可以去墾丁找家民宿。

M: Now you're talking. 這樣才像話。

Q: How will the couple spend their weekend? 這對夫妻將如何渡過他們的週末？

A. They'll visit Lugang and stay in a bed and breakfast.

他們將去參觀鹿港，並且住一家民宿。

B. They probably won't spend too much money. 他們可能不會花太多錢。

C. They'll spend the entire weekend there. 他們會在那裡渡過整個週末。

D. They want to go down to Kenting. 他們想要去墾丁。

1. 本題是夫妻或情侶之間的對話，題目是問他們將怎麼做，也就是「如何渡週末」。

2. 答題線索是在 We could find a bed and breakfast in Kenting? 和 Now you're talking. 最後一句表示贊成去墾丁的想法。

3. 關鍵詞彙：bed and breakfast「提供床和早餐的民宿（簡稱為 B&B）」、Now you're talking.「這樣才像話。」　　　　　　　　**◯答案 D**

35 W: Hi, Henry. 嗨，亨利。

M: Hi, how are you, Carol? I haven't seen you in a long time. How's Annie?

嗨，卡洛，你好嗎？我有很長一段時間沒有看到妳了。安妮還好嗎？

W: She's doing well. Yeah, she's taking her college entrance exam today.

她還不錯。對了，她今天參加大學聯考。

M: Is that why you came to the temple?

這就是為什麼妳要來寺廟的原因？

W: Actually, I came because my company lost a big contract this month.

其實，我來是因為我的公司這一個月失去了一張大訂單。

M: Sorry to hear that. 很抱歉聽到這件事。

W: We'll bounce back, but it's been a tough month.

我們會捲土重來，但是這一個月很辛苦。

Q: Why is the woman at the temple? 這位女士為什麼在寺廟裡？

A. She wants to pray that her daughter gets into a good university.
她去拜拜，希望她女兒可以考進一所好大學。

B. She wanted to meet Henry there to discuss business.
她為了要和亨利談生意而去那裡。

C. She lost one of her contacts at the temple. 她在寺廟裡丟掉了一個隱形眼鏡。

D. She wants her company to have better luck in the future.
她希望她的公司在將來運氣更好。

1. 本題情境是朋友在外面巧遇的對話，內容是在聊近況和來寺廟的原因，題目是問來寺廟的「目的」。

2. 答題線索是在 I came because my company lost a big contract this month. 透露出公司的現況與來寺廟的原因。

3. 關鍵詞彙：college entrance exam「大學聯考」、bounce back「重新恢復；捲土重來」。

> 答案 D

㊱ W: Hey, how long have you and Lori been dating? 嘿，你和蘿莉約會多久了？

M: It'll be two years in November. 到 11 月時就兩年了。

W: Wow! So are you going to pop the question? 哇！那麼，你要求婚了嗎？

M: I'd like to ask her to marry me in November. 我想要在十一月時向她求婚。

W: Aren't you romantic? 你不是很浪漫嗎？

M: Yeah, but my parents have to meet her first. They hope she can visit during Chinese New Year, so I'll have to wait until after the holidays to propose.
我是啊，但是我的父母親要先見見她。他們希望她可以在農曆新年期間去拜訪他們，所以我必須等到假期後才求婚。

W: Let me know how it turns out. 要告訴我結果如何喔！

Q: When will the man likely propose? 這名男子可能何時求婚？

A. In November. 在十一月。

B. They want to get married in November. 他們希望在十一月時結婚。

C. During Chinese New Year. 在農曆新年期間。

D. After his parents give their approval. 等他的父母認可之後。

1. 本題情境是朋友之間的閒聊,內容是在談論男方與他女朋友的婚事,題目是要我們推論男方「求婚的時間」。

2. 答題線索是在 but my parents have to meet her first 和 I'll have to wait until after the holidays to purpose.,我們可以得知男方要等父母親見過女方才會求婚。

3. 關鍵詞彙:pop the question「(口語說法)求婚」、turn out「結果是」、propose「(動詞)求婚」、approval「認可;允許」。 ●答案 D

③ M: Nancy, can you help me slice the vegetables? 南西,妳能幫我切蔬菜嗎?

W: I wanna help Grandma cook the dumplings. 我想要幫奶奶煮餃子。

M: Paul is helping Grandma. 保羅正在幫奶奶。

W: But he helped her yesterday. 但是他昨天幫過了。

M: Nancy, please do what you're told and stop complaining.
南西,請做我告訴妳的事,不要抱怨。

W: I'm sorry. 對不起。

Q: **Who is cooking the dumplings? 誰正在煮餃子?**

A. Nancy and Paul will help their grandma. 南西和保羅將會幫他們的奶奶。

B. Grandma is cooking the dumplings by herself. 奶奶自己正在煮餃子。

C. Nancy is helping her father. 南西正在幫她的父親。

D. **Paul is helping his grandma cook the dumplings. 保羅正在幫奶奶煮餃子。**

1. 本題是居家的對話情境,本題是考細節,題目是問「誰」正在煮餃子。

2. 答題線索是在 Paul is helping Grandma. 而且爸爸還說 please do what you're told and stop complaining 表示就是這樣決定,不要再說了。

3. 關鍵字彙:slice「切開」。 ●答案 D

③ W: Does it have an MP3? 它有 MP3 嗎?

M: Yeah, it can store about 200 songs. It also has a camera and a video recorder. Let me show you.
有,它可以儲存大約 200 首歌。它也有照相機和錄影功能。讓我展示給妳看。

W: This is probably too expensive. 這個可能太貴。

M: If you sign up with our mobile network provider, you pay only NT$1,200.
如果妳和我們的電信公司簽約,妳只需要付台幣 1,200 元。

W: Sounds reasonable. How about text messaging? I know that can be costly.
聽起來合理。那簡訊如何?我知道那可能會很貴。

M: You get your first 30 messages free, and each additional message is just NT$1.
前面 30 則免費，每增加一則只要台幣 1 元。

W: Hmm, can you show me the video recorder function?
嗯，你可以展示給我看錄影的功能嗎？

Q: What is happening in this conversation? 這段對話中發生什麼事？

A. The woman is paying her phone bill. 這位女士正在付電話帳單。

B. The woman is checking out a video recorder. 這位女士正在看錄影機。

C. The woman is looking at a cell phone. 這位女士正在看手機。

D. The sales clerk is showing the woman an MP3.
銷售店員正在展示 MP3 給這位女士看。

1. 本題情境是銷售員與顧客之間的對話，題目是考我們「主旨大意」。

2. 答題線索是在 If you sign up with our mobile network provider, you pay only NT$1,200. 我們可以知道這位小姐正在電信公司看手機。

3. 關鍵詞彙：store「儲存」、sign up「簽訂」、text message「簡訊」、costly「昂貴的」、additional「額外的」。　　　　　　　　　　　　　答案 C

39 M: You ate the entire bag of candy? 妳吃了整袋的糖果嗎？

W: Yeah. 是的。

M: Do you wanna go out and get more? I'm sure people are still handing out candy.
妳想要出去拿更多嗎？我敢肯定人們還在發糖果。

W: But my clown make-up is all messed up. 但是我的小丑妝已經弄花了。

M: That's okay. You'll just look like a messed up clown.
沒有關係。妳只是看起來像一個弄花臉的小丑。

W: I like the way you think. 我喜歡你思考的方式。

Q: What holiday is this? 這是什麼節日？

A. It's Christmas. 是聖誕節。

B. It's Chinese New Year. 是農曆新年。

C. It's Double Ten Day. 是雙十節。

D. It's Halloween. 是萬聖節。

1. 本題的情境是居家的對話，題目是問對話的「時機」。

2. 答題線索是 I'm sure people are still handing out candy. 和 But my clown make-up is all messed up. 這兩句話提到糖果和妝扮，所以我們可以推論出這是萬聖節。

3. 關鍵詞彙：entire「全部的」、hand out「分發」、make-up「妝扮」、mess up「弄糟」。　●答案 D

40 W: What are you getting Mandy for her birthday?
你要買什麼東西給蔓蒂過生日？

M: I have no idea. Do you have any good suggestions?
我不知道。妳有什麼好建議嗎？

W: What's your budget? 你的預算是多少？

M: I was thinking around NT$1,000. 我想大概台幣 1,000 元左右。

W: Wow! Mr. Generous! 哇！慷慨先生！

M: What? That's not enough? 什麼？這樣還不夠嗎？

W: How about this shirt for NT$1,200? 這件襯衫台幣 1200 元怎麼樣？

M: I like it! You want one, too? 我喜歡！妳也想要一件嗎？

W: Really? 真的嗎？

M: Yeah, right. 才怪，怎麼可能。

Q: How much will the man spend? 這位男士會花多少錢？

A. He'll spend a total of NT$2,400. 他全部將會花台幣 2,400 元。

B. No more than NT$1,000. 不超過台幣 1,000 元。

C. He's spent time shopping for Mandy. 他已經為蔓蒂花時間買東西了。

D. He'll spend NT$1,200. 他將會花台幣 1,200 元。

1. 本題情境是兩人在討論買禮物，題目問男方會「花多少錢」。

2. 答題線索是在 How about this shirt for NT$1,200? 可知他會花多少錢，而最後一句 Yeah, right.「才怪，怎麼可能。」我們得知這位男士只會買一件。

3. 關鍵字彙：budget「預算」。　●答案 D

41 W: I really like this apartment. What about the utilities?
我真的很喜歡這個公寓，水電、瓦斯怎麼算？

M: The rent includes the water bill, cable fee, and the monthly security guard fee.
租金包括了水費、有線電視費和每月的管理費。

W: How about the electric bill? 電費呢？

M: No, that's not included. The deposit is two month's rent.
沒有，沒包含在內。押金是兩個月的房租。

W: Is it okay if the deposit is one month's rent? 可以只押一個月的房租嗎？

M: No. 不可以。

W: That's too bad. 那太糟糕了。

Q: Why won't the woman rent the apartment? 為什麼這位女士不會租下這個公寓？

A. The electric bill isn't included in the rent. 房租不包括電費。

B. The man won't let her rent the apartment for only one month.
這位男士不會讓她只租一個月的公寓。

C. She wants to look at a few others first. 她想先看看其他的。

D. She can't afford the deposit. 她負擔不起押金。

1. 本題是房東與來看房子的房客之間的對話，題目是問不租這個公寓的「原因」。

2. 答題線索是在 Is it okay if the deposit is one month's rent? 和 That's too bad. 這兩句話透露出女方只能負擔得起一個月的押金。

3. 關鍵詞彙：utility「（水電瓦斯等）公共用費」、cable fee「有線電視費」、security guard fee「管理費」、electric bill「電費」、deposit「押金」。　　●答案 D

㊷ W: Why the long face? 為什麼擺臭臉？

M: My girlfriend just stood me up. She called and said she had other plans.
我的女朋友放我鴿子，她打電話來說有其他的計畫。

W: Look at the bright side. 要看事情的光明面呀。

M: What bright side? 什麼光明面呀？

W: Now you have time to take me to a movie.
現在你就有時間帶我去看電影啦。

M: Are you pulling my leg? 妳是在跟我開玩笑吧？

W: Let's go, handsome. 帥哥，走吧。

M: Lucky me! 我真幸運！

Q: How does the man feel? 這位男士有什麼感覺？

A. He feels depressed. 他感到沮喪。

B. He feels disappointed. 他感到失望。

C. He's a little confused. 他有一點困惑。

D. He's pretty excited. 他相當興奮。

1. 本題情境為朋友之間的對話，題目是問男方的「感覺」。

2. 答題線索是在 Now you have time to take me to a movie. 這句話為女方的提議，由男方的回答 Lucky me! 可知，男子很開心。

3. 關鍵詞彙：long face「悶悶不樂的臉色；臭臉」、stand someone up「放某人鴿子」、Are you pulling my leg?「你是在跟我開玩笑吧？」。　　　➡答案 D

㊸ M: Attention passengers. Flight 70 will be delayed one hour. We apologize for any inconvenience.

各位旅客，請注意。第 70 航班將會延誤一個小時。造成不便，我們深表歉意。

W: Excuse me, sir. Why will the flight be delayed?

對不起，先生。為什麼這班飛機會延誤呢？

M: They're just double-checking the landing gear.

他們只是要再次檢查起降裝置。

W: Do we have time to go shopping? 我們是否有時間去購物？

M: Sure. Just be back in about 45 minutes. 當然。只要大約 45 分鐘內回來。

W: By the way, is there a telephone around here? I need to call my husband right away.

對了，這附近有電話嗎？我要馬上打電話給我老公。

M: Just over there, ma'am. 夫人，就在那邊。

Q: What will the woman likely do next? 這位女士接下來可能會做什麼事？

A. She'll go shopping. 她將會去逛街購物。

B. She'll notify her husband of the delay. 她會通知她丈夫班機延誤的事情。

C. She'll get something to eat. 她會找點東西吃。

D. She'll stay in the boarding area and do some shopping.

她將留在登機區買點東西。

1. 此對話情境為旅客和機組人員的對話，考的是「細節」問題，題目是問這位女士接下來會「做什麼」。

2. 答題線索在 By the way, is there a telephone around here? 和 I need to call my husband right away. 我們得知這位女士接下來會打電話給她老公。

3. 關鍵詞彙：passenger「乘客；旅客」、apologize「道歉」、inconvenience「不方便」、right away「馬上」。　　　➡答案 B

44 W: We just don't get along that well anymore. 我們相處不再那樣融洽了。

M: Why don't you tell her to leave? 妳為什麼不告訴她，要她離開呢？

W: We've been roommates for almost a year. 我們已經當了將近一年的室友了。

M: Yeah, but you said she plays music late at night and leaves her clothes all over the place.

是啊，但是妳說她在深夜放音樂，而且將衣服散落滿地。

W: I live in a pigsty! 我生活在豬圈裡！

M: Tell her to take a hike. 告訴她，要她離開。

Q: What are the man and woman discussing? 男士和女士在討論什麼？

A. They seem to agree about what should be done.

他們似乎都同意應該要做的事。

B. They're talking about where to take a hike. 他們正在談論要去哪裡登山。

C. **They're discussing the woman's roommate.**

他們正在討論那名女子的室友。

D. They're not happy living together. 他們住在一起不快樂。

1. 本題是朋友之間的對話，內容是談論女方和室友的問題。題目是問對話的「主旨大意」。

2. 答題線索是 We've been roommates for almost a year. 我們可知是有關室友的問題，而從 but you said she plays music late at night and leaves her clothes all over the place，我們了解到問題有多嚴重。

3. 關鍵詞彙：get along well「相處融洽」、pigsty「豬窩」、take a hike「希望別人離開」。

◯➔ 答案 C

45 W: I can't wait for summer vacation! 我等不及要放暑假了！

M: Only twenty more days. 只要再 20 天。

W: I'm flying to Japan on the 16th. 16 號時我會飛往日本。

M: Oh, I wish I could tag along. My dad's taking me to Taitung on the 20th.

喔，我真希望可以跟去。我的爸爸 20 號會帶我去台東。

W: Aren't you going to a summer camp there?

你不是要去那裡的夏令營嗎？

M: Yeah, I'll stay with some relatives for a week, and then I'm off to camp.

是啊，我會住在親戚家一個星期，然後我再去營地。

Q: **When will the boy leave for summer camp? 男孩何時會去夏令營呢？**

A. A week after he graduates. 畢業後一個星期。

B. On the 16th. 16 號。

C. He'll leave before he visits his relatives. 他拜訪親戚之前就會離開。

D. **On the 27th. 27 號。**

1. 本題是小男孩和同學之間的對話，題目是問小男孩「何時」去夏令營。

2. 答題線索是 My dad's taking me to Taitung on the 20th. 和 I'll stay with some relatives for a week, and then I'm off to camp. 由這兩句話我們知道，他 20 號會先去台東，再過一星期後才去夏令營。

3. 關鍵詞彙：tag along「跟隨」、be off to「離開前往」。　　　　⊙答案 D

朗文全民英檢贏家策略—中級聽力測驗
Longman Strategy Series for GEPT—Listening Test (Intermediate)

作　　　者	Jason Buddo & 謝璿蓁
發　行　人	Isa Wong
主　　　編	陳慧芬
責　任　編　輯	陳慧莉
協　力　編　輯	官芝羽、華韻雯、林欣頤
封　面　設　計	黃聖文
發行所／出版者	台灣培生教育出版股份有限公司
	地址／231 新北市新店區北新路三段 219 號 11 樓 D 室
	電話／02-2918-8368　傳真／02-2913-3258
	網址／www.pearson.com.tw
	E-mail／reader.tw@pearson.com
香　港　總　經　銷	培生教育出版亞洲股份有限公司
	地址／香港鰂魚涌英皇道 979 號（太古坊康和大廈十八樓）
	電話／(852)3181-0000　傳真／(852)2564-0955
	E-mail／hkcs@pearson.com
台　灣　總　經　銷	創智文化有限公司
	地址／23674 新北市土城區忠承路 89 號 6 樓（永寧科技園區）
	電話／02-2268-3489　傳真／02-2269-6560
	博訊書網／www.booknews.com.tw
學校訂書專線	02-2918-8368 轉 8866
版　　　次	2012 年 8 月二版一刷
	2013 年 12 月二版二刷
書　　　號	TT259
C　O　D　E	978-916-001-045-6
定　　　價	新台幣 320 元

本書相關內容資料更新訊息，請參閱本公司網站：www.pearson.com.tw

23143
新北市新店區北新路三段219號11樓D室
台灣培生教育出版股份有限公司　收
Pearson Education Taiwan Ltd.

Switch
on to
learning

ALWAYS LEARNING

PEARSON

★資料請填寫完整，謝謝！

書名：_____

ISBN: _____

讀者資料

姓名：_____ 性別：_____ 出生年月日：_____.

電話：(O)_____ (H)_____ (Mo)_____.

傳眞：(O)_____ (H)_____.

E-mail：_____.

地址：_____.

教育程度：□國小 □國中 □高中 □大專 □大學以上

職業：1.學生 □

　　　2.教職 □教師 □教務人員 □班主任 □經營者 □其他：_____

　　　　任職單位：□學校 □補教機構 □其他：_____

　　　　教學經歷：□幼兒英語 □兒童英語 □國小英語 □國中英語 □高中英語
　　　　　　　　　□成人英語

　　　3.社會人士 □工 □商 □資訊 □服務 □軍警公職 □出版媒體 □其他_____.

從何處得知本書：

　　□逛書店 □報章雜誌 □廣播電視 □親友介紹 □書訊 □廣告函 □其他_____.

對我們的建議：

_____

_____

_____

_____

感謝您的回函，我們每個月將抽出幸運讀者，致贈精美禮物，得獎名單可至本公司網站查詢。
讀者服務專線：02-2918-8368#8866
http://www.pearson.com.tw　　E-mail:reader.tw@pearson.com